Praise for the novels of Cassie Ryan

"From the first erotic word to the last sensual line, *Ceremony of Seduction* weaves a spell around its reader and doesn't let go."
——*Joyfully Reviewed*

"An incredibly creative read. If you're looking for a sexy escape, you'll find it here."
——*Romantic Times*

"Ms. Ryan creates a bold and beautiful world . . . I highly recommend it."
——*Night Owl Romance*

"An amazing journey between two worlds. Definitely a book that, once opened, won't be closed until the final page has been read."
——*Kate Douglas*

The DEMON *and* the SUCCUBUS

CASSIE RYAN

BERKLEY SENSATION, NEW YORK

THE BERKLEY PUBLISHING GROUP
Published by the Penguin Group
Penguin Group (USA) Inc.
375 Hudson Street, New York, New York 10014, USA
Penguin Group (Canada), 90 Eglinton Avenue East, Suite 700, Toronto, Ontario M4P 2Y3, Canada
(a division of Pearson Penguin Canada Inc.)
Penguin Books Ltd., 80 Strand, London WC2R 0RL, England
Penguin Group Ireland, 25 St. Stephen's Green, Dublin 2, Ireland (a division of Penguin Books Ltd.)
Penguin Group (Australia), 250 Camberwell Road, Camberwell, Victoria 3124, Australia
(a division of Pearson Australia Group Pty. Ltd.)
Penguin Books India Pvt. Ltd., 11 Community Centre, Panchsheel Park, New Delhi—110 017, India
Penguin Group (NZ), 67 Apollo Drive, Rosedale, Auckland 0632, New Zealand
(a division of Pearson New Zealand Ltd.)
Penguin Books (South Africa) (Pty.) Ltd., 24 Sturdee Avenue, Rosebank, Johannesburg 2196,
South Africa

Penguin Books Ltd., Registered Offices: 80 Strand, London WC2R 0RL, England

This book is an original publication of The Berkley Publishing Group.

PRINTING HISTORY
Berkley Sensation trade paperback edition / April 2011

Library of Congress Cataloging-in-Publication Data

Ryan, Cassie.
  The demon and the succubus / Cassie Ryan.—Berkley Sensation trade pbk. ed.
    p. cm.
  ISBN 978-0-425-23906-3 (trade pbk.)
1. Demonology—Fiction. I. Title.
  PS3618.Y33D45 2011
  813'.6—dc22
                        2010052533

PRINTED IN THE UNITED STATES OF AMERICA

10 9 8 7 6 5 4 3 2 1

ACKNOWLEDGMENTS

Thanks to my awesome agent, Paige Wheeler, and my fabulous editor, Kate Seaver, for following through on this second book in the Sisters of Darkness series. They rallied the troops to overcome obstacles and moved this project through on schedule like the wonderful professionals they are.

To my critique buddies—Erin Quinn, Jordan Summers, and Kayce Lassiter—my eternal gratitude for your help and support in getting the final touches put on this story.

As for all the friends, family, coworkers, and fans that have been there for me these last few months with cards, letters, food, labor, prayers, and positive energy for healing . . . you humble me with your loving and caring hearts. You brought food to my family, you packed our belongings and showed up with trailers and trucks to help us move, you showed up in the dark to work a yard sale, and you let me know I wasn't alone. Thank you!

For the fabulously skilled and talented staff and volunteers at the Scottsdale Health Care Osborn Medical Center, there are no words to express my undying gratitude for all you have done for me and for my family.

Bree, my best barista friend, you truly rock, girl! What didn't you do?

My father, David, and my sister, Amy, have shown me how truly priceless the love and support of family can be. I love you both.

Finally, my thanks and love to Jon and Darian for your love and support. Your faith in me never wavered and I could not have come half the distance without the two of you cheering me on. You are my life and I couldn't have done any of it without you guys!

1

"Not what I expected. But a lovely prelude to our relationship."

Sunk deep in a relaxing hot bath, Amalya glanced toward the doorway to find a stunning stranger in a very expensive Italian suit devouring her with an amused hazel gaze. Irritation and surprise warred inside her and she bit them back. "I'm sorry. Did we have an appointment, Mr.—" She remained in her reclined state with her head resting back against the bath pillow and her arms resting along the sides of the ridiculously large claw-footed tub as she waited for him to fill in the blank as she mentally reviewed her calendar.

There were no appointments for today, and the Madame hadn't informed her of any pop-ups, which was why she'd slept in this morning and was now lounging in the tub.

After all, even succubi liked to relax on their days off.

"Levi." His rich voice with a definitely upper-crust British accent softly echoed around the spacious bathroom as he walked forward uninvited. He grinned as he crouched and reached out to rub some strands of the long blond hair she'd pinned on top of her head in between his fingertips. "Soft and lovely." His inflection told her he meant more than just her hair.

Surprised at the man's bold actions, Amalya resisted the urge to define her personal space. Instead, she mentally shifted into work mode.

She cocked her head to the side and reached out to touch his hair in the same manner he had hers, smiling when he raised his brows as if she'd surprised him. His hair was soft to the touch, the color of rich milk chocolate, clean cut, but longer on the top where it fell over onto his brow. She traced one finger down his sideburns, which were worn long and ended even with the bottom of his earlobes.

He was definitely good looking, attractive with a strong jaw and rich hazel eyes that sparked with amusement.

He intrigued her.

A glowing aura of nearly white energy surrounded him like a pulsing mist. Amalya wasn't in need of energy, having just entertained a client last night, but this man's presence tasted human with an undertone of something exotic she couldn't quite place. Her skin began to ache—the succubus equivalent of a stomach growl, telling her he would give her a surge of energy better than any she'd had lately among the stream of humans and lower-level supernaturals. Not to mention he was interesting, and she had a feeling she would very much enjoy spending some time with this mystery man.

Everything that made it well worth working on her day off.

"So what *did* you expect, Mr. Levi?" she asked with a small smile.

"Levi is my given name." His gaze devoured her face as silence fell between them as if he were trying to put his thoughts into words. "Perhaps someone older?" His lips quirked up at the edges.

A lie.

Amalya bit back a smile. Each succubus had a gift and hers was being able to discern truth from lies. Not the most powerful gift among her people, or even her three sisters, but one she'd grown to rely on over the millennia—and millennia was how long she'd lived.

From the way Levi's eyes sparkled, he knew it.

His grin widened as he slowly stood and reached into the inside pocket of his jacket. "The Madame gave me this." He held up a black old-fashioned ladies' fan, and a spurt of surprise threaded through Amalya that she hoped hadn't shown on her face.

Each different color of fan represented what the client had paid for and what he expected from his time with her. A very simple tool that kept all talk of money out of the bedroom and part of a philosophy that had made Sinner's Redemption one of the most profitable legal brothels not only in Nevada, but in the world. The black fan meant this man had paid with an open account and he had deep enough pockets to cover whatever he wished to go on inside this room or out.

"My apologies, Amalya. I've caught you off guard." He bowed from the waist as if they were in Victorian England, but the intense hazel gaze that bored into hers held no apology, only delight, intrigue, and anticipation.

"Not at all," she lied, glad most others didn't share her gift. "I must not have received the Madame's message to expect a client. If you'll give me a moment, I'll get ready." She sat up and braced her hands on the side of the tub so she could stand.

"Don't." His voice sounded like more of a request than a statement and she stilled and glanced up at him.

He laid the fan aside and crouched again next to the tub, making the room feel very small as he loomed next to her. "Please don't be angry with the Madame. She didn't know of my arrival until just a few minutes ago, and I asked her not to disturb you." He smiled— the first genuine smile she'd seen from him, which made him look younger and more vulnerable. Now that she'd seen the real man behind the mask, he'd never be able to fool her with his masked expressions again. "And now I'm glad she didn't."

Amalya sensed no danger—no special succubus talents needed. Pure female intuition honed over a long life. Not to mention that Jethro, her longtime friend and the bodyguard for Sinner's Redemption, wouldn't have let Levi through if he were any danger to her. She'd saved Jethro's life years ago when a stray demon had cornered him in the alley behind Sinner's Redemption. Amalya had been wounded in the rescue and nearly died herself, but Jethro had given his own sustenance to bring her back. Since then he'd become a trusted ally, privy to the truth about who and what she was. Jethro would take a bullet—or a demon, as was more likely—for her. And Amalya would do the same for him.

She had been in Hell's version of Witness Protection for just over seven hundred years. She couldn't afford to let down her guard when the demon she'd helped lock away still had plenty of contacts within the human realm and would relish the chance to torture she and her sisters for the rest of eternity.

She searched Levi's face, finally meeting his deep hazel gaze squarely. Pure logic told her there was something more going on here than a rich playboy who wanted some time with her. "What can I do for you, Levi? Really."

"It's what I can do for *you* that brings me here."

The truth of his cultured words hit her like a slap before he stood and took off his suit jacket. "Do you mind if I join you? It seems a shame to waste a perfectly good bath, don't you think?"

Amalya wanted to make him explain his odd statement but figured he'd get around to it in his own time. Years of isolation from her sisters and her own kind had taught her patience.

She studied Levi and debated saying no. She'd never let anyone join her in the bath before—for her, baths weren't sexual. A silly distinction for a succubus to make since she'd had partners in just about every other scenario, location, and position before. But there was definitely something about this man that enticed her and made her want to share even this private sanctuary with him.

She mentally shrugged and relaxed back against the tub. "By all means. There are extra towels just behind that door."

He smiled and opened the door to her spacious walk-in closet, pulling a large green towel off the shelf and hanging it on the hook next to hers. He toed off his shoes and loosened his tie. "You know, I don't think I've bathed with anyone since I was a child. Baths have always been my private thinking time."

She smirked at the irony of his statement and raised one brow earning a short laugh from him.

"Touché. Apparently, we are very similar creatures, Amalya. And for interrupting both your day off and your private time, I promise to make it worthwhile."

Amalya didn't bother to censor the laugh that bubbled up from her throat. "You're very sure of yourself, aren't you?"

He stilled and met her gaze directly. "Yes. I have no doubt I can give you everything you need."

She frowned at the strength of the truth in those few words. They hadn't been said as a boast but almost as a sad fact.

Pure instinct made her add, "I have no doubt you already know I'm a succubus and everything that entails . . ." By which she meant that time spent with her would drain some of his energy.

He smiled slowly. "I'm well aware and not worried in the least, my beauty."

A weight lifted from her and she sighed as anticipation slid through her. She hadn't realized what a relief it would be not to have to hide what she was. Even supernaturals tended to try to forget to some extent what she was during their time together.

What would it be like to just be herself with no secrets for a while?

Fascinated by the man in front of her, Amalya allowed herself to relax as Levi continued to undress.

He draped his suit jacket and tie over the closed toilet lid before turning back to her and unbuttoning his expensive, designer shirt.

A surge of delight tripped through her. He seemed eager to be with her—not the well-known courtesan from Sinner's Redemption, but her. Which she knew was probably only her imagination, but she held on to the sensation anyway.

Each opened button of his shirt revealed a new tantalizing glimpse of firm skin dusted with crisp, dark hairs, and Amalya, riveted in place, couldn't seem to look away.

Arousal slid through her like fine Cognac, a slow warmth that built in intensity until her nipples hardened under the hot water and familiar slickness formed between her labia. Apparently, her body wholeheartedly agreed with her decision to suspend her day off.

When both sides of Levi's shirt hung loose to reveal a strong line of firm, male flesh, his hands quickly moved to the button of his slacks.

Amalya tightened her fingers on the porcelain to keep from pushing out of the tub and taking over the simple task. Apparently, his quick, hurried movements weren't even fast enough for her. She smiled and mentally chided herself for acting like a teenager in a backseat after prom.

So much for all her hard-earned patience.

Levi lowered his zipper and she found herself moistening her lower lip with her tongue as impatience snapped through her to see what was hidden underneath the fine, dark fabric.

When she glanced up into Levi's face, he was smiling.

Heat seared into her cheeks as she realized she'd been caught staring.

"There's no need to be embarrassed for looking, Amalya. I fully plan on returning the favor once you're not hidden in all that water." He hooked his thumbs in the waistband of his slacks and slid them off along with his dark silk boxers in one fluid motion.

Amalya frowned as Levi bent over to pull the slacks off each foot, blocking her view of his newly revealed body. He was magnificent thus far, and she was impatient to know if his cock matched the rest of the package.

She huffed out a small breath of frustration, laughing at herself in the process. How long had it been since she'd been this anxious to see a man's cock? Three thousand years? More? She couldn't remember, which was answer enough.

Levi straightened and tossed his slacks on top of his other clothes, then slipped off his shirt and gave it the same treatment.

Amalya sucked in a breath as her gaze devoured him.

His entire body was a study in male beauty. He was fit and trim with long legs, muscular thighs, a flat stomach, and a long, thick cock that stiffened to attention under her perusal. He wasn't circumcised, which was rare in this day and age—especially here in the United States where the bulk of her business originated, but since most of her existence had been spent during times when that practice was rare, she appreciated the fine arts of pleasuring a man with foreskin still attached.

Her mouth watered as she imagined taking his hard length between her lips and running her tongue over the taut skin while she sucked him.

As her vivid mental fantasy continued, she ran her gaze over every inch of him within her sight while Levi stepped into the water, settling his large body against the other end of the tub and tangling his legs with hers.

The water level rose to within an inch of the top edge of the tub and a large sigh escaped Levi as he relaxed back and grinned at her.

Suddenly self-conscious for the first time she could remember, Amalya mentally shook herself and pulled out her full work arsenal. "You mentioned there was something you could do for *me*, Levi." She traced her toes up his inner thigh until she gently brushed against the heavy sac that hung just under his cock. "Why don't you show me?"

Levi's hazel eyes darkened to nearly black and his balls tightened against his body making a small surge of triumph snake through Amalya. She'd hated the sensation of being off balance, she liked being the one in control when it came to sex, and she knew exactly what men wanted and how to give it to them.

Without warning, Levi reached out and pulled her across the tub until she straddled him, his hard cock caught between them, nestled against her stomach and burning into her skin like a dark promise. She glanced up to find herself so close to him she could see the small scar that ran just over his right eyebrow. Her heart beat thickly inside her chest as his energy aura pulsed against her in a tempting thrum. Before she could gather her wits and think of something seductive to say, he pulled her firmly against his chest and captured her mouth with his.

The faint taste of warmed whiskey filled her senses as did the scent of something exotic, musky, and very male.

Amalya melted against him as he captured her lips in a slow, but surprisingly firm caress. His arms came around her holding her close but, rather than crushing her to him, gave the impression that she was someone to be treasured.

He sucked gently at her bottom lip, nibbling and teasing without breaking the sensual dance of their kiss.

Surprised and impressed not to be the one doing the leading, Amalya sighed against his lips and laid her palms flat over the muscled male chest in front of her.

He settled her against him more firmly, gently caging her hands between them as he explored her mouth and reactions with lips and teeth and tongue, then artfully repeated those actions that pulled an unwitting sigh, gasp, or shudder from her.

He slowly and expertly kissed her into breathlessness as she enjoyed the sensations of his mouth against hers, and his hard body beneath her. She gave herself up to the unexpected arousal he ignited, wrapping her arms around his neck and spearing her fingers into his silky hair as he continued to kiss her.

One of his large, warm hands cupped her cheek, his thumb feathering a slow, wet line back and forth across her cheek as he thoroughly explored her mouth. She gasped as the first wave of his strong, clean aura knifed into her, absorbing into her pores and converting into usable energy inside her.

Amalya closed her eyes tight against the wave of light-headedness that assaulted her from the sudden influx of strong energy—the succubus equivalent of brain freeze—and greedily kissed him back, wanting more.

Her pussy ached and she ground against his cock as the scent of their arousal perfumed the air around them, overpowering the strong aroma of vanilla and lavender from the bath salts.

Levi growled low inside his throat and in a quick motion cupped her ass in one of his large hands, then lifted and impaled her.

A long moan ripped from Amalya's throat as her body stretched to accommodate his generous girth. She slowly sank down on him until they were pelvis to pelvis and he filled her completely.

Levi stilled, and Amalya appreciated the moment to allow her body to adjust. It showed consideration for her as a person that he treated her not just as a warm body to fuck—something she didn't often find in her profession.

She brushed a quick kiss over his lips before she leaned back and began to move. Not wanting to waste the exquisite full sensation he gave her, she ground against him, rubbing her clit against the crispy hairs that covered his pelvis while her sensitive nipples rasped against his chest with each movement.

Levi's hands gripped her hips, but he let her lead, keeping her gaze as she rode him and he hardened further inside her.

Amalya set a slow, steady rhythm, refusing to move faster when their breathing became raspy and Levi's fingers tightened against her hips. She continued to move, torturing them both until the world fell away and only this one room and the two of them existed for her.

Curling heat of arousal snaked through her limbs as Levi's dark gaze bored into her own.

When the first drop of pre-come leaked from Levi's cock and came into contact with the inner walls of her pussy, a hard blast of energy surged through her and she stiffened on top of him. Her pussy clenched around him as her body absorbed the life-giving energy he offered.

As her borrowed power surged through her, she faltered and Levi moved his grip to her ass, guiding her to continue the same movements she'd begun, which drove her hard toward a peak that seemed to surge forward in a dizzying rush.

The sound of his harsh breathing merged with hers inside the small room, and it blended with the sounds of sloshing water and the rushing that sounded inside Amalya's ears from her blood rocketing through her body.

She tried to speed her movements, to meet the urgency of that edge that stayed just out of her reach, but Levi held her firmly, keeping the pace she'd started and torturing her until small whimpers of need spilled from her throat and she dug her nails into his shoulders in a silent protest.

"Patience, my beauty." His words were a harsh rasp as he began thrusting up inside her with each movement. A small scream of surprise ripped from her throat as the tip of his cock firmly made contact with her cervix again and again until Amalya was sure her body would break apart from the intense pleasure shooting along every nerve ending and threatening to overload her brain.

When she was sure she couldn't take any more, a hot surging warmth began deep inside her and spilled out into her body, seductive and enticing, until it engulfed her, blanking her mind and leaving her euphoric and boneless.

Almost distantly she heard Levi's soft cry of completion and felt the hot spurt of his release as he came inside her.

Her body absorbed Levi's essence, feeding the spreading warmth.

Tiny aftershocks quaked through her. Each one equaled an ordinary orgasm, and they continued to rock through her until they blended together to become surreal in their intensity. She lost track of time as the sweet bursts spread liquid ecstasy through her veins until she was sure she'd never be able to move again.

When awareness returned, she was slumped against Levi's chest, her face buried in the crook of his neck, her arms bonelessly draped over his muscled shoulders.

She sighed against his neck and tried to make her brain cut through the fog of endorphins and the tiny aftershocks of great sex that still twitched through her whenever she moved. The only real movement she could manage was tracing her fingers over his shoulder. When her fingers found a metal medallion on a chain, she stilled.

Amalya frowned, unable to raise her head yet. She didn't remember him wearing a necklace when he'd undressed, but her attention had definitely been on other things. She wasn't surprised she'd missed it, especially since the medallion had hung down his back rather than over his chest.

She closed her fingers over it, tracing the etching and wondering what it said.

When the sharp essence of her mistress, Lilith the Queen of the Succubi and Incubi, tingled against her fingertips, shock stabbed through her and she forced herself to sit up and meet Levi's dark gaze.

She pulled the medallion around to the front where she could see it and ice churned through her blood, chasing away the boneless euphoric sensation of just a moment ago. The medallion was sterling silver with faded ancient Hebrew characters inscribed on it that roughly translated to the current-day equivalent of "Temptation"— fitting and ironic for a succubus.

However, the last place she'd seen this necklace was hanging around the neck of her queen.

Why did Levi have this?

Dread pooled inside her stomach and she swallowed hard against all the horrible possibilities that flashed through her mind like a macabre old-time silent movie.

Movement from the doorway made Amalya snap her head around to find Jethro standing in the entranceway, a fully packed duffel in his hand.

"Is she fully energized?"

Fully energized? If she were any more energized, she'd blow the roof off the entire building!

She glanced between the two men. Anger and irritation snapped through her as she realized Jethro was talking to Levi and not her. She stiffened, and with as much dignity as she could maintain while still sitting impaled on Levi's cock, she demanded, "What the hell is going on here?"

Levi met her gaze. "I think it's time for the second part of what I can do for you, my beauty."

Amalya scrambled off Levi's lap, not caring if she snapped off his cock in the process. She stood at the other end of the tub, the water sluicing off her as she turned to face Jethro. "What's going on?"

Her friend met her gaze squarely and she thought she saw a flash of guilt before the familiar calm mask fell across those deep blue eyes—which definitely didn't bode well for the situation.

"Jethro," she said in a low tone of warning.

"Get dressed, Amalya," Levi said smoothly as he stood, "and we'll explain everything."

Amalya held out a hand to stop Levi's words and stared at Jethro, piercing him with her steady gaze until he nodded.

"According to Levi, Semiazas has escaped his prison. Lilith sent Levi to bring you back to her lair."

"It could be a trap."

Jethro sighed. "I thought of that, but Lilith sent him with more than just that medallion. She told me facts to convince me to help him. And he has a lot of information. He says two bounty demons are moving this way. One pestilence and one famine. Amalya, we can't take a chance on it not being true."

"Why did he tell you this instead of me?" she asked Jethro, pointedly ignoring the naked man in the tub.

Levi answered anyway. "We'll need Jethro's help in making it back to Lilith. It was necessary I gain his trust. Plus, Lilith told me you would be more likely to trust your guardian than a stranger. We don't have time to discuss this further. Now that you have the energy you'll need, we have to get out of here. "

Amalya took several long seconds to absorb the shock of their words.

She'd known this day would come. Semiazas would either serve his entire term and *then* hunt down her and her sisters, or he would escape early with the same result. She'd had no illusions that this would end otherwise, but that didn't make it any less terrifying. She raised her chin as she stepped out of the tub, grabbed a towel, and began drying off in rough motions. "My sisters?"

"No word." Jethro sounded apologetic.

"How close?" Levi stepped out of the tub and Amalya pointedly turned away so she wouldn't have to see his muscled body or remember what he had felt like moving inside her.

Jethro set down the full duffel and stepped inside Amalya's closet as he spoke. "We've got maybe ten minutes, give or take. They must have someone on the inside because we had no early warning on this." Anger vibrated just under the surface of his deceptively calm voice. He came back into the bathroom holding a full set of Amalya's casual clothes which he gently pushed into her arms. "Get dressed quickly." He met her gaze for a long moment and then brushed a warm finger over her cheek before he turned to face Levi. "Meet me at the side entrance when you're done."

Amalya hurriedly dressed in the jeans, tank top, and sneakers Jethro had chosen for her, then pulled the clips from her hair, letting her long, blond hair spill around her shoulders. She finger brushed the tangles out as she turned to find Levi already dressed and watching her.

"Amalya," Levi began as he dried off. "We needed you at full strength for the trip ahead and this was the best way to get it done quickly."

"It?" Anger and embarrassment moved through her, both fighting for dominance. She stiffened and glared up at him. "You mean you both decided that the poor, weak succubus couldn't be trusted with very important information that concerns her, so you took matters into your own hands to trick me into sex, supposedly for my own good?"

Levi picked up the duffel off the floor, seemingly unaffected by her words or her anger. "Is it better if I paid a lot of money for the privilege of fucking you than Jethro and I making sure you would be ready before we begin this very dangerous journey?"

His reasonable tone grated against her nerves and she stared at him with all the hatred and revulsion she could muster as the full slap of betrayal surged through her. This man had given her the best orgasm of her entire life, she'd shared her private time with him and even her real self, and it had all been an act, a job assigned to him by Lilith.

"Regardless of what you may think of me, Levi, I'm neither a fool nor a woman who is ashamed of what she is or what she does. So fuck off." She started to step away and then stopped short. "You may have considered it a freebie, but the fuck in the tub will definitely cost you, no matter what you thought when you got into this."

Levi's smug chuckle echoed gently around them. "I have very deep pockets, my beauty. Don't worry about that."

She glanced back over her shoulder as she hurried down the hall to find Jethro. "I never said it would cost you money, now did I?"

2

"Let's try this again, shall we? I can smell the damned succubus all over you, so now I just need to know where you last saw her." Semiazas had grown tired of the man's brave but ignorant act. He just wanted answers.

The man held his hands up in front of him as the putrid stink of fear poured off him in noxious waves. "I told you, I don't even know what a succubus is, so I'm not sure who you mean. If you'll just—"

Semiazas darted forward much faster than the human's eyes could track to wrap the fingers of his right hand around the man's throat.

When the man clawed at Semiazas's tight grip, the demon smiled and lifted the human off the ground until his polished Italian loafers flailed above the hardwood floor.

"Let's make this easier. Who have you fucked in the past several days?" Semiazas grinned and allowed the illusion of flames to flicker inside his eyes. Granted, it was all a bit 1970s horror movie but decidedly effective in his experience.

Understanding lit the man's eyes as he tried hard to swallow past Semiazas's grip. With a dramatic sigh, Semiazas lowered the man until his shoes touched the ground and then loosened his grip only enough to allow the human to speak. "Now. Where is my succubus?"

"I bought whores at each of my business stops. But I don't know what a succubus is," the man hissed through the limited air Semiazas let get past his grip.

Anger snaked through him and he tightened his hold on the man's throat until cartilage and flesh gave way like a ripe tomato squeezed too tight. He enjoyed the small surge of power that snaked through him at the fear and pain swimming in the man's dark eyes.

The sickening gurgle that rose from around the man's crushed throat sent frustration and disdain searing through Semiazas but definitely not a penchant for mercy. "I've been very patient. And if you really knew me, you'd understand that's not really one of my stronger points, if you get my meaning." Semiazas leaned close to the man's face and snapped his neck, enjoying the muffled crunch as bones and vertebrae snapped.

A spurt of evil glee speared through him but quickly faded when the now lifeless body slumped in his grip.

Semiazas cursed. He'd forgotten he wasn't torturing the human in Hell, which meant rather than unlimited regenerations while the man continued to feel everything acutely, now he was just a rotting meat suit.

Semiazas opened his fingers with a sigh and let the corpse drop to the floor in a heap.

Torturing and extracting information in the earthly realm had been so much easier in the Dark Ages when people were more superstitious and fearful of everything. He'd still killed and maimed, but that had been for pure enjoyment after they'd given up whatever information he'd needed at the time, if any.

He turned his wrath toward the demon who had taken the form of the dead man's roommate. "Tell me you found something before I strip your flesh off a piece at a time and send you back to Hell in a shoe box."

The demon in human form met Semiazas's gaze and nodded once. "He just returned from a four-stop business trip—San Diego, Phoenix, Vegas, and Santa Cruz. The scent of the succubus is faint, so it might have been several days since he's seen her. I'll backtrack to see if I can find anything on his credit card statements, but I'm betting he paid cash from the large wad he withdrew from the bank before he left." The demon shrugged. "Apparently, he and my host only shared an apartment to split rent, not because they were friends or confided in each other."

Semiazas fisted his hands at his sides trying to corral his temper. Regardless of what he'd threatened, killing his demons only poofed them back to Hell, which would force him to go round up more who were willing to work for him. And since he had stripped the flesh off several previously, the pool of demons who fell into that category was beginning to thin. So it was better to save his physical wrath for the humans, who were expendable and populated the planet like goddamned rabbits.

"Your Grace, he may not have known who you were referring to. Most humans wouldn't know a succubus if one bit them on the ass."

"Fine," Semiazas snapped. "If you think you can do better next time, I'll leave you to it. But find me results soon or you'll think the torture you've endured for the past millennia in Hell was a holiday next to what I'll do to you."

The demon paled before he dissipated.

Semiazas wiped his bloody fingers on the curtains and then straightened his shirt and tie before sucking in several large breaths to try to expel the last of the adrenaline surging through his system.

He had more work to do to ensure his plan played out smoothly, and getting sidetracked by his emotions wouldn't help him reach his goals. Although once he had those four succubus at his mercy . . . He let the thought trail off as images jumbled together inside his mind of what he could spend the rest of eternity doing to them.

* * *

Amalya hurried down the hallway after Jethro past rooms that she might never see again. A few women glanced up or waved as Amalya passed, and she tried her best to appear calm and happy, so as not to worry them. These women had become her friends and surrogate family, even though she had always been apart from them because of what she was. They had at least made her welcome and as much as possible treated her as one of their own.

The sound of Levi's sure footsteps behind her made her quicken her pace.

Damn both men for treating her like she was too weak to make her own decisions!

She just wished she couldn't smell the unique musky scent of Levi's arousal that still clung to her skin and hair. It was a constant reminder of how much neither man trusted her judgment. Embarrassment and anger surged through her to flame heat into her cheeks as she rounded the corner and nearly ran into Jethro's muscled chest.

He reached out to steady her and then motioned Levi forward. "Time to prove your skills, Ashford. They're closer than we thought."

Amalya frowned as she glanced between the two men, finally realizing that Ashford must be Levi's last name.

Jethro handed a leather-wrapped bundle to Levi who unrolled it to reveal a dozen wicked-looking silver daggers with polished black handles.

"Thanks for watching over these for me." Levi's tone made it clear he hadn't voluntarily given them up as he pulled each blade out of their bundle and slipped them into tiny sheaths all over him that Amalya would never have guessed were there if she hadn't watched him.

Jethro pulled out both his concealed carry guns and checked them—for ammunition, Amalya assumed. She didn't like guns and never had any desire to find out more about them.

Still angry with Jethro, she glared up at him. "Do you have mine?"

Levi stared at her as if she'd suddenly grown two heads. "Your what?"

She refused to acknowledge his question and instead held out her hand as Jethro laid her sterling silver single-action switchblade in her outstretched palm. She'd had to use it last week on a supernatural customer who had gotten a bit out of hand, and unfortunately, the trigger mechanism had been damaged in the process. Jethro had used his network of contacts to have it fixed for her.

The four-inch switchblade might not be a dozen daggers or a gun, but it had saved her enough times over the few hundred years she'd carried one that she usually felt naked without it.

Levi laid a hand on her shoulder. "Do you even know how to use that thing? Those can be dangerous."

Amalya shrugged away from his grip and opened her mouth to tell him exactly where she'd like to use her blade right now, when Jethro stepped around her to stand toe to toe with Levi.

"Let's get one thing straight right now, Ashford. I would never put Amalya in danger, which is why I'm going with her. In fact, if Lilith hadn't sent you, your ass would've been relegated to the parking lot the first time you walked through those doors."

The tension in the room skyrocketed until both men's anger vibrated against Amalya's skin like thousands of tiny ants. She glanced between them braced for more male posturing when Levi smiled and visibly relaxed. "I like you already, Jethro. I'm glad Amalya has had someone to watch her back all these years. But as I said before, you're not needed on this trip."

"Too damned bad. Because I'm not leaving Amalya's side. Take it or leave it . . . Your Grace."

Amalya stared between the two men trying to figure out the derisive nickname Jethro had just used, but her thoughts were cut short when Levi raised one dark brow as if surprised by the taunt. However, his manner told her whatever it meant, there was truth to it.

"All right then . . . peasant. Just don't get in my way of protecting her."

"You either." After another few tense seconds, Jethro relaxed, nodded, and stepped back, as if the two men had just exchanged some type of unspoken male agreement. "By the way, she's fully proficient with that blade, so I'd watch pissing her off any further if I were you."

Amalya slipped the blade into a special pocket she'd had sewn into her bra and glared back and forth between the two men. "Don't forget I'm still angry at you too, Jethro." She took a last look around the back room of Sinner's Redemption. "Wait, what about the others?"

"It's you they want." Jethro laid a gentle hand on her shoulder. "The sooner we're away from here, the safer they'll be."

Amalya wasn't so sure, but she'd demon-proofed the building the best she could when she'd first come to work here. And the women knew enough about what she was and what existed outside the realm of humanity to take care.

Amalya took a deep breath, opened the door, and rushed outside toward the staff's private parking area.

The two male shouts of protest from behind her only spurred her forward.

The bounty demons could be here any minute and she was done letting the men take the lead.

The hot Nevada sun shone down prickling against her skin after the air-conditioned climate inside. Her steps faltered as she noticed a fine misty fog floating around the edges of the building. She frowned and started forward to investigate when the Madame of Sinner's Redemption, Celine, stepped out of the limo that was used to ferry VIPs back and forth, her long red hair spilling over her shoulders, her face set into a concerned frown. "Amalya! Why are you still here?"

Amalya stepped forward to take the Madame's outstretched hands. "We're just leaving. Take care of yourself, Celine. I'll miss you." Amalya pulled the older woman into a quick hug before releasing her and stepping back.

"Maybe once everything dies down you could come back." Celine's green eyes filled with tears and she blinked them away. "You and your sisters. You would all be welcome."

Amalya grinned as she sniffed back her own tears. "I'd like that."

"Now go. Hurry." Celine pressed a set of car keys into her hands. "Take the truck, it's faster and has four-wheel drive."

The men had caught up with her and pulled her toward the truck parked next to the limo as Jethro took the keys from her hand and tossed them to Levi. "Your knives can't be used in a driving fight—you drive."

"Hey!" Amalya protested. "I'm perfectly capable of driving, you know." Before she could protest further, Jethro picked her up and slid her across the bench seat before he jumped inside the truck and pulled the door closed behind him. Levi slid into the driver's seat next to her, cutting off her renewed protests.

The truck roared to life and Levi backed out, nearly running over Celine in the hasty maneuver just as two large bounty demons came around the back of the building.

The pestilence demon was entirely covered in mottled black skin with maggots and worms crawling along its flesh in a constant sea of putrid motion. Thousands of jagged sharklike teeth glistened with venom in its huge mouth.

The famine demon was nearly seven feet tall and seemed to be made up of bones draped in dried-out corpselike skin that hung on its scarecrow frame in tatters. Its face was drawn and gray and its limbs like sticks, but Amalya knew better than to rely solely on its appearance. Any demon was dangerous, but especially bounty demons.

The two demons grabbed Celine by either arm and began to pull. "Come out and play, little succubus, and we'll let your boss go." The voice of the famine demon seemed to echo inside her thoughts as if she was in a large, empty cavern, and her skin crawled from the uncomfortable sensation.

"No!" Amalya leaned over Jethro trying to reach the door, but he held her back.

"Go, damn it," he barked to Levi.

The truck peeled out peppering Celine and the two demons with dust and gravel as Jethro captured Amalya in an iron grip.

Panic welled up in her throat and escaped in a small scream as the dust from the tires obscured the three forms they left behind. "Let me go. We can't just leave her to those things!" Hot tears burned at the backs of her eyes and she blinked them away, angry with herself for not insisting Celine come with them when she had the chance.

Jethro held her close, rocking her slowly against his hard body while Levi drove away from the place that had sheltered her for the past century.

"Amalya." Levi's voice was a soft command and she raised her head from Jethro's shoulder to look at him.

"I never told the Madame why I was here. She only knew I was a paying customer with deep pockets."

The truth of Levi's words hit her like a hard slap and she flinched.

Back in the parking lot, Celine had known she was leaving, and the urgency for her to be gone. If Levi hadn't told Celine, that meant her friend had been the one to sell her out to the bounty demons.

The pain of betrayal sliced through her like a white-hot knife to the gut and she wrapped her arms around her middle in silent defense. "No." Amalya shook her head again. "Jethro must've told her." She glanced up at Jethro, wordlessly begging him to confirm her thoughts. Anything to make it so Celine, the woman she'd loved like a sister, hadn't betrayed her.

Jethro sighed. "I'm sorry, Amalya."

As the truth of Jethro's words vibrated against her skin like a tiny warm hum, Amalya took a deep breath, shoving all her roiling emotions deep inside her where she could examine them later. Now wasn't the time to fall apart. Right now, she had to focus on getting to Lilith's lair and reuniting with her sisters. She'd worry about everything else when those two things were done.

She sat up straight, keeping as much distance as the small space would allow from the men on either side of her.

Amalya had allowed herself to grow comfortable over the past century, and if she was to survive now, she had to get back to the mind-set of always being alert and looking over her shoulder. "What's next? Where's the nearest safe portal?" It had been several centuries since she'd been back to the queen's lair, or even seen her sisters. Portals were part of the natural landscape of the universe and tended to creep or even move long distances over time. The ones she frequented in the past had most likely moved a considerable distance by now.

"That is going to be something of a challenge." Levi turned onto the main freeway, expertly maneuvering around the other cars quickly without bringing unwanted attention. "Your sister, Jezebeth, has already made it to Lilith's lair, but now the demons are watching all the portal points for the rest of you."

"You've seen Jezebeth?" Amalya turned to face him as hope blossomed inside her chest like helium.

"No." Levi cast her a quick glance before returning his gaze to the road. "Lilith mentioned it."

Jethro turned in his seat to glare at Levi. "You told me there was no word of her sisters."

Levi shrugged. "I didn't have more time to waste giving you the play-by-play when we needed to get Amalya out of there."

Anger vibrated around Jethro. "Bastard, you—"

"Stop it. Both of you." Amalya glared back and forth between them. "What's done is done, but from here forward, I need the truth from everyone." She remembered her time with Levi back in her bathroom and how everything he'd said had been true—but he still hadn't told her the entire story. "And that means no manipulations and half-truths. We have to trust each other to get through this. Agreed?"

Slowly, both men nodded and she turned her attention back to Levi. "What else do you know about my sister that you haven't told us?"

Levi maneuvered around a slow moving block of cars and merged into the fast lane. "Jezebeth and her companion, a writer named Noah Halston, made it back to the lair yesterday."

"Noah Halston, as in the horror writer?" Amalya had read several of his books. They'd given her nightmares for days afterward, but she'd always bought each book as it came out and usually read them in one sitting. "Why would Lilith send a horror writer to protect Jez?"

"Apparently, he was a good choice since she made it back in one piece." Jethro glanced toward Levi. "Better than some snobby Brit."

"This snobby Brit is perfectly capable of guiding Amalya safely to Lilith's lair without your mouthy arse along for the drive." The curse sounded odd coming from Levi's mouth and delivered in his upper-crust British accent. "It's not too late to let you out here."

Jethro laughed. "Such common language, Your Grace."

Levi's lips quirked. "As you just pointed out, I'm still a bastard."

"Stop it." Amalya gritted her teeth. "We need to concentrate on finding a safe portal point, not on bickering among ourselves." She glared at both men before turning her gaze out the front window where she scanned the freeway for any sign of demons. "What exactly did Lilith say when she sent you?"

Levi pulled the necklace out of his collar so it draped down over his tie. "She gave me this to make me immune to the effects of your succubus nature and told me to bring you back quickly and safely to her lair."

The words were all true, but pure female intuition told her there was something unspoken left hanging between them. "And?"

"And that's all she told me."

Amalya turned to glare at Levi's profile. "Then what *aren't* you telling me?"

He never took his gaze off the road as he continued to thread through slower-moving traffic and took the interchange toward a connecting freeway. "It's nothing Lilith told me."

Jethro huffed out a derisive laugh. "So much for the total honesty and trusting each other."

Levi glanced at both of them before returning his gaze to the road. "It may not even be true. It's only a rumor." He laid a gentle hand on Amalya's leg and she fought against the comforting warmth that slid through her from the contact.

She stiffened under his touch until he moved his hand. She bit back an audible sigh of relief from the release of the unwelcome sensations of closeness. "Then tell us and we'll decide together if it's pertinent to us getting back to the lair."

Levi gave a Gallic shrug. "The rumors are that someone is trying to jump-start Armageddon."

"What does that have to do with Amalya and her sisters?"

"Maybe nothing." Levi glanced at Jethro. "But I don't know of anyone else powerful enough or angry enough in the demonic realm to call the horsemen except for Semiazas."

"What about Lucifer?" Jethro countered.

Amalya shook her head. "No. He wants the world to continue. If Armageddon comes and the world is no more, then he and the other fallen don't have anywhere to go."

"Agreed." Levi shifted in his seat and tapped the steering wheel with one finger as if it helped him think. "It just seems a large coincidence that Semiazas is the most likely candidate, and he's also the one after the four sisters. And there are *four* horsemen."

Something tickled at the back of Amalya's mind, but she couldn't bring it into focus. "What are you saying?"

Levi sighed. "I'm not sure. But there are no coincidences—especially when supernaturals are involved. And especially when the supernaturals involved are high level."

Jethro waved away the comments. "Since we don't know any of that for sure, let's stick to the problem at hand. How do we find out where all the portal points are and choose one that will give the least resistance for us to pass through?"

Amalya's temples began to throb as if her thoughts didn't want to coalesce inside her mind. She glanced up through the front wind-shield in time to see a sudden wall of misty white fog looming in front of them. She wondered why there was more here than there was back at Sinner's Redemption. From a purely scientific perspec-tive, Nevada weather wasn't right for fog or mist. "What's—"

Her words were cut short when Levi swerved to the side, shifting into four-wheel drive and cutting across the grass strip of land that separated the freeway from a nearby cotton farm.

The sounds of screeching tires and crunching metal rose behind them snaking icy fear through Amalya's belly. The mist was causing the cars to crash into one another. Where was it coming from?

As they hit the edge of the farm and their tires went up and over the large berm that separated the farm from the strip of land the city owned next to the freeway, Amalya cringed at the sounds of crunching under the tires that told her they were ruining the nearly grown crops. She wasn't ready to trade her life for the cotton, but she felt for the poor farmer who would have the aftermath to con-tend with.

Fuzzy nearly translucent shapes were scattered across the farm in front of them, and Amalya blinked to bring them into better focus. They almost looked like . . . people.

"Shades," Levi supplied.

Jethro braced his arm against the front dash as they bumped along over the farmland. "Shades of what?"

As the figures came into closer view and the SUV drove right through them, Amalya was able to make out some of their features. "Shades of the dead," she said as understanding began to dawn. "Earthbound spirits."

"What the hell?" Jethro craned his neck to study the next one they passed by. "Are they dangerous?"

Levi navigated around a water line and headed toward the

gravel road that ran between two fields. "Not necessarily, but as we saw back on the freeway, they can be a distraction, which can cause problems."

Amalya rubbed at the small throb that had begun at her temples. The mysterious mist was shades and drivers swerving to avoid them were causing terrible accidents. She spoke her next thought aloud. "And if people can now see the shades, then they might be able to hear them as well, which could cause mischief."

"Define mischief."

She cringed as they drove through the shade of a small child. "All of the shades have some type of issue that's kept them from moving on. Some are confused, some stayed to watch over a loved one, some are angry or want revenge, and many more are afraid they won't get into Heaven for the things they've done, so they choose to stay."

Jethro ran a hand through his hair, leaving behind a sexy, sandy blond tousled look that made Amalya smile. "So, can anyone share why there are suddenly a bunch of ghosts with issues everywhere?"

"They've always been here." Amalya thought about how lonely it must've been for them, walking the earth with very few of those alive able to see or even sense them. "Just most beings aren't able to see them."

Jethro sighed. "So what do we do now?"

The SUV fishtailed as Levi took a sharp right past a large red barn and guided them onto the road that ran past a rustic two-story farmhouse. A wall of white fog speared up in front of them and Levi cursed as the truck passed through the thick mist, then sputtered and died.

Hard, cold urgency speared through Amalya and she unbuckled her seat belt. "Get to the farmhouse."

Jethro grabbed her arm. "What's going on?"

She popped open his seat belt buckle and met his blue gaze. "Trust me. Run."

Levi jumped out of the car and helped Amalya out, urging her ahead of him.

Glad Jethro had chosen tennis shoes for her to wear, she dodged around the eerie ethereal forms that rose in front of her or suddenly appeared in her path.

A slimy, cool sensation chilled her shoulder and she cringed away only to have the same eerie touch slant across her belly and down her legs. She ran harder, the uncomfortable sensation slapping her again and again on various parts of her body and her energy slowly siphoned away by contact with the shades.

She blinked hard and stumbled as a sudden wave of lethargy washed over her.

Shades often took energy from the living in order to manifest or in some way affect the physical world. But she'd never heard about them being so aggressive.

The sound of one of the men stumbling behind her sent a flash of hot panic through her gut and she slowed to turn back and help them.

"Run, damn it," Jethro rasped. "We'll catch up."

Amalya turned to find Jethro on his knees in the dirt, a thick wall of shades closing in from all sides—so thick she couldn't make out their individual features. Levi was only a few steps behind, but it was clear from his slow movements and the glazed expressions on both men's faces that neither man would last much longer without help.

Being drained of all her energy wouldn't kill Amalya, or so she hoped, but it could kill a human and a half human within minutes.

Such a state would leave her more vulnerable to beings that

could kill her, but hopefully if the men were safe, they could figure out something to restore her long before that happened.

Amalya spread her arms wide, opening her energy and pushing it forward so it surrounded her like a solid blanket, turning herself into a spotlight beacon for the shades.

As she'd hoped, the wall of entities began to float toward her and leave the men. "To the farmhouse. Find salt," she yelled as she darted forward, away from the farmhouse and back toward the road.

Cursing behind her confirmed the men didn't approve of her plan, but since they obviously didn't have anything better, they'd just have to follow her lead. Hopefully one of them would know what to do with the salt once they found it.

Amalya ran full-out, dodging as many shades as she could and trying not to sprain her ankle as she ran over the furrows that striped along the cotton field. The nearly grown cotton stalks scratched against the sensitive skin of her arms, snagging against her jeans and slowing her progress until she stumbled. She windmilled her arms trying to catch her balance but lost the fight as she fell on her knees in the dirt.

A large wave of ice slid through her as if she were being slowly dipped into arctic waters. She had a moment to hope that Jethro and Levi had made it to safety, another quick moment to hope her sisters were still safe, and then her awareness slid away.

3

The Archangel Uriel stared across the street at the seedy bar called the Badass Café. The two-story brick building was tucked into a strip mall between an adult bookstore and a massage parlor that offered much more than massages to anyone who could pay. A combination of heavy metal and classic rock blared from the storefronts, making the sidewalk vibrate beneath his feet.

A cold, drizzled rain pattered against the sputtering streetlights so the only real illumination came from the glaring neon signs over each establishment, strobing over the swirling sea of humanity that spilled out of all three doorways and onto the sidewalk out front.

Ignoring the hostile looks cast his way, Uriel stepped in between two parked cars to make his way across the street. He'd tracked another journal to this place, which meant he would soon be one step closer to understanding the Armageddon prophecies.

Strong fingers closed around his arm as something hard and metal pressed into his side.

Uriel froze. A bullet wouldn't kill or even incapacitate him, but it would be damned inconvenient to deal with right now. He had been so focused on retrieving the journal, he hadn't bothered to think that coming to this part of town wearing a designer suit and an expensive-looking trench coat might bring him unwanted attention.

Stupid, he chided himself. He knew better but had let the prize of the journal blind him to that probability.

He turned to look at his assailant. The man was Caucasian with a touch of something exotic that gave him an olive complexion, high cheekbones, and full lips that would instantly label him as the much sought after "bad boy" by most women. He wore a grimy black leather jacket that reeked of Jack Daniel's and his eyes were bloodshot and wild. He looked about thirty, but from the energy aura that surrounded him, Uriel would bet he was much younger.

"Welcome to Hell, pretty boy. Hand over your wallet."

Uriel raised an eyebrow as he stared down at the man. "I don't carry a wallet. I'll give you one chance to move on, but that's all I have time for right now."

A gravelly laugh accompanied the barrel of the gun being pressed harder against Uriel's ribs. "Listen, rich man, this is *your* last chance before I blow a hole in your side. Hand over the wallet. You don't want to test my patience." A frantic edge crept into the man's voice as he glared at Uriel.

Uriel stared into the man's dark eyes and peered closer, opening his senses so he could see inside the man's soul.

Knowledge, pain, and darkness rushed forward in an icy, murky flood telling Uriel everything about the man before him.

Uriel sighed and shook his head. An addict. What a waste.

The man stumbled as the effects of the soul gaze kicked in, freezing him in place.

Uriel steadied him and, with his free hand closed his fingers around the gun, pointing it away from his side.

Uriel touched the man's forehead calling forward the dark addiction that held him.

The addiction resisted, digging in and refusing to release its hold on its host. It had existed inside this man for years and resented giving up someone it had worked so hard to master.

Many humans thought addiction was an actual demon that lived inside them. And while addiction did share many traits with the demonic realm, it was created purely by human free will and had to be destroyed the same way.

Except when one of the Heavenly Hosts stepped in, although even with that intervention, addiction couldn't totally be banished without human consent.

Uriel concentrated, calling the addiction forth until it loosened its hold and finally seeped through the man's forehead and pooled in Uriel's hand like a baseball made of thick black tar.

The man in front of him whimpered, the only reaction to Uriel's sudden intrusion.

A small sense of triumph curled through Uriel and he closed his fingers around the ball, crushing it until it shattered, sprinkling to the wet ground as black specks of dust. "Henry," Uriel said using the name he'd plucked out of the man's mind during the soul gaze. "I'll take the gun. You need to go home."

Henry loosened his grip on the gun and Uriel slipped it inside the pocket of his jacket.

Henry stumbled back but seemed unable to go farther. "Who the hell are you?"

"Who I am doesn't matter. I've taken the addiction from you, but you'll have to make the choice not to use again. I can't affect free will." Uriel pointed north toward where Henry lived with his pregnant wife. "Go. That's all I have time for tonight."

"Who the fuck are you?" Henry's pain-wracked question was a mere whisper, but Uriel heard it easily through the blaring Metallica coming from just across the street.

"I'm your second chance." He met Henry's gaze again for a long moment. "Don't waste it." Uriel walked across the street not bothering to watch to see what Henry would do. He'd given up long ago letting human choices get to him. Too often they took their second chances or even third, fourth, or forty-fourth to make the same poor choices again.

Uriel would always hope this one would be different, but sometimes it was best if he kept the hope and didn't bother to find out for certain. He was afraid that the actual statistics might be much too discouraging to ponder.

He walked purposely through the crowd, which parted before him. He wasn't sure if it was because they'd seen his run-in with Henry or if they felt his presence. There were some sensitive humans among the crowd who hadn't ruined their gifts by drowning them with alcohol and drugs. He'd bet most of them were just very adept at sensing the predator versus the prey, which was how they survived.

When he reached the open doorway to the Badass Café, he ducked inside.

A thick haze instantly assaulted him from all sides, a suffocating combination of tobacco, various types of drugs, and the smoke from the dry ice machine that sat under the DJ's booth. Uriel sent a silent thanks to his Father that he didn't have to breathe to survive, and he planned on putting that into action unless he had to speak, which unfortunately required him to breathe to force air through his vocal chords.

Sometimes taking human form definitely had its drawbacks.

He threaded his way through the gyrating crowd until he made his way to the bar. Patrons parted on either side to let him through.

The bartender handed out a drink and then turned a bored gaze toward Uriel. "Cop?" he yelled to be heard over the music.

"No." Uriel shook his head in case the bartender had trouble hearing him.

"Then you're looking to get your ass kicked wearing that in here." The bartender motioned to Uriel's suit. "Hell, even if you were a cop, you're asking for it."

"Duly noted. I'm looking for T-Bone." Which was the name of the contact who had acquired the journal.

"And who are you?"

"Uriel," he said simply and resisted the urge to use a soul gaze to find the information he wanted. He could subdue the entire room if need be, but causing that much of an obviously supernatural disruption within the human realm would only add to the growing hysteria. Ever since the shades had appeared and portions of the oceans and even some lakes had begun to boil, all those with a doomsday message were cashing in on the growing fear. A crowd mentality among the greater part of the human population would only ensure more people were hurt or killed, which is something Uriel hoped to avoid.

The bartender studied him for a long moment before motioning to a man at the end of the bar who looked like the poster boy for "I just got out of prison." He was at least three hundred pounds of solid muscle. His head was smooth shaven, a tattoo of a skull and crossbones done in green on the back and sides of his skull. One-inch black gauges that looked like intricate hubcaps stretched his earlobes and there were no fewer than twenty piercings peppering the rest of his face and neck.

Uriel was thankful for his supernatural vision, otherwise he wouldn't be able to see much besides a murky figure at the end of the bar past all the smoke. He materialized a hundred-dollar bill inside his jacket pocket and then slid it onto the bar toward the bartender before edging through the crowd toward the man he assumed to be T-Bone.

The man eyed him suspiciously as he closed the distance between them but didn't budge from his stance where he leaned indolently against the bar, an open bottle of Budweiser next to his elbow.

"T-Bone?" Uriel asked when he made it close enough to be heard over the music.

"Depends," came the surly answer as the man gave Uriel an up-and-down glance and sneered at what he saw.

"I'm Uriel. I'm here for the journal." He tried to ignore the incessant tickle at the back of his throat from all the combined smoke he'd just inhaled in order to speak.

"Do you have payment?"

"Do you have the journal?" Uriel countered.

T-Bone smiled revealing a gold front tooth with a glittering diamond set into it. "What makes you think I won't just take the payment, buttercup, and send you packing?"

Uriel bit back his impatience and met the man's gaze, glad he didn't have to steady him when the man used his leaning stance on the bar to hold himself upright.

A cold rush of fear, bravado, and survival emanated from the man along with all the details of his life.

This wasn't T-Bone but a bouncer of sorts for the real fence. This man had been wrongly accused of a robbery as a teen and was put into the prison system to survive, or not, on his own. He'd responded by bulking up, becoming a bully, and training himself how to be a predator. Weakness of any type reminded him of himself back when he'd first been tossed into jail, so he tended to react violently to any sign of it in anyone else—a psychological need to destroy what he hated about his old self.

"Sidney, I need to see T-Bone, now."

The man's eyes grew round and then narrowed into a glare as he straightened and stood toe to toe with Uriel. "Who the fuck are you? I don't know any Sidney."

"Sidney is your name. Your *real* name."

Fists double the size of Uriel's clenched at Sidney's sides. "You don't know shit about me, man."

"I know you were innocent of that burglary that landed you in the system when you were sixteen. I also know what you had to do to survive, especially when not even your family would stand behind you. I know the terror you felt and still feel but lock away until you think no one sees it and ever will."

Sidney threw a right hook hard enough to knock any human on his ass.

Uriel reacted quickly, ducking back and catching the oncoming fist in his palm the same way he would catch a baseball.

The sudden stop of motion reverberated back down Sidney's arm and the first metallic stench of fear emanated from him. No human would notice since Sidney had honed his reactions over the years purely to survive. But Uriel was definitely not human.

Sidney dropped his hand and studied Uriel for a long moment. "Who the fuck are you, man? How do you know who I am?" The last sentence was said so softly that no one save a supernatural would be able to hear it.

Uriel softened his gaze. "I'm someone who wants to barter in good faith for the journal. Once I have that, I won't remember you at all." The implication that Uriel wouldn't share his knowledge of Sidney's real name or anything else hung between them like a tangible promise.

Sidney stared back at Uriel as if measuring the truth of the unspoken words. Uriel was impressed Sidney would even meet his gaze after undergoing the soul gaze. Most beings were leery of looking at him after that. But then, Sidney had trained himself to show no fear and face things head-on—something that had allowed him to thrive in his new circumstances.

After several tense seconds, Sidney nodded, but he continued to boldly hold Uriel's gaze. "Down the hall, the room just before the bathroom. Tell him Diesel vetted you." He glared at Uriel as if daring him to say anything about the name he'd been dubbed with back in prison.

"Thank you . . . Diesel." Uriel materialized another hundred-dollar bill inside his pocket and slipped it to Sidney as he started past him.

Sidney laid a hand on Uriel's shoulder. "If you ever come here again, man, dress the part. You stand out like a lone virgin in a whorehouse dressed like that."

Uriel grinned. "Duly noted. It does tend to make people underestimate me."

Sidney huffed out a laugh and shook his head. "Get outta here, man." He chucked a thumb over his shoulder toward the hallway where T-Bone waited.

Uriel walked down the hallway sidestepping a man who had passed out and looked like he'd been rolled off to one side to sleep it off. When he reached the door Sidney had indicated, Uriel slowly turned the knob and pushed the door inward. A slice of light spilled from the open doorway along with the promise of cleaner, clearer air.

Uriel stepped inside to find a man who looked like a cross between

Harry Potter and an accountant. The spindly man wore rumpled unmatched clothes, round dark glasses, and a persistent frown. He sat behind a desk with a large calculator, a state of the art computer, monitor, and several neatly stacked books and ledgers.

He glanced up as Uriel stepped inside closing the door behind him. "Diesel vetted me. Are you T-Bone?"

The man nodded, his Adam's apple working overtime in his skinny throat. "And you are?"

"Uriel. I've come for the journal."

T-Bone leaned back in the office chair, which squeaked as it reclined. He held a well-chewed pencil between the tips of the fingers of both hands and studied Uriel, careful not to meet his gaze. "What's it worth to you?"

"What would you like?"

"I'd like a lot of things that someone like you could provide." His gaze stayed squarely on Uriel's chin.

Uriel smiled. T-Bone's aura told him that the man in front of him was very sensitive and somehow knew about the soul gaze. "Someone like me?"

"An Archangel. If you were just a human, we'd be talking dollars, drugs, guns, or something else tangible. But with you, I think we're on a different barter scale." He shrugged. "After all, if I have something that an Archangel can't get on his own, then it's got to be very rare and valuable."

Uriel sat without being invited. The stained chair was as uncomfortable as it looked and Uriel suspected it was that way on purpose to give whoever sat here a distinct disadvantage. "What type of things did you have in mind. Even as an Archangel some things are not within my power to give."

"And some you won't. I totally understand." T-Bone leaned forward, the office chair squeaking again with the movement. "What

I want is purely personal and won't affect anyone else's free will, won't endanger the balance between good and evil, and according to my research, is definitely within the purview of one such as yourself."

"Your research?" Uriel raised a single brow as he waited for T-Bone's answer. Other than the Bible and some scattered sources, there were only myths and legends with bare snippets of truth about him in them.

"The journals."

"You have more than one?" Uriel asked calmly.

T-Bone shook his head. "Only the one in my possession. But the information the previous one contained is still available for a price."

Uriel nodded not surprised the information still existed even though he'd recovered that journal. The information age made it highly improbable that purely laying hands on the journal itself would stop the information from getting out. But having the original did ensure he was dealing with the correct translations and the original text that they held.

"I'm not interested in secondhand information. Only the original journals interest me."

Anticipation sparked inside T-Bone's eyes and his expression turned shrewd. "I have one journal in my possession and I can contact you if any others come into my hands . . . for a price."

"Which is?"

"I've been blessed with brains and an awareness of some things beyond the purely human realm. However, I was saddled with this body."

"You want a new body?"

"Not all of it. I only want certain parts enhanced if you get my meaning."

Uriel frowned. "You want me to enhance the size of your penis."

"Yeah, man. Skinny white guy with book smarts isn't exactly a chick-magnet scenario." He held his hands out to his side, palms up. "If I go for the whole package overhaul, I'd have too much explaining to do and I'd have to fight to prove my dominance. When other guys see a big guy, they always want to kick his ass to prove where they are in the pecking order. I have no desire to get into all those pissing contests. I'm the brains and I know how to make a shitload of money, and the big guys respect that. But if I have something substantial to offer the ladies . . ."

Uriel nodded as the entire picture came clear. "You do understand that size really isn't everything? Skill, patience, and the willingness to be a very giving lover play a large part." He shook his head at the odd turn the conversation had taken.

T-Bone waved away Uriel's advice. "I get that, man. But without the lure, not very many ladies will even give me the chance to hone my skills, if you know what I mean. I can pay for play, but I'd like a woman to be there willingly. Besides, I'd like the chance to build up that skill on my own, if you know what I mean." T-Bone gave Uriel a leering grin that told him the man needed to hone more than just his sexual skills.

Uriel bit back the urge to explain the dichotomy between T-Bone wanting a woman to desire him for himself and the necessity to have a "lure" to pique her interest. But Uriel needed the journal, and what T-Bone asked was easily within his ability to grant it. He didn't have time to debate the philosophical issues or wisdom of wishing for a larger cock with a fence named T-Bone. "Do you have the journal?"

T-Bone unlocked his top desk drawer and pulled out a slim leather journal with a worn blue cover. He held it up and wiggled it back and forth in the air between them. "Right here. Do we have a deal?"

"If that is the journal I seek, then we have a deal." He held out his hand and waited until T-Bone laid the journal on his outstretched palm. As soon as he touched it, he knew this was the right journal. The words written within had power and just like the other one, that power beat against his hand in tangible waves.

For appearance's sake, he flipped through the pages, impatient to find some time to spend reading the journal and deciphering its messages.

He glanced across the desk at T-Bone as he secreted the journal away inside an inner pocket of his suit jacket. "Imagine what you'd like vividly inside your mind and it will be yours. But make sure that's what you really want. There is no return policy on a gift such as this."

T-Bone grinned and stood as he held out a hand to Uriel. "I've been imagining exactly what I'd like for a long time." He shook Uriel's hand with a clammy palm and weak grip. "Nice doing business with you. How do I contact you if I find another journal?"

"A simple prayer using my name will be enough to summon me. Good luck." As Uriel closed the door behind him, he heard the distinctive sound of a zipper unzipping and shook his head, glad he would miss the unveiling.

4

Semiazas.

Uriel sensed him as soon as he stepped out into the hallway. The fallen's energy signature was as familiar to Uriel as Raphael's or Gabriel's or Michael's. After all, until the mutiny against their Father, in which Semiazas followed Lucifer, Semiazas was a cherished brother and friend. But too many eons of betrayal and bad blood stood between them now to ever reconcile things back to the way they had been.

Resigned to the conflict ahead, Uriel walked down the hallway past Sidney and back into the waiting bar.

Semiazas stood in the center of the room, a caricature of a biker badass. The strobing neon lights from the bar signs flashed illumination over him at different intervals, making him look even more menacing.

Whereas his normal form was tall and graceful, the one he resided in now was stocky and bulky, easily two times Diesel's size and muscle. His normally dark medium-length hair was now close cropped and tattoos covered every inch of exposed skin including his face and neck. He wore black leather from head to toe including shit-kicker boots, which reminded Uriel of Raphael's normal outfit of choice.

The humans had stepped back away from Semiazas leaving a several-foot clear circle around him. A quick gesture from Semiazas and the thumping music died away leaving only a strained silence inside the close-packed bar.

"Uriel." Semiazas sketched a courtly bow, which looked odd in his present form. "I've been waiting for you. All that business with T-Bone's cock all cleared up?"

A titter flowed through the watching crowd at the obvious implication.

"Did you let him have a test run? Is that what took you so long in there?"

Unconcerned with the glances and derisive sounds sent his way, Uriel kept the demon's gaze while staying alert to every person in the bar. "What can I do for you, Semiazas? I have pressing business elsewhere."

Semiazas laughed. "I'll just bet you do." He thrust his hips forward several times as if air humping someone in front of him. The appreciative crowd laughed but kept the volume low as if afraid to miss any of the byplay between the two.

Uriel sighed. The necessity of dealing with Semiazas's dramatics grated on his nerves. Semiazas had always been this way, even before the fall, although he'd gotten even more irritating since then. "Interesting costume. A little cliché, don't you think?"

"You don't like it?" Semiazas glanced down at himself as if admiring a new suit. "It works for Sidney over there." He gestured toward the man who stiffened and glared as the crowd laughed and jeered.

Sidney started forward and Uriel held out a hand, stopping the man's forward motion. "He's mine, Diesel," he said pointedly using the man's chosen name.

Sidney didn't look happy about it, but he slowly nodded and stepped back. "I'll take whatever's left of him when you're done, man. Besides, I want to see a dude fight in those fancy threads you've got going on."

The crowd laughed, a general murmur of agreement flowing around the room.

Uriel knew Semiazas hadn't come for the journal. The information contained inside had already made its way into the world. His reasons for being here had to be for something else, although with Semiazas the reason could be anything between something of huge significance all the way down to pure boredom. "What do you want, Semiazas?"

"I want so many things, none of which you are either willing or able to give me." He shrugged, dark amusement shining in his eyes. "Why is that, Uriel?"

"Because you want things you've no right to." Uriel knew he shouldn't be drawn in to a banter session with Semiazas, but he wanted to try to find some way to diffuse the violence he knew the demon was trying to incite inside the tiny bar.

"You know what I think?" Semiazas countered. "I think it's because you're frustrated. Frustrated because you don't have the mojo to keep your woman happy. Is that why she left you for a woman?"

The resulting "oooh" from the crowd ratcheted the tense atmosphere, and Uriel sighed at the senseless violence he knew was coming regardless of what he did in the next few minutes. Semiazas wanted nothing less than a bloody, violent bar fight.

"Is that what forced you to come here and let a skinny-assed geek like T-Bone bend you over a desk to get off?"

The jeers from the crowd reached a full-scale frenzy until Semiazas held up his hand to quiet his growing group of supporters.

"This is between you and me. Leave everyone else out of it." Uriel meant the humans who stood to be hurt from the coming conflict, but he knew to the crowd it sounded like he was defending himself against Semiazas's accusations.

"But they're very much a part of this, Uriel. Lilith has had to resort to fucking Gabriel full-time, you know. In fact, they're together right now. Two beautiful women." He grabbed his crotch and rubbed his hard cock through the tight leathers. "I can just picture all those ripe, lush curves pressed together as they both wished you had balls enough to wade in and fuck them both properly."

The taunt hit home, and without thinking Uriel tossed back, "At least I'd be welcome between either of their thighs if I chose. Didn't Gabriel ban you from her bed long ago? And Lilith has never even offered."

Semiazas's form wavered as actual fire flashed from his eyes. Uriel had definitely pressed the right button to throw the fallen off his game.

The crowd of humans took a collective step back as an aura of pure evil crackled through the bar. Even those with no sensitivity probably felt the neck ruffling sensation that was hardwired inside every human to recognize evil.

Semiazas's form solidified as he gained control of his temper. "That was because Gabriel still doesn't see the truth, but she will. All of you soon will. But right now it's down to you and me . . . brother."

Uriel's temper flared. "Don't ever call me that. You've no right," he bit out.

"You can't choose your family, or deny them, Uriel. No matter how much our Father wishes it so."

"Enough." Uriel made a slashing gesture in the air in front of him. "I'm done with this, Semiazas. This fight is between you and me. Leave everyone else out of it."

"*You don't make these rules. I do . . . brother,*" Semiazas said inside Uriel's mind. Out loud he said, "Free will is a wondrous thing." He grinned, his gaze locked onto Uriel's face. "To every person here who brings me a piece of Uriel, I'll give a thousand dollars."

There was a split second of shock as the crowd digested the meaning behind Semiazas's offer before they began to close in on Uriel from all sides, separating him from Semiazas with a sea of humanity.

Uriel cursed under his breath as he materialized his twin daggers. The same daggers that had meted out the justice his Father had decreed since well before the very first human had walked the planet.

His anger flared and he let loose his power that he usually dampened so he blended in better walking among the humans.

Energy crackled the air so thick every person in the room now knew he was something more than he'd first appeared, but that did little to thin the surrounding crowd. "Think about what you do and make your choice. No mercy will be given if you choose this path freely." As soon as his words died away, he anchored his left foot and kicked out in a wide arc with his right driving back the crowd while he slashed out with his daggers, slicing a path around him and felling several humans in the process. Those left standing lunged back just out of his reach as the injured crawled or were pulled back away from the battle.

The crowd around him thinned only a little now that he'd proved himself capable of fighting back. Although the biggest and strongest found their way to the front, the others hoping to take advantage of any injuries those in front of them could inflict on him.

Uriel resisted the urge to glare at Semiazas. The effort would be wasted and he had enough to keep him busy right here. Someone jumped him from behind, knocking him forward into those unlucky enough to try and attack from the front.

Uriel let his anger flow and began to fight in earnest. Reaching back, careful to keep his grip on his dagger, he grabbed the man still clinging to his back. He yanked the man forward, over his head and tossed him into the crowd in front of him, knocking them back. Others closed in, but Uriel let his instincts take over, kicking, punching, dodging, slashing in a fluid motion that only millennia of fighting could bring.

It took less than a minute to scatter the sea of human bodies around him and make his way to where Semiazas had stood, but not surprisingly, the fallen had disappeared.

Uriel sensed movement behind him and whirled to find Sidney grabbing his would-be assailant by the back of the jacket and delivering a hard knee to the gut. The man's air whooshed out and Diesel dropped him to the ground.

Uriel met Sidney's gaze. "Thank you."

Sidney stepped close and held out his hand. "You're the first person to ever say I didn't do that robbery all those years ago. I hadn't realized how much it would mean to me to have someone . . . anyone say that. I'm in your debt."

Uriel shook Sidney's hand. "Let's call it even." He nodded toward the man Sidney had just downed.

"You could've handled him yourself. Just call it a token gesture of thanks, man."

Uriel nodded his agreement and walked out of the bar, stepping over injured humans who still cluttered the path. Outside, everyone gave him a wide berth and he strode across the street back to where he'd started.

He had the journal, now he needed to shut himself away and study its entries. He should go straight home and get to work.

But something else vied for his attention besides the weight of the leather journal in the breast pocket of his suit coat.

Memories of Semiazas's taunting words about Lilith and Gabriel rang in his ears churning acid through his gut. Which was exactly what the fallen had hoped to do—distract Uriel.

"Damn it. It's fucking working."

* * *

The Archangel Gabriel materialized just outside Lilith's quarters and knocked lightly, anticipation jangling inside her belly. She hadn't seen Lilith in nearly twelve hours, and the Queen of the Succubi and Incubi had become something of an obsession for her over the past few days.

With all the odd happenings lately, Armageddon might be coming sooner rather than later, so Gabriel vowed to take what happiness she could before the end of the human realm came.

The door in front of her opened to reveal a stunning succubus with long chestnut hair that fell in waves past her well-shaped ass. Her eyes were the color of rich milk chocolate and her skin held the ethereal perfection all the succubi shared.

"Jezebeth." Gabriel nodded in greeting. The succubus before her had been the first of the four sisters to make it back safely to Lilith's lair with her protector, Noah.

Jezebeth nodded and dropped her gaze—a sign of respect. "Gabriel. Please, come in." She held the door wide and stepped back so Gabriel could enter.

Lilith sat in an overstuffed chair near the fire, her feet tucked up under her, her black hair pinned on top of her head as if she soon planned a dip in the swirling hot springs that graced the back corner of her quarters. Sexy, long tendrils of hair had escaped the clip to wisp around Lilith's heart-shaped face, and Gabriel tightened her hands into fists to keep from plunging her fingers into the silky mass while Jezebeth was still in the room.

Gabriel's recent time spent in Lilith's quarters had to be a well-known "secret" among the denizens of Lilith's lair, but Gabriel wouldn't tarnish Lilith's authority by flaunting it in front of anyone, especially since Lilith had been through enough already during her long existence.

The Archangel Uriel had interceded for Lilith back at the Garden of Eden and vowed before God that he would keep her supplied with sustenance so she could survive. To further complicate matters, relations between the Archangels and any other nonhumans, including each other, were forbidden. It had been difficult for Uriel to reconcile his two sets of vows until he'd found a loophole. He facilitated sexual sessions between Lilith and others, including humans, demons, and a whole host of other supernaturals. He watched and pleasured himself but didn't participate. The sexual energy he gave off from his completion was more than enough to feed Lilith and still technically stayed within the boundaries of his vows.

The complicated relationship between Uriel and Lilith meant both had spent countless miserable millennia owing to Uriel's adherence to his vows before God.

Finally, last week, Lilith had decided she'd hurt Uriel and herself enough and had asked Uriel to send Gabriel to her . . . alone.

The past week had been the happiest Gabriel could remember. And while she still harbored guilt over enjoying relations with another supernatural, she had found her own loophole. Since she and Uriel were close, Uriel had bid her come and care for Lilith as he would himself, which gave her leeway inside that same loophole Uriel had used.

Lilith glanced up, and as her gaze met Gabriel's, a slow smile spread across her face.

The intensity in that dark gaze sent slivers of arousal stirring across Gabriel's skin and she licked her lips as her nipples tightened into hard buds and moisture slicked between her thighs.

Lilith slowly stood, the yellow, flowing dress she wore offering tantalizing glimpses of the soft curves beneath. She glanced toward the succubus who had answered the door. "Jezebeth, let me know as soon as you have more information about what we discussed. Leave us now."

"Yes, my queen." Jezebeth slowly backed out of the room, shutting the door behind her and leaving Gabriel alone with Lilith.

When silence fell between them, the sexual tension in the room skyrocketed, buzzing against Gabriel's skin like static electricity. She walked slowly forward, enjoying the sudden musky scent of Lilith's arousal that perfumed the air. "I've missed you."

Lilith grinned and quickly closed the distance between them, sliding her arms around Gabriel's waist and smiling up at her across the two inches that separated them in height.

Gabriel molded Lilith's soft curves against her own and slowly lowered her face until their lips were so close, she could feel Lilith's warm breath against her mouth. The scent of gardenia and cinnamon that always clung to Lilith filled Gabriel's senses and she sighed as she gently brushed her lips over Lilith's.

The succubus immediately opened for her, wordlessly begging for more, and Gabriel dipped her tongue inside to tease and explore.

Lilith tasted of dark, forbidden spices—unique and tempting—and Gabriel cupped Lilith's cheeks, deepening the kiss, enjoying the small tremors that rocked the smaller woman in front of her.

A small moan sounded inside the room and Gabriel wasn't sure if it had come from Lilith or herself. And right now, she didn't care. The recent time apart from Lilith had been spent aching for the queen's touch and the exquisite sensation of the succubus's mouth against her own.

Lilith traced a path along Gabriel's rib cage until she found the front buttons of Gabriel's fitted shirt. As the fabric of her shirt loosened, Gabriel unhooked the clip holding Lilith's hair and freed the wavy mass to fall around Lilith's shoulders. She speared her fingers into the silky waves enjoying the vivid memory of how the soft weight had felt rubbing against her bare skin.

Lilith peeled the shirt from Gabriel's arms, forcing her to drop her hands as the shirt fell to the floor and left her bare from the waist up. As the cool air hit her breasts, her nipples puckered and she ached for the succubus's touch.

Gabriel reached forward and pulled the tie at Lilith's neck that cinched the flowing dress and held it up. The yellow fabric loosened and slowly slithered down over Lilith's full breasts, pausing, as if purposely teasing Gabriel and hiding Lilith's bare skin from view, before it gave way, sliding down the rest of those sensuous curves and leaving her gloriously naked to Gabriel's hungry gaze.

She allowed herself to look her fill for a long moment, savoring the anticipation of what was to come.

Lilith smiled and cocked her head to the side, backing toward the oversized bed as she beckoned Gabriel closer. "I couldn't wait for you to come back. I've been fantasizing about this all day."

Gabriel caught up just as the backs of Lilith's legs bumped against the mattress. Impatience and urgency snapped through her and Gabriel pulled Lilith close, her breasts pressing against the plush softness of Lilith's. "I much prefer the reality." She wrapped one arm around Lilith and captured her mouth as she slowly lowered her backward onto the bed.

The mattress gave under their combined weight, cradling them as Gabriel sank against Lilith's soft curves. She slid one knee between Lilith's thighs so her full weight didn't press down on her.

The scent of their combined arousal permeated the air, sending fresh spurts of excitement through Gabriel until her clit ached and she realized almost absently that she'd begun to gently rock her hips, gently riding Lilith's thigh while they continued their kiss. The exquisite friction against her sensitive clit sent sparks of desire shooting through her.

She edged her thigh forward so that with every movement it would rub against the sensitive hardness of Lilith's clit.

Gabriel's breath came in short gasps, and she quickened her movements as her own clit throbbed with each exquisite contact against Lilith's silky-soft thigh. Arousal tightened deep inside her gut until only the urgency to reach the orgasm that hovered just beyond her reach drove her movements.

Lilith seemed to welcome the hard, unforgiving movements, tightening her grip on Gabriel, the sharp pain of the queen's nails biting into Gabriel's back seemed to pull her arousal tight, pushing her over the edge until white-hot pleasure exploded through her. Dimly she heard Lilith cry out beneath her and a sharp stab of pain sliced through her shoulder before easing down into a dull ache that blended with the maelstrom going on inside her.

As reality slowly returned, Gabriel became aware of the strong, new scent inside the room.

Arousal . . . but although it was familiar, it was not her own or Lilith's.

She braced her elbows on either side of Lilith and pushed up to look behind her, already knowing what she would find.

Uriel.

Lilith's soft curse from underneath her made Gabriel stiffen and push up off the bed to stumble away from the queen.

Lilith slowly sat up, her lips still swollen from Gabriel's rough kisses, but her pain-filled gaze was only for Uriel.

5

Awareness slowly tickled at the edges of Amalya's consciousness, urgently beckoning until she forced open her eyes. She winced as pain scraped across her eyeballs as if someone had installed sandpaper on the inside of her eyelids while she slept.

When the pain cleared along with her mind, she realized she lay on the floor of what looked like a very posh office. A large dark cherry desk loomed to her left and plush, soft carpet met her fingers when she wiggled them against the floor.

The last thing she remembered was running through the cotton field to draw the shades away from the men.

What had happened to Levi and Jethro?

Urgency forged with icy fear snaked through her to pool deep inside her belly. She forced herself to sit up, nearly banging her head on the edge of the desk.

"Welcome, little succubus."

Amalya stiffened as a wave of power ruffled along her skin raising the hairs on the back of her neck and sending a shudder wracking through her. She slowly raised her chin to peer over the desk, already dreading what she would find.

Lucifer's piercing green gaze met her own and she gasped, scrambling up and away until she stumbled against something hard and fell backward into an overstuffed leather chair. After a split second of swallowing back the urge to run, she took a deep breath and let it out slowly, hoping her composure hadn't totally deserted her. "How did I get here?"

Her voice sounded reasonably calm, and she raised her chin as her confidence grew by a tiny fraction.

Lucifer's long blond hair flowed around a handsome, pale face. He had an ethereal beauty but would never be considered feminine. The well-formed body, smooth, deep voice, and the compelling presence he exuded marked him as decidedly male and unmistakably powerful. "You're near death. You're on the other side. In the administrative offices of Hell to be exact." He gestured vaguely around him.

Amalya frowned and sat forward in her seat as anticipation spilled through her chasing back her fear. No one technically knew what happened to succubi upon their deaths. Neither Heaven nor Hell seemed overly eager to claim them. "So, succubi are demons? We are denizens of Hell?"

His full lips curved as if he enjoyed keeping her in suspense. "No sarcastic remarks about Hell having administrative offices? I'm both disappointed and impressed."

She raised her brows, an impatient gesture she only realized she'd done when he mirrored the gesture as if mocking her.

"Sadly, you aren't my creature, although I would be happy to take you and all of your kind under my wing if Lilith and the Archangels would only agree." He leaned back, an expensive gold pen suspended between both his hands where he rolled it idly back and forth using both thumbs and index fingers. "However, until that day comes, let's just say when I sensed you leaving the earthly realm, I pulled your spirit this way so we could have a small chat."

She sighed. In true supernatural fashion he'd told her nothing definitive.

Was there a class on how to be vague that all supernaturals had to take before being admitted to the human world? She mentally waved away his comments. "Are Jethro and Levi all right?"

He gave a dismissive shrug. "They were ten minutes ago in human time, but I haven't kept track beyond that. It's you I'm interested in . . . Amalya."

At the sound of her name from those beautifully sculpted lips she stiffened in her seat and glared across the desk into his amused green gaze. "And I would be a much better conversationalist if I knew they were all right." Her words were soft and nonthreatening, but she infused them with certainty.

She held her breath as she waited for an outburst of anger. After all, Lucifer wasn't known for his patience and sparkling personality.

When the room filled with his dark, rich laugh, Amalya sat back in her chair, confusion eroding her certainty like rushing water against a sand castle.

"It always amazes me how those who are technically on the lower end of the power chain are usually so much stronger of character than those on the upper end. It does actually make what I do more enjoyable." He tapped the end of the pen against his smiling lips before dropping it on his desk and lacing his fingers in front of him. "And my Father mistakenly thinks the humans are the most fascinating beings He created."

When Amalya didn't offer any comment, he continued, his expression a mask. "Yes, both men you mentioned are currently alive. Is there anything else you need to know before we can resume our conversation?"

Cool relief slid through her. They were alive. Now all she had to do was figure out how to find her way back to them without running into the shades again and winding up right back here. When she realized Lucifer still watched her closely she raised her chin and met his gaze. "Are you aware Semiazas has escaped his prison?"

Lucifer's expression never wavered. He pierced her with his too-perceptive green gaze and Amalya shrugged away the sensation that he could see straight through to her soul—especially since it wasn't clear if succubi even *had* souls.

"Maybe when this is all over, I'll answer both those questions for you, little one, but right now time runs too short for small talk."

She started. Both questions?

She ran through the conversation in her mind, realizing he meant both the question about Semiazas and her internal wonderings about succubi having souls. Could he read her mind?

An impatient frown darkened his expression. "Yes, little one. You currently reside in my lair. My power base is here, so I can read strong thoughts that come my way."

Then something else Lucifer had said came clear.

Small talk?

Lucifer considered Semiazas escaping and tracking her and her sisters down for revenge small talk? She bit back the churning ball of anger that filled her chest. Lucifer was the only being that could control Semiazas. She had to remind herself that angering the prince of darkness wouldn't be a good move at this point.

Maybe she was becoming too much like her sister, Reba, but if the situation weren't so dire, she might enjoy lashing out instead of bottling the anger that currently churned inside her like acid.

Amalya took a deep breath, battling back her anger until she was confident she could control her emotions. "All right. Why am I here?"

"I need you to keep your word."

"My word?" Shock slapped at her as she searched her memory for anything she could've said that might have been construed as a promise. High-level supernaturals operated by their own set of rules, which they often made up as they went along. "My word about what?"

"Such a low opinion of us. Although I'm sure a well-earned one in most cases." He shrugged. "If you'll take my hand, all will become clear."

Amalya eyed Lucifer's long-fingered hand as she would a poisonous predator ready to strike. When she glanced up, his expression seemed to mock her, although it was probably only her own pride. After all, he'd admitted she wasn't his creature, and since she was beginning to think that she and her sisters, once reunited, might have to return to ask for his help with Semiazas, it wouldn't do to anger him now.

She steeled herself for his touch and reached out to take his hand. As soon as her skin touched his, knowledge and memories came rushing back, crashing over her in crippling waves.

She saw herself inside Lucifer's lair, a gilded room full of opulence and self-importance—totally unlike even the affluent office space she'd just left—and knew she was reliving a forgotten experience.

Power prickled against her skin stealing her breath until she had to force air into her lungs and blow it out slowly just to keep it from overpowering her.

"Welcome, ladies."

Amalya started at the respectful greeting and glanced to the side as her hands were clasped from both sides in a silent show of comfort and support.

She squeezed each hand lightly recognizing the familiar presence of her sisters on either side of her.

Amalya swallowed against the vertigo that came with this too vivid memory and instead enjoyed the sensation of having her sisters around her again. She hadn't seen them in over seven hundred years, so even though this was only a memory, she clutched it to her like a comfortable blanket.

"That is something we'll soon find out, Jezebeth."

Amalya frowned wondering what question Lucifer was answering. She turned to glance at Jezebeth, who had paled.

"Yes, within my lair, I can pick up strong thoughts from others."

Apparently, I'm not the only one who fell into that trap.

Lucifer's green gaze met hers and a quick smirk curled his lips as if to say he'd heard her thought too. The intensity of all that awareness concentrated on her sent a wave of power biting at her skin in tiny little stings that morphed into one large discomfort.

When he finally dropped his gaze to motion off to his side, the sensation receded and Amalya sighed as cool relief slid through her.

"Michael, join us."

Amalya frowned as the name he'd spoken registered.

Michael?

As in *Archangel* Michael?

Her sisters gripped her hands tighter as confusion sent Amalya's thoughts spinning. What had they gotten themselves into?

A large Archangel with a muscular, sleek build, mocha skin, and piercing green eyes joined Lucifer. Standing side by side, their eyes were identical, even though the rest of their features were very different. They were a study in dark and light, but while Lucifer's power bit at her making her resist the urge to shudder and cringe away, Michael's power flowed over her in a seductive, enticing warmth. Amalya wondered why Lucifer's power hadn't felt like that back inside his office, but her musings were cut short when Michael spoke.

"Greetings, followers of Lilith." Michael's deep voice washed over her, calming her and chasing back her fears. When her sisters' grips on her hands loosened, she knew they were experiencing the same thing.

"We have come to ask—"

"We already know why you're here." Michael's voice was kind but firm as he cut off Jezebeth's words, the calming effect of his presence increasing until Amalya felt boneless and relaxed.

Lucifer paced a slow path back and forth in front of them giving the impression of languid, slow movement, while still seeming impatient. He moved like liquid sin, but the eerie energy pouring off him was enough to remind her that for all his beauty, there was something evil lurking beneath that handsome exterior. "Ladies, we are well aware of Semiazas's activities, and they will be curtailed ... for now." He stopped in midstride and met each of their gazes in turn.

Amalya bit her tongue against demanding to know what "for now" meant. She squeezed Reba's hand, hoping the small gesture would remind her headstrong sister that if there was ever a time for them to be diplomatic and not anger either Michael or Lucifer, now was the time.

"Why only for now?" Jezebeth's clear voice rang through the large room echoing Amalya's thoughts, and she was sure Reba's and Galina's too.

Lucifer cast Jezebeth an impatient look and the edges of Michael's lips quirked as if he were trying to hide a smile.

"Semiazas will be imprisoned for his crimes, but there are bigger things at work here, ladies." Lucifer raised one eyebrow as if making sure he wouldn't be interrupted again.

Amalya clamped her lips closed, resisting the urge to do just that.

"Prophecy," Lucifer said slowly. "Armageddon prophecy to be exact."

"Fuck."

Amalya snapped her head toward the sound of Reba's quick curse, but since she agreed with the sentiment, she didn't bother to shush her, not that shushing Reba ever did any good.

Lucifer laughed. "Very eloquently put, Reba. From the expressions on your sisters' faces, I'd say they agree with your very astute assessment."

Reba scowled and Amalya tightened her grip on her sister's hand. Things needed to move along before one or more of them said something to set off the powerful demon or Archangel in the room, which meant all of them would end up dead.

Jez took a deep breath and let it out slowly before she spoke. "Do you think we could move past the dramatic theatrics and get on with why exactly we're here, since I don't think it's for the reason you agreed to meet with us?"

Amalya stiffened as she waited for the reaction to her sister's strong words.

Lucifer's green eyes narrowed and this time it was Michael who laughed, the warm sound echoing through the large room like a sudden wave of spring. "Calm yourself, brother. They have every right to know what they are agreeing to."

Lucifer didn't look like he would agree, but finally he nodded. "All right, ladies. Here's the situation. Armageddon could be at hand."

"Could be?" Amalya didn't realize she'd spoken until she heard her own voice and all her sisters turned to look at her.

Michael smiled. "Yes, *could* be. If it comes to pass is up to you four." He held up a hand to stop Lucifer from speaking, and once Lucifer gave a small nod, Michael continued. "The four horsemen have been imprisoned in Atlantis at the bottom of the Aegean Sea since before the beginning of your recorded time. If they are released, then Armageddon begins, and the outcome is decided at the expense of untold human suffering."

"The horsemen?" Jez's voice was laced with just as much disbelief as flowed through Amalya as she tried to make sense of Michael's words. "As in Pestilence, Death, War, and Famine? *Those* horsemen?"

"Exactly." He nodded as if Jez were a prized student.

"Excuse me, my lord," Galina interrupted politely—the only one of them so far to remember the respectful address. "But what do Armageddon and the horsemen have to do with us? We only came to warn you of Semiazas's activities before he kills off the entire human race on earth."

And us, Amalya added to herself.

Lucifer snorted and Amalya bit her lip as she remembered he could pick up her thoughts. "No one wants Armageddon to come about—not me, not Michael, and certainly not our Father. This world is a playground for those of us who rebelled and a grand naïve experiment for those who didn't."

Michael cast Lucifer a long-suffering look, but remained silent. This seemed like a familiar argument between them.

"Don't you see?" Lucifer continued. "Rather than flip the switch and risk the entire thing, we want to exercise the loophole and use a test group, as it were, to prove the world is worth saving."

"And *we're* the test group?" Jez's last word ended on a squeak.

Michael held up a hand. "You have to willingly take on this responsibility and the contest will be between you four and Semiazas. He will be imprisoned for his crimes and as soon as he is free, he will hunt the four of you down to seek revenge, which is the beginning of the Armageddon prophecies."

Jez swallowed hard. "What happens then?"

Michael exchanged a glance with Lucifer before continuing. "We will separate the four of you to protect you the best we can until the prophecy begins, and then only our Father, Lucifer, and I will know of the contest. The four of you will have to make your way to safety, find each other, and prevent Semiazas from releasing the horsemen, however you can."

Reba snorted. "Yeah, that sounds like a walk in the park. Can't we just do something easy like turn the world inside out or get Lucifer to make up with Daddy?"

Amalya squeezed Reba's hand until her sister turned to scowl at her. Reba's temper would get them all killed if she weren't careful.

When a charged silence fell over the room, Amalya held her breath and snapped her gaze toward Lucifer to wait for his reaction. When he laughed and slowly clapped his hands, she gritted her teeth as she waited for all of them to be killed where they stood. "Bravo. That's just the kind of spunk and fire all four of you will need to win through this." His heavy gaze settled on Reba and he raked a sensual gaze over her from head to toe. "Perhaps when this is decided, little one, you'll come back and pay me a visit."

"Not likely," she bit out, making Amalya and, she was sure, Galina and Jez cringe.

Lucifer only smiled and exchanged a look with Michael that told Amalya there was much more they weren't being told. "There is always a way to win through, ladies, but"—he held up a finger—"there is a catch that I think you missed."

Silence descended and Amalya held her breath as she waited for another comment from her sisters, which thankfully never came.

Finally Lucifer smiled, making him look like a hungry predator studying his next meal. "None of you will know about this—your memories will be removed. You might find clues along the way, but your choices must come from free will and selfless actions. Any allies you make along the way can help you, but neither Michael nor I can directly interfere other than to enforce the rules."

"Rules?" Jezebeth found herself asking.

Michael nodded. "If any of the four of you fail—Armageddon begins. Any of the four of you can kill Semiazas if you can, but not before all four of you have stopped the horsemen. And Semiazas can not die at the hand of anyone else. Otherwise—"

"Armageddon begins." Jezebeth's words were soft and resigned. "And you said we have to willingly sign on for this. What if we don't? What if we refuse?"

Lucifer spread his hands wide. "Armageddon begins."

Anger roiled through Amalya—something that happened more and more often lately—as Jez snorted. "So we have no choice."

She exchanged a glance with her sisters, seeing the same frustration she felt mirrored in their expressions.

"There is always a choice," Michael said softly. "You may not like the options, but there is always a choice."

A wrench of vertigo pulled Amalya nearly in two and she sucked in a breath to keep from throwing up as she realized she was back in Lucifer's office sitting in the same chair she'd been in when she'd taken his hand.

6

Levi scowled after Amalya even as his logical side told him she was correct in staying behind. The action went against both what he'd promised Lilith about protecting Amalya and his male pride. But he was already light headed from the dozens of shades sliding through him and stealing his energy, the eerie icy sensations making his skin clammy and his vision swim as he forced one foot in front of the other. If he died, he definitely wouldn't be able to protect her.

The sound of Jethro just behind him told him Amalya's ploy to draw off the shades seemed to be working. So, not willing to waste her effort, he gritted his teeth and ran toward the farmhouse.

As he reached the front steps, Levi risked a glance behind him and had to dodge out of the way as Jethro pushed past him toward the front door. He raked his gaze over the farm, but from this vantage, he couldn't see Amalya. Fear merged with protective anger inside his gut and he let adrenaline surge inside him.

He turned to find the front door of the farmhouse standing wide and he ducked inside, allowing a quick second for his eyes to adjust to the gloom. When they did adjust, the light from the front door only barely penetrated the deep gloom inside the room. He cursed as he realized the farmer and his family had probably drawn all the curtains and blocked off all the windows against the shades, not realizing that wouldn't stop them.

"Straight ahead, and watch out for the farmer. His body is on the floor just in front of the kitchen."

Jethro's words sent a chill of foreboding quaking through Levi to blend with the clammy sensation that still clung to his skin from the shades. He didn't want to see proof that the entities could kill when Amalya was still out there at their mercy.

Levi edged forward until his loafers bumped against what must be the farmer's body. Then he sidestepped and headed forward again, carefully placing each foot in front of the other and reaching out with his hands until he saw a faint glow from what he assumed was the kitchen.

"I found two fifty-pound bags of salt in the cellar and put them on the table. None of the electricity works. It was most likely cut off at the breaker."

As Levi edged farther inside the kitchen, he could just make out Jethro's features, illuminated by candlelight. "We'll worry about the breaker after we've saved Amalya. Let's find the bathroom."

"Can't taking a piss wait? She's still out there." Anger laced Jethro's words, but Levi ignored it.

"We need to dissolve the salt in the tub."

Understanding flashed across Jethro's features, and Levi's respect for the man edged up a notch. At least Amalya had the good sense to have a bodyguard who not only adored her enough to lay down his own life for her but was intelligent and quick too.

Jethro hefted a bag of salt over his shoulder and disappeared through the doorway leaving Levi to hurry behind, using the edge of the candlelight to watch his footing. When they reached the living room, Levi carefully made his way back toward the front door and then felt along the front wall until he found the heavy curtains that covered the front windows. When he yanked and the curtains refused to budge, he traced his fingers to the edge until he felt the slick thickness of duct tape.

He bit back a growl of frustration as he pulled one of his daggers from a sheath just inside the waistband of his slacks and sliced open the line of thick tape. Now that he could grab hold of an edge of the curtain, several hard yanks ripped down the heavy cloth, pulling it rod and all to the floor and letting bright sunlight stream in.

He closed his eyes tight until the light through his lids didn't make him wince and then opened them to see the insides of a quaint farmhouse decorated in the Southwest style.

A creative curse from Jethro made him smile. He might've begun to respect the man, but that didn't mean he was ready to accept his presence on this trip quite yet. This all would've been easier if it were just he and Amalya.

"Thanks for the warning, Your Grace." Sarcasm dripped from Jethro's voice as he trudged to the upper floor.

"Any time," Levi called back as he jogged up the stairs after him. "Makes it easier to navigate, doesn't it?"

Instead of an answer, the sound of running water guided him up the stairs, down the long hall, and toward the spacious master bedroom. The room was filled with sunlight, a testament to Jethro taking the time to rip down the curtains that hung over the window like Levi had done downstairs. This room was more homey and less fashionable. Framed pictures of many different sizes covered every available surface, and the furniture looked comfortable rather than stylish.

Quick steps took Levi to the four-poster bed where he pulled off the multicolored quilt and then stepped inside the master bathroom.

Jethro was busy dumping the five-pound bag of salt into the slowly filling garden tub.

Impatience bit at Levi like hounds nipping at his heels, but he kept a tight rein on the sensation. He dropped the quilt onto the floor and used the nervous energy to look out any window he could find searching for Amalya. As each new view offered nothing but fields or road, he cursed under his breath and moved on to the next.

Finally, he pulled open the curtains in the guest room down the hall and saw her. She lay limp among the nearly grown cotton stalks, a swirl of white mist still surrounding her. Levi clenched his fists as impotence twisted with fear inside him. The fact that the shades still surrounded her meant she was alive, but that didn't mean she would be for long. He wasn't familiar with succubus anatomy, so even though he knew she could take more damage than a human and live, he didn't know how soon that line would be crossed.

"Ready."

Jethro's call from down the hall was followed by the sound of water splashing and more colorful curses from the man. Levi entered the bathroom in time to see Jethro step out of the tub still fully clothed, dripping salt water onto the hardwood floor.

Levi stripped off his suit jacket and tossed it aside before he stepped inside the tub and sank under the water. The cold hit him harder than the slap of the shades had. Now he knew why Jethro had cursed.

Thanks for the warning, he thought, and knew it had been revenge for the sudden sunlight from the curtains downstairs. He surfaced with a gasp, more in protest from the cold, wet clothes that clung to his skin than from holding his breath.

As soon as he stepped out of the tub, he grabbed the quilt and shoved it into the water, wetting it and allowing a few seconds for the salt water to penetrate the cloth. He picked it up, still dripping and started for the door. "Salt the window and door frames," he called over his shoulder to Jethro as he tried to hurry his steps, but his wet loafers threatened to slide out from under him on the well-waxed hardwood floor. When he hit the carpeted stairs, he jogged down the steps two at a time, the banked adrenaline now surging freely through him and urging him forward.

He could imagine Jethro's angry reaction at being left behind to ready the house, but once Amalya was brought back, they needed someplace to recover that was safe from the shades. Not to mention that since his maternal side added something not quite human to his DNA, Levi was sure he could survive against the shades longer than Jethro who was a hundred percent human.

Levi chafed at the necessity of slowing down when he reached the bottom of the landing and more hardwood floor, but after several deliberate steps he made it to the front porch and shifted into an all-out run.

He increased his pace, ignoring the slap and sting of the cotton stalks that thrashed against his legs over the uneven ground, even though he nearly slipped and fell several times. Men's dress shoes just weren't made for running through cotton fields.

As he rounded the building, his breath left him in a quick rush. Amalya still lay unmoving, the mist of shades around her growing brighter as they siphoned her energy.

As he neared, the shades noticed him and a few advanced toward him. When they reached him, they seemed to cringe away, their translucent forms undulating as if in pain or discomfort.

The cool relief that slid through him was short lived as he glanced past them toward Amalya's still form. He'd never actually had to use salt water against shades, and he was glad this information hadn't just been an old wives' tale.

He reached through the mist to spread the wet comforter on the ground next to Amalya, crushing cotton plants under its weight. The shades scattered back as they shied away from his touch but stayed close as if a small force field surrounded him.

As he moved, they undulated with him, zeroing in on Amalya's still form as if they sensed they were about to lose their prize.

He gently lifted her and laid her on the comforter.

His gut clenched at the clammy feel of her skin, but he reminded himself it could be him after his dip in the frigid garden tub upstairs. He shoved everything else out of his mind except getting Amalya safely back to the farmhouse.

Using the free end of the blanket, he covered Amalya and rolled her in the excess cloth to ensure none of her body was exposed to the touch of the shades.

A low, uncomfortable vibration filled the air around him, making his stomach roil and his head throb as he hefted the bulky bundle in his arms and started back toward the house. As the low rumbling hum increased, Levi realized the sound came from the shades.

The mist began to swirl around him like an angry cyclone as he hurried back over the uneven ground with the bundle containing Amalya's limp form firmly in his arms. As the vibration in the air around him increased, the sensation that his stomach was going to turn itself inside out made Levi clench his jaw against the sudden bite of bile on the back of his tongue.

He rounded the side of the house determined to make it inside without succumbing to the side effects of the angry shades.

The mist swirled faster and faster around them turning the air opaque and sending a crippling wave of vertigo cutting straight through Levi. He stumbled and fell to one knee, swallowing hard to keep from retching. Sucking in large breaths of air in an attempt to calm the roiling inside his head and stomach, he clenched his eyes tight and frantically tried to think of a way past the shades.

"Levi! Can you hear me?"

Relief speared through him as he turned to orient on Jethro's voice, keeping his eyes firmly shut. "I hear you. Keep yelling."

Levi slowly stood, hefting Amalya's limp form into a better grip before he started forward, following Jethro's voice until his foot bumped something hard.

"Stairs," Jethro called, and Levi smiled as excitement surged through him giving him another burst of strength. If he'd made it to the stairs, he could make it the rest of the way.

The swirling and rumbling increased until it felt like the air was a tangible force, and with every movement he pushed through solid gelatin.

He lifted one foot slowly and firmly placed it on the bottom stair before transferring his weight and pulling his foot up behind him. Never had six stairs seemed like such a daunting task before, but with the dead weight of Amalya in his arms, urgency pushed him forward.

"Incoming."

The words had a split second to register inside his brain before a wall of icy water hit Levi, leaving him sputtering and tasting salt.

When he blinked away the water that had splashed into his eyes, Levi found Jethro standing ten feet in front of him in the doorway to the farmhouse holding a silver bucket.

Levi dashed toward the doorway.

As soon as he passed the door frame, the heavy sensation he'd fought against disappeared and left him stumbling against the sudden lack of resistance. He fell to his knees, careful not to drop Amalya as the door slammed shut behind them.

* * *

Amalya blinked across the desk at Lucifer as the overwhelming sensation of reliving the vivid memories slowly died away leaving her exhausted.

"Welcome back." Lucifer's expression was intense but left Amalya unsure of his mood. He still held her hand and she tried to tug it back, but her body refused to respond to the command. His fingers were warm and strong around hers and she wondered again that she didn't feel the biting sensation of his power in such close proximity with him.

"I'm holding my power in check. You're already weak, and that would only debilitate you further, not to mention make this meeting much more difficult to complete."

He let go of her hand and she left it suspended in the air for a long moment before her brain kicked in and allowed her to lower it to her lap as the implications of those memories burned through her. "So why tell me all this now? I thought we were supposed to know nothing of this."

Lucifer's lips quirked so slightly that if Amalya hadn't been watching, she wouldn't have noticed. "I will follow the rules scrupulously. Once you leave here and go back into the human realm, your memories will fade."

"Then why tell me in the first pl—"

He cut off her question with an impatient wave. "You're being called back. We will meet again." He smiled. "I look forward to it."

As if he'd suddenly let down the shield keeping his power in check, a neck-ruffling wave of energy flowed toward her, biting against her skin and making her cringe away.

A tugging sensation from deep inside her gut made her gasp as it slowly grew in intensity. At first she thought it was due to the sudden flash of Lucifer's power, but then his words penetrated and she realized she was being pulled back to the human realm.

The urgency from within her memories came back to her with startling clarity. She cast about for some way to keep the memories that Lucifer had restored and said would soon fade when she returned to the human realm.

She closed her eyes and concentrated, chanting a mantra over and over under her breath as the tugging turned into a wrenching that threatened to pull her inside out.

Wave after wave crashed over her, battering her until she was certain she'd never survive the journey back.

Was this what birth and death felt like? If so, she was glad she'd been created rather than this chaos of pain and discomfort that held her in its grip now.

Time lost all meaning as pain turned into agony and became her entire world. She clenched her fists, the slight pinch from her nails biting into her palms almost a relief next to the other sensations tearing through her. Through it all she continued to chant, holding on to the tendrils of memories that tried to fade into the abyss.

When the sensations finally receded, she immediately wished for the wrenching to return. The sudden absence of agony was such a shock to her system, she wasn't sure she would survive it.

Shivers wracked her body, and she felt as if her core had been turned into ice. Every body part felt numb and achy, as if it might no longer be attached and functioning.

Distantly she became aware that arms held her and cold, naked skin pressed against hers. The unknown presence rocked her slowly as hands chafed her arms and legs, which slowly brought some semblance of warmth back to the surface, and along with it prickles of pain and awareness.

Slow chanting filled her ears, but she couldn't make out the words and wished they would stop. They were an annoying buzz that only added to the cacophony of sensations assaulting her overtaxed system. But somehow she knew they couldn't stop, and she resigned herself to the monotonous noise.

"Amalya?" Levi's voice sounded softly next to her right ear making her realize Jethro must be the second body she felt on her left. His voice held a thread of concern as well as relief and she sent a quick prayer of thanks that both men seemed to be safe.

She nodded in answer to his question, rocking harder in their grip, unable to answer as the chanting slowly crystallized inside her mind.

Four succubi must stop horsemen to save all.
Four succubi must stop horsemen to save all.
Four succubi must stop horsemen to save all.

As soon as those eight words seeped inside her consciousness, she realized it was her own voice she heard all around her.

She stiffened as a hard stab of premonition pierced deep.

Something tickled at the edge of her consciousness but stubbornly remained just out of her reach. She sucked in a large breath and willed herself to stop speaking.

After several more repetitions, the words died away and the sudden quiet in the room was nearly deafening inside Amalya's pounding head. Her tongue was dry and tired as if she'd been saying those words over and over for quite some time.

She tried to remember what happened or even how she'd ended

up here between Levi and Jethro feeling as if she'd been trampled by a herd of angry elephants, but a thick haze of lethargy lay over her mind edging her toward sleep. "So tired," she pushed out through chapped lips before she closed her eyes and gave herself up to the darkness.

7

Amalya woke to find herself warm but very weak. She was draped against a hard male chest, an exotic musky scent filling her senses, while hot water lapped gently against her lower back.

Levi.

She was in a bathtub straddled across Levi.

If she had any energy at all she would've stiffened and pulled away purely on principle. She still hadn't forgiven either man for lying to her, regardless that they'd obviously saved her from the shades.

"Amalya?"

She tried to raise her head, to hold on to some semblance of her pride, but her skin and even her hair ached—a definite sign that she needed energy. Now. And from the very hard cock that lay trapped against her stomach, he could definitely provide it.

Instinctively, as if sensing sustenance nearby, slick moisture formed between her labia as her clit hardened, pressing against the hard male body she straddled. Her nipples budded into tight peaks where they were pressed against him and her pussy throbbed in anticipation and need.

She sucked in a breath as she gathered the strength to speak. "Need you. Inside me."

Levi gently raised her head until their gazes met, the green flecks in his dark hazel eyes mesmerizing her. His dark hair had fallen down onto his brow and she was glad she could barely move because the urge to touch the lush softness and brush it back off his forehead was strong.

The energy aura that surrounded him was still a pulsing mist of white but weaker than she'd seen it last. He still hadn't fully recovered from his own bout with the shades, not to mention whatever he'd done while she'd been unconscious.

And even worse—she was relieved to see him.

"Are you sure?" Concern laced his voice and impatience and irritation snapped through her.

She wanted to scream at him, and although the urge pricked at her, she bit it back, not willing to waste her energy.

Now he chose to ask her opinion when she could barely move? When she'd been quite healthy back at Sinner's Redemption, he'd thought nothing of tricking her into sex. But now that she needed it, he'd turned chivalrous?

Men!

He bit back a grim smile and then nodded as if he'd heard her unspoken thoughts. He leaned forward to kiss her.

Amalya jerked away from him, nearly falling backward into the water.

Kissing was an intimate act, and after cheapening everything a bath had previously meant to her, she wasn't ready to give him that much, even if it would help restore some of her energy. "Inside. Only."

A small muscle ticked in Levi's jaw as first shock and then anger flowed across his handsome features. He met her gaze and then nodded in a quick, curt motion.

He settled her against him again so her cheek lay flat against his chest. Something hard and metal pressed between them and she realized it was the medallion he'd received from Lilith. Most likely that's what kept her from taking too much energy from him—although it would serve him right at this point if she drained him dry.

She tried to feel bad over the vindictive thought but couldn't quite bring herself to. Betrayal still burned just under her anger, which made it unlikely to heal quickly, even with his current bout of chivalrous, though misplaced, intentions.

One large hand cupped her ass and lifted her until she felt the head of his cock nudge between her thighs. She tried to wriggle, impatient to have him inside her, but her body refused to respond and instead she had to wait as Levi slowly lowered her onto his thick shaft.

He held her firmly, giving her body plenty of time to adjust to him. She sighed as she stretched to accept him, the slow, torturous sensation of his cock sliding inside her like small electric shocks inside her system. His energy thrummed against her skin, beckoning to her as her own slick moisture coated him until he filled her and they sat pelvis to pelvis. The head of his cock pressed firmly against her cervix, sending tiny bursts of arousal through her with each breath.

She found the energy to shift her hips, taking him even deeper and making them both gasp.

Levi's strong hands closed around her hips, holding her in place for a long moment while he sucked in large, deep breaths.

Good, she wasn't the only one so affected by this arrangement.

There was something decidedly erotic about him taking her when she couldn't move or help—something similar to being tied up while a lover pleasured her. Of course, Levi wasn't her lover, she reminded herself forcefully. He was a means to an end, a client who had paid well at Sinner's Redemption and a man who would help her and Jethro make it safely to Lilith's lair.

Several long seconds later, Levi blew out a long, slow breath before he used his grip on her hips to grind her against him, ripping a moan from her throat and coaxing the first hot drop of pre-come from Levi.

As the life-giving essence hit her internal walls, a small explosion of energy surged through Amalya as her body greedily absorbed what was offered and converted it to usable energy inside her.

Levi slowly lifted her, sliding his cock nearly out of her before impaling her again in a slow, torturous movement that made Amalya whimper with impatience.

"Relax, my beauty. Let me pleasure you." His deep voice feathered against her like a dark caress, making her shiver.

Damn it! She wanted him fast and hard. She wanted him to come inside her and replenish her energy so she could regain the distance between them that her anger and hurt demanded.

Instead, Levi touched her tenderly, as if she were precious, drawing out her pleasure, and his own, while giving her the energy she both craved and needed.

After several minutes of the exquisite, slow torture at Levi's set pace, Amalya's body began to slowly respond to her wishes and she was able to sit up on her own. She anchored her hands on Levi's shoulders as she began to set her own pace.

However, when she began to move, rather than the quick, frenzied passion she thought she wanted, she kept the torturous slow pace he'd begun as she met and held Levi's dark gaze.

He watched her, his gaze burning into hers as if he memorized every second.

The intimacy of the gaze pierced her deep and she mentally set space between them. She closed her eyes, her work persona clicking into place as she remained impassive and apart from him. She leaned back, lifting her wet hands to her breasts, tweaking her aching nipples as she rode Levi's cock.

He was just a means to an end. She needed his come and that was all.

She repeated those two sentences like a mantra.

He hadn't earned anything else.

Her gift tried to tell her the lie of her own thoughts, but she shoved it aside.

"I'm not your bloody blow-up doll." The anger vibrating in his voice bit against her skin like an accusation, but she ignored him and continued to ride.

One strong arm came around her, pulling her close and tipping her against him. In a quick move, he pushed up and stood, lifting her, still impaled on his hard cock, and forcing her to wrap her legs around his waist for balance. Dripping water across the floor, he walked into the bedroom and then gently but firmly laid her on the bed, pinning her under his weight.

Amalya began to protest, but then he thrust hard inside her ripping a gasp from her throat as searing arousal shot through her, scattering her thoughts.

That first hard thrust was followed by another and another until Levi was pistoning inside her, causing a cascade of sensations to explode through her and swell into a growing maelstrom.

Through her haze of arousal, a single coherent thought found its way through. He was using her as she'd tried to use him mere moments ago—as a means to an end.

Amalya's anger stirred, feeding the growing pleasure that churned inside her ever tighter. She should be happy that he'd decided to keep his emotional distance as she'd dictated, but emotions and logic rarely saw eye to eye.

Amalya had spent millennia keeping distance, and she'd match her experience against Levi's any day. If he wanted to play, she was more than ready.

She tightened her grip on his shoulders, digging her nails in deep and enjoying the way his cock hardened even further inside her. More pre-come hit her internal walls and her body greedily absorbed it, sending an explosion of exquisite sensations through her while Levi continued to thrust inside her.

When her vision cleared, she opened her eyes to find Levi's eyes closed, his expression closed off as if he were masturbating.

Irritation snapped through her and she shoved the sensation away, forcefully reminding herself that this was what she wanted. A devious desire for revenge snaked through her and she smiled to herself as she widened her thighs, welcoming him deeper.

His gasp and sudden moan sent satisfaction spiraling through her. *So, the man isn't granite after all.*

Levi increased his speed, driving into her so hard that any human woman would be bruised and sore afterward. Instead, Amalya tightened her inner muscles around him, enjoying the slap of his testicles against her sensitive slit as he pounded into her. The scent of their combined arousal perfumed the air, a sweet musk that both teased and beckoned.

Just as Amalya neared her own orgasm, Levi's movements became frenzied and urgent, his harsh breath chuffing out as if he'd just run a marathon and he was eager to cross the finish line.

Anticipation of both her release and needed sustenance spread through her and she dug her fingernails into his shoulders again, holding on as if he could anchor her to the earth.

The extra friction met his hard cock and Levi cried out, stiffening over her as his hot seed spurted inside her.

Amalya's body greedily absorbed Levi's essence sending her over the edge with her own orgasm and also igniting dozens of white-hot explosions inside her.

Her vision flashed with white stars, and waves of pleasure crashed over her until she thought she would drown.

Finally her screaming lungs reminded her to suck in a much-needed breath and she blinked open her eyes as Levi pulled out of her and turned away from the bed.

He swallowed hard before speaking over his shoulder. "You've had your sustenance now, love. Jethro is downstairs if you fancy a more leisurely fuck or even a meal."

His words were calm, but Amalya could sense the thin thread of anger that rode just under them.

She lay on the bed, her thighs still spread and the moisture from her arousal and orgasm still wet against her inner thighs as he walked out the door without looking back.

Guilt wormed its way deep into her gut as she realized how she'd treated Levi, but she shoved it back. It was about time he realized how it felt to be on the other end of such treatment. She refused to let his little exercise in guilt and shame bother her. After all, she hadn't asked him to come on this trip and provide for her. She and Jethro would've made it to Lilith's lair fine on their own.

They didn't need Levi and his overblown ego.

Liar! her internal voice mocked her once again.

She shoved it aside, unwilling to entertain for even a moment that Levi's heavy-handed ways were a necessary evil to get her to Lilith's lair safely.

She pushed up to sitting, surprised to find herself still weak, although being able to move was a huge improvement. The walk to the bathroom was stilted and slow, but she managed it and then sank down on the toilet to clean up. Long after she was finished, she sat as weariness closed over her like a heavy blanket.

She had energy but could use more, not to mention food, water, and sleep.

Finally when her legs began to fall asleep, she forced herself to stand and venture back inside the bedroom where her clothes lay on an armchair. It took all her willpower to pick up each garment and slip it on, and in the end, she decided to go barefoot rather than spend the extra effort to put on her shoes.

If Levi thought she would beg for his help again, he would be disappointed. Instead, she concentrated on placing one foot in front of the other until she found the main staircase where she was forced to sit down on the top stair to rest and recover from the exertion of dressing and making it this far.

Levi's come had brought her back from the brink of death, and she couldn't help but be grateful for that. But she'd saved his life first, so now she supposed they were even.

"That doesn't give him the right to be a haughty bastard," she muttered under her breath as frustration and irritation swirled through her.

She thought about calling for Jethro to ask for his help making it down the stairs, but she refused to give Levi the satisfaction of seeing her ask for help from anyone. Instead, she stretched her legs until her feet hung over the step below her. Then she scooted her ass forward until her feet landed on the step two below her and she could lower herself down one step.

It took her nearly twenty minutes of slow scooting and lowering to finally reach the bottom of the long stairway, especially since she was forced to stop frequently to rest and recover her strength. She

tried to make as little noise as possible and was grateful when neither of the men came to investigate.

She leaned against the banister, her strength entirely gone. Her
eyelids were heavy and a long sleep sounded like a very good idea
even though her stomach rumbled reminding her that she also
needed food and water to help her recover.

But in the end, the lethargy that stole over her won out and
she turned sideways on the bottom stair, resting her back against the
side banister and stretching out her legs across the bottom step as she
resigned herself to a quick power nap here on the cold hardwood.

8

Levi walked away from Amalya with anger churning inside him like a volcano ready to erupt. He had been surprised and angry when Amalya had shied away from his kiss in the tub. She couldn't still be upset about him not telling her who he was up front, could she?

He shook his head, dismissing the thought. She was an intelligent being and surely she'd reconciled herself to the necessity of that before now. After all, if she hadn't been at better than full strength, she might well have not survived the run-in with the shades.

As it was, it had taken both he and Jethro to warm her up enough so she wasn't shivering before they could undress her and get her in the tub.

And then she'd refused to kiss him!

He bristled at the uncomfortable memory.

He might not know a lot about succubi, but he did know kissing was a valid way of transferring energy, which she was still badly in need of if her pale features were any indication. He shook his head and padded down the hall naked since all his clothes were still inside the room where Amalya lay. A few steps took him to the guest room where he pulled open the closet praying the farmer kept extra clothes in here.

Levi wasn't a modest man by nature, but he also didn't relish the notion of going downstairs to discuss the next steps with Jethro in his current state of undress.

He was relieved to find the closet jam-packed with clothes, and from the stale, musty scent that greeted him, none of them had been touched in quite a while. He flipped through the odd assortment— jackets to Halloween costumes and everything in between—except a pair of trousers that might fit him.

He'd just begun to think giving up would be the best strategy when on the very last hanger he found a pink terry-cloth robe. He grit his teeth and bit back his pride as he pulled it off the hanger and held it up in front of him. Whoever had worn the robe had been very short and very round, but thanks to their girth, it looked like it would fit, although he'd have to be very careful about bending over.

Ignoring the mothball scent that clung to the fabric, he slipped on the robe. It wrapped around him easily but only fell to just above his knees. If he bent over, he'd give someone a ball's eye view. But at this point, he'd rather suffer wearing this than returning to the room where he'd left not only his clothes but also Amalya and the urge to shake her until she saw reason.

What was it about her that unsettled him? He was normally unflappable, especially with women, but from the very first time he'd laid eyes on her, she'd gotten under his skin and pulled reactions from him that no one had since his childhood.

Once he'd realized the extent of her rebellion in the tub, he'd tried to beat her at her own game, but the little minx had neatly turned the tables on him—no doubt from all the skills learned in her profession. He had to admit, she'd surprised him, and broken his hard-won control at the same time.

He would admit some grudging respect for her if it hadn't severely bruised his ego in the process. The damned woman had been at death's door. Didn't she realize he'd only been trying to restore her energy?

He huffed out a long breath and squared his shoulders as he headed downstairs, braced for Jethro's reaction to his colorful attire.

When he entered the kitchen, he found the man cooking, which meant the electricity was back on.

Without turning, Jethro asked, "How is she?"

"Stubborn woman," Levi mumbled in answer as he took a seat at the kitchen table and tried in vain to find a sitting position that didn't leave his bare ass on the cold wooden chair.

Jethro turned to glance over his shoulder and Levi gritted his teeth as the man did a double take. "I'm not sure I want to know about your wardrobe choice, but I am concerned about Amalya," he said finally before turning back toward the stove.

Jethro's amused voice did little to calm Levi's churning emotions. "She's still weak."

"Unable to give her enough energy, Your Grace?"

Irritation snapped through Levi at Jethro's mocking tone and he glared at the back of the shorter man's head. "Stop calling me 'Your fucking Grace.'"

Jethro turned to give a courtly bow coupled with a knowing smirk. "As you wish, my lord." He dropped pasta into the boiling water on the stove and stirred it with a long-handled spoon.

"Bloody American," Levi ground out.

Jethro laughed and answered as if Levi hadn't spoken. "As you can see, the electricity is working. I put the farmer's body in the laundry room so Amalya won't have to look at it. Beyond that, I don't have any wonderful ideas how to get past the shades once we're all recovered." He shrugged. "So I figured we'd eat and sleep on it and then figure out what to do."

Levi shook his head even though Jethro couldn't see him. Lilith had made it very clear that time was of the essence, and the shades appearing everywhere seemed a bad omen that only added to his urgency. "We don't have that kind of time."

Jethro laid the spoon on the counter and turned to lean against the cabinets, crossing his arms in front of him. "I don't see as we have much of a choice unless you have any bright ideas. You and I weren't much match for the shades before, and you've just said Amalya is still weak."

Dread curled inside Levi's stomach as he realized their only way forward. He scrubbed his hand over his face, trying to ignore the weariness that had taken up residence inside his body. He'd originally thought he'd gotten the better end of this deal with Lilith to escort Amalya in exchange for information on his father. Now he was beginning to think Lilith had known from the start any information Levi originally received would be hard earned. "I'm going to call in an old debt and hope it helps more than it hurts."

"Is that before or after you find the matching slippers for that getup?"

Levi scowled and stood. Facing Amalya and retrieving his clothes was beginning to look like the lesser of two evils here. "How soon until the food is ready?"

"About twenty minutes."

Levi nodded and walked out of the kitchen with as much dignity as he could muster barefoot and wearing a pink terry-cloth robe. When he stepped inside the living room and turned toward the stairs, he stopped short.

Amalya sat on the bottom step sound asleep, her legs stretched out in front of her, her back resting against the banister. He wasn't sure how she'd made it this far. She'd been weak and pale when he'd left her and figured she'd fall asleep instead of dress and try to make it down the stairs.

You've had your sustenance now, love. Jethro is downstairs if you fancy a more leisurely fuck or even a meal. The words he'd flung at her as he left replayed through his mind like an accusation, making him wince.

"Damn, I really am an ass sometimes," he whispered to himself as he gently picked up Amalya and nestled her close to his chest as he carried her up the stairs.

She sighed in her sleep as she curled against him, her head resting against his chest as he cradled her.

He'd lashed out at her because she'd wounded his ego. He hadn't thought she would risk life and limb by trying to navigate the stairs before she was ready. She'd even dressed—in her own clothes, which was more than he could say for himself.

He smiled as he reached the top of the stairs and turned toward the bedroom. She continued to surprise him, and she'd earned his grudging respect several times over, which was more than he could say for most beings, and sadly, that included most supernaturals.

He laid her gently on the bed and she immediately curled onto her side, cuddling into the pillow like a small child, her fist tucked under her chin, her knees drawn up as if she were cold.

Levi pulled the covers up over her and carefully tucked her in. When he was finished, he straightened and allowed himself a few minutes to study her. In sleep she looked innocent and very young, regardless of the fact that she'd been created back before the Bible was written.

Her golden eyelashes lay like delicate lace against her cheeks and her full lips were slightly parted.

A warm tendril of tenderness stole through him and he gave into the urge to brush a strand of hair away from her face. Her skin was warm and silky under his fingertips, her hair a soft spill that he remembered burying his fingers in as she rode him that first time back at Sinner's Redemption.

His cock hardened instantly at the sudden erotic reminder and Levi shook his head. He reacted like a randy schoolboy around her, which he'd not experienced since . . . well, since he *was* a randy schoolboy.

He forced himself to turn away and cross the room to where his clothes lay over the ottoman. Grateful to be rid of the pink robe, he dropped it to the floor and quickly dressed, careful to check that all his blades were where they should be before he cast one last glance over his shoulder at Amalya and turned to head toward the guest room.

Once there, he sat cross-legged on the floor, the hardwood cold through the fabric of his still damp slacks. He took a deep breath, ignoring the internal voices that reminded him he had promised himself he would never do this again.

A quick mental image of Amalya lying pale and cold as death in the cotton field outside with shades surrounding her cemented his resolve.

He slid the dagger out of the sheath in his sock and wrapped his palm around the cold blade. In a quick motion he slashed his palm, hissing against the sting of the sharp cut.

As his blood welled into the wound, he closed his eyes and spoke. "Caldriel, by your blood that runs through my veins, I summon you."

Static electricity snaked over him, raising all the hairs on his body in a flesh-crawling rush. He shuddered against the sensation and took deep breaths as he held up his open palm, offering the inducement for the summons and hoping the price he'd have to pay wasn't too steep.

Energy began to swirl inside the room gaining power and momentum. It spun until the sound of the curtains flapping against the window cut through the howling of the wind. Power prickled against him as if he stood too close to an ungrounded electric cable and he clenched his teeth together as the basic human urge to flee from such a sensation ripped through him.

He stubbornly remained as still as possible, weathering the storm and defying the consequences for what seemed like hours.

Abruptly the world around him fell silent and the sensation of power slowly receded until he felt the warm, wet sensation of a tongue lapping at his wounded palm.

He opened his eyes to see a stunning brunette with his same color hair and clear, green eyes making one more pass over his palm with her tongue before she straightened and faced him. Her expression showed impatience twined with concern that he remembered well from his childhood.

He smiled and flexed his now fully healed palm as he took in her modern appearance and tried to reconcile it with the last time he'd seen her over one hundred years earlier. Times, fashions, and styles had changed and she never failed to keep pace.

"Obediah, why did you summon me? You're lucky I was alone. I can't be seen disappearing into thin air at the queen's garden party. Not to mention you could've attracted some dangerous visitors by advertising your blood ties to me." Her cultured British accent washed over him, the perfect blend of condescension and arrogance. That kind of unquestioned authority had been commonplace in Regency England but in modern times seemed sad and misplaced.

He wondered if he sounded the same to others. If so, no wonder

Amalya had taken offense to his making decisions for her. The fact that he'd come by the behavior and attitude honestly did little to make him feel better.

He'd lived the life of the rich noble. He'd spent many years in the unforgiving role of Obediah Levi Spencer, Duke of Ashford. But when he'd stopped aging in his late twenties, his mother had been forced to admit that the anomaly had nothing to do, biologically speaking, with the previous Duke of Ashford.

He sighed and rose, towering over his mother's five-foot-seven frame. "Summoning you was necessary. I apologize for interrupting such an important event as the queen's garden party."

She raised one brow, the only sign she'd registered his dry sarcasm. "Have you reconsidered your decision?"

He huffed out an impatient breath. "No, I have not. I need your help."

She glared up at him, the vast height difference serving as no impediment for her displeasure—not that it ever had. "And what would induce me to help you when you refuse to see reason?"

"I had hoped that the life of your only son would be reason enough. You may enjoy endlessly being reborn as your own offspring in the eyes of the British nobility, but I prefer to live my life on my own terms."

"At least your father was loyal."

Anger flashed through him and he grabbed her arm and stepped close, towering over her. "Don't ever call him that. We both know Ashford wasn't my father, no matter how often I wished him to be."

Her eyes flashed fire—actual fire—something he knew others rarely ever saw and lived. To get her to show her demon side was a feat he generally excelled at but had long ago tired of.

He slowly released her and took one step back. Not out of fear but chagrin that he'd let her goad him into actually laying a hand on her. Two things he did value from the time period of his upbringing were honor and manners—both of which his mother paid little heed.

"If you'd wanted loyalty, Mother, you should have gotten a dog. But then I suppose that's how Ashford let you treat him all those years, anyway."

She brushed a hand over the sleeve of her dress where he'd grabbed her as if he'd soiled her designer garment. "What is it you want, Obediah? I have a life to return to that obviously doesn't involve you."

The hurt in her voice had long ago ceased to work on him once he'd realized what a master manipulator she was. He ignored it and met her clear green gaze. "My two companions and I need a way safely past the shades."

"Shades?" Genuine surprise flashed across her features that sent cold hard worry settling inside his gut. His mother knew all the latest gossip both human and supernatural. If he'd surprised her, that meant this was both a recent development and still unknown, which in supernatural terms meant more dangerous.

"What shades?" Her form flickered and then solidified, telling him she'd flashed outside to investigate and returned. The fact that he saw the flicker at all was a testament to his half-supernatural heritage.

"Bloody hell." She frowned. A sure sign that she was unhappy with what she'd found. Even though she was a demon who would never age, his vain mother wouldn't risk frowning which might eventually cause a wrinkle between her smooth brows. "When did this start?"

"The first I saw of them was several hours ago."

She pursed her lips, another mannerism he'd rarely seen from her. "They appear to be more dense near cemeteries but are quickly spreading elsewhere, anywhere they can draw energy." She raised her gaze to his. "Even if I could transport you and your companions out of this house, the shades will continue to be drawn to you. *Especially* with your energy levels, no matter how well hidden."

Levi raked his fingers through his hair and paced away from her as he cast about for a way for his mother to help. She was his last hope to keep the three of them from dying inside this house.

"I don't have the power to keep the shades from you. But I know someone who does."

The resignation and even the tinge of fear in her voice made Levi snap his gaze to hers as icy foreboding chilled him. "Someone who would be willing to help me?"

She winced and dropped her gaze.

"Mother." He spoke the single word sharply, discomfited by her display of reluctance and fear—something he'd *never* seen from her. "Who?"

She sighed and reached up to the long silver chain that ringed her throat and plunged down between her breasts. She fished the necklace out to reveal a bulky ring that Levi instantly recognized.

"The ring of Ashford?" The ring had the coat of arms of the Duke of Ashford etched into it; in older times it was used to impress the wax seals on letters and other official correspondence. He'd left it along with the other items from his old life when he'd walked away.

"The dukedom is yours and ever shall be. Regardless of your own lack of interest, I've been running your affairs in your absence and keeping up appearances as needed."

Levi shook his head at her audacity. However, he couldn't even bring himself to be surprised by her actions. Appearances were everything to her, and thanks to her special circumstances, she'd had many years to hone hers . . . and apparently, his.

She unclasped the necklace and slid the ring off the chain. "You'll need this." She held out the ring and Levi reluctantly took it.

"Who am I supposed to summon now, Mother?"

He'd said it in jest so was surprised when she answered. "Use the same incantation you did to summon me, but leave out my name."

The implication was that whoever he summoned would be someone else who shared his blood.

Cold, hard shock stole his breath and he stood frozen to the spot as he stared at his mother as if seeing her for the first time. He tried to speak several times before he was finally able to push words past his lips. "But I thought my father was human. Just not Spencer." He resisted adding that humans couldn't be summoned like supernaturals could, not to mention that Thomas Spencer, the duke of Ashford, had died long ago. A fact that still hung between them like a bitter accusation.

Caldriel raised her chin and met his gaze with a hauteur worthy of the queen herself. "I never said your biological father was human."

"You may not have said, but you bloody well let me assume."

She gave a Gallic shrug. "Even I cannot summon him, and he will have to choose to appear or not. But if you show him the ring, he'll be able to surmise the rest." She suddenly appeared uncomfortable, and a thought niggled at the back of Levi's mind.

"He doesn't know he has a son, does he?"

When his mother wouldn't meet his gaze, that was answer enough. "I wish you luck, my son. The appearance of the shades isn't a good omen. The end times could be nearer than we'd like. If you finally see sense and want to live the rest of your days as you should, you know how to find me."

Levi studied her for a long moment and something like pity filled him. She'd spent her entire long existence making a place for herself within the human realm. If the end times came and all of that was erased, all her efforts would have been for nothing.

He shook his head, the familiar weariness of being in his mother's presence weighing him down. "Mother."

She glanced up to unwillingly meet his gaze.

"Thank you."

Surprise flashed across her features before she disappeared leaving the scent of sulfur and smoke behind.

Levi refused to let himself think too much before he sat on the floor cross-legged once more, ready to perform the summoning ritual for the second time today.

The fact that who he thought he was—half human—had just been ripped asunder, would have to wait for him to examine it when they were out of danger. For now, he had more urgent matters to attend to.

Excitement curled through him and he chuckled at the thought of a nearly three-hundred-year-old man being excited to finally meet his father. Especially if said father had caused such fear in his mother.

He sighed as he picked up his weapon where he'd dropped it earlier and wrapped his hand around the cold bloodstained handle. With a deep breath for courage, he pulled the blade across his flesh, cutting deep. The sharp pain centered him and he held up his palm, laying the ring next to the welling cut as he closed his eyes and concentrated.

Please let me not regret this.

"By your blood that runs through my veins, I summon you."

At first, nothing happened, and disappointment had just begun to curl inside him when the familiar static electricity crackled over his skin raising all the hairs on his body and bringing energy and power to swirl through the room in a breath-stealing maelstrom. When silence finally fell around him, someone plucked the ring from his upturned palm and Levi opened his eyes to look up at who or what had answered his summons.

"Hello . . . Father."

9

Semiazas materialized in the parking lot of Sinner's Redemption and raked his gaze over the remains of the late Madame, Celine, that still lay just outside the side door on the hot blacktop. She'd literally been ripped in two with both pieces of her head still sporting the beautiful long, red hair he remembered from their last meeting.

He pushed at one piece of the grisly remains with the toe of his shoe. "Pity." She was definitely more fun alive than dead. The woman had been destined for Hell after a lifetime of unrepented debauchery that included a very long, creative list of sins. She'd recently been diagnosed with some terminal disease or another and had suddenly begun to think about the afterlife.

Humans had an amazing penchant for only worrying about the afterlife when it was too late to do anything worthwhile about it. Which actually was one of the reasons humans were so much fun to play with—a shortsighted set of beings.

However, Celine was smarter than most. Rather than some last-ditch attempt to make it to Heaven in the limited days she had left, she'd contacted a bounty demon with information on one of the missing succubi in exchange for leniency when she reached Hell.

Hoping to collect the bounty for themselves, two bounty demons had taken her up on her offer. Sadly, Celine had forgotten to ask for leniency here on earth, so her death had been a particularly gruesome and painful one. Her last act of helping the succubus bitch escape would probably lessen her punishments in Hell but hadn't earned her any appreciation from Semiazas. The woman had better hope she was never under his sole power or she would spend eternity regretting her last decision.

Semiazas nodded in greeting as several human men walked by without a glance toward the grisly former Madame's remains. The bounty demons had left an aversion field around the body until Semiazas could come and examine the site himself. They'd gone on to track the succubus but at least had been smart enough to alert him. If he'd heard about the incident from anyone but the two of them, he would've been peeling more demon flesh—and bounty demons could last a long time before expiring and poofing back to Hell.

Semiazas had already tried to pick up the succubus's energy signature himself, but it was as if something had erased it as soon as it passed by. He shrugged. That's what bounty demons were for. They could do the legwork and bring him his prize.

In the meantime, he had work to do. He straightened his tie and jacket and walked toward the front entrance whistling happily.

As he neared the front doors, something burned against his flesh and he jumped back to find the leg of his pants singed and smoking, the flesh beneath stinging.

A demon barrier.

The little bitch had shown the whores how to set up a demon barrier. And a powerful one if it had been able to injure Semiazas. He'd be impressed if he weren't already so angry with those four damned succubi. They'd cost him seven hundred years of imprisonment, and he would spend four times that long ensuring they regretted it.

He examined the exterior of the building finally seeing the faint pearly white shimmer that marked the edge of the barrier. Now that he knew it was there he could recognize it easily.

It took not only a great amount of rare knowledge, but several years and the combined energy of many individuals well steeped in their faith to erect one of these. There had to be several races of supernaturals involved.

Had the Archangels been in on this?

If so, Semiazas would think it highly amusing. Archangels making a whorehouse a safer place for humans? He laughed and shook his head. Michael would probably spout something about temptation having a place in their Father's world along with free will and all the rest. Michael liked to see things in shades of gray, or "a rainbow of possibilities" as he would often say. But Semiazas knew there was only black and white.

Anyone who was against him was his enemy. Everyone else was his to use as he pleased.

Simple. Easy.

He shrugged and slowly smiled as anticipation curled through him like a promised treat. There were always ways around demon barriers, and he'd just made it his goal for the day to find one.

He walked back around to the parking lot and meandered, waiting. There were always opportunities if one knew where to look.

Nearly an hour later he'd found it.

A car slowly pulled into the parking lot, sliding into a space precisely. The man stepped out and straightened his perfectly pressed black button-down shirt.

The man was in his late thirties, tall and thin, but with enough muscle that marked him as someone who either liked to use the gym or dabbled as a weekend warrior at some sport or other. His aura was mottled enough to show his early life had been spent well, but as the years went on he'd dabbled into the darker areas.

Semiazas smiled as his gut told him this was the one.

He hung back as the man stood in the parking lot deciding if he should go inside or not. Semiazas enjoyed the byplay of emotions that ran across the man's features. The sad sap who actually believed the tripe he'd been taught over the years had convinced himself that sex was a sin, so therefore by choosing to go inside, he truly believed he was actually choosing to do wrong. Which made it a sin against himself and his own morality.

Delicious.

Semiazas loved self-inflicted stupidity.

The human population would be surprised to find that consensual sex among two unattached adults by itself wasn't considered a sin by their Father. The prudes who had drafted the Bible had definitely added quite a few of their own touches, including diminishing women's roles. And to add a wonderfully ironic twist, most of those so-called prophets had broken pretty much every commandment they'd had the audacity to write.

If the human population ever decided to stop being sheep and actually listen to that little voice of common sense and morality that the Father had created inside each of them, Semiazas and all of the fallen would die of boredom.

But Semiazas knew that would never happen. Humans, by definition, were fallible and excelled in proving him right.

The man Semiazas had been watching squared his shoulders and walked forward toward the entrance of Sinner's Redemption.

Now that the decision had been made and the man was open to the guilt of his upcoming actions, the picking was ripe.

Semiazas dematerialized, phasing himself inside the man and pushing the existing consciousness aside. There was a flash of surprise from his host, but then he cowered back as he realized who and what Semiazas was.

The pathetic fool actually thought he deserved this possession because he'd been about to walk inside a whorehouse. Semiazas laughed, enjoying the echoing sound it made inside his new host. He opened his thoughts showing the man the truth.

For a long moment nothing happened, and then came the anger.

Yes! Here was something Semiazas could work with.

All those years of repression were about to be made up for in a few short hours.

Semiazas now had access to everything Ronald knew, but poor Ronnie was a silent bystander who didn't have a brake pedal on his side of the body.

It would've been easier had the fool been drunk or high, but Semiazas wasn't going to question the gift that was offered. Besides, being the one to let the man know the ironic truth had been a fine treat all on its own.

When they were done, poor Ronald here would remember every delicious moment of what Semiazas had planned for this place.

He experimentally moved his arms and legs, getting used to his borrowed body. When he was sure he could function comfortably, he brushed a hand down his already perfect shirt and straightened. "Showtime," he whispered almost as a dare to the demon barrier he approached.

Ronald here was a good enough soul that he should be able to trick the barrier. Most demons wouldn't be able to embed themselves deeply enough to fool the damned thing, but Semiazas was one of the originals. Hell, he'd been next in line after Lucifer and Michael until he'd decided the Son and not the Father had the right idea about the universe.

He walked to the front entrance again, and this time passed through without incident. As the door chimed overhead he grinned and hoped Ron had brought his credit cards.

"Welcome to Sinner's Redemption, sir. Have you been here before?"

Semiazas turned to find a stunning redhead with the best store-bought curves money could buy. Her upgrades were classy enough that if Ron were riding solo, he would've mistakenly believed them all to be stock. But Semiazas knew better.

Not that he minded.

Fucking a refurbished model did have its advantages. "This is my first time here," he said with a wink. "But I'd like to see how many of the services I can avail myself of in one sitting."

The woman smiled and motioned him into a small sitting room. "I'm Melanie. I can help you find the perfect woman and discuss options for your time here." She gestured for him to sit and when he did, sat across from him.

"I spoke to Celine on the phone, is she here?"

Melanie's smile never faltered, which meant none of the whores knew about their Madame yet. "She's out for the day, but you're in good hands. What type of woman are you looking for?"

Semiazas sat back in his chair, enjoying the give of the expensive leather. "I like all women, and I think I'd like several at the same time. Is that allowed?"

Melanie smiled. "Absolutely. Why don't we call a conference and have all the women come out and meet you. But first, why don't we talk about your budget so I know what options to look for."

Semiazas shifted and fished Ronald's wallet out of his back pocket. Right there with several other cards he found the black and platinum cards. A quick delve into Ronald's consciousness told him the man had a near-perfect credit rating and unlimited credit on a few of these cards in his hand.

Perfect.

He pulled out a black card and handed it to Melanie. "No budget. I have the means to pay for anything you can offer, and I'm in the mood to partake."

To Melanie's credit, he couldn't detect any outward reaction, but the sudden scent of her arousal that permeated the room told him enough. She disappeared into the back office with his card and returned with a black Victorian ladies' fan.

"Take this with you when you greet the ladies." She smiled. "Are you ready to meet everyone?"

Semiazas hesitated for effect, pulling a little of Ronald's real personality in just for fun. "Now that I'm here, maybe I could start slow and just build up to meeting all of them?" He made sure there was a slight waver of nerves in his voice.

Melanie smiled gently and reached out to touch his arm. "No problem at all. If you'll head into the main hallway, you can knock on any open doors. A less threatening way to meet the ladies might be one at a time."

Semiazas blew out a slow breath as if suddenly relieved. "Thank you so much. I appreciate you being so wonderful." He stood and she did the same. "I don't suppose that you have a room down that hallway as well?"

Melanie's lips stretched into a smile. "Mine is at the far end of the hall. I'll be there in a few hours when someone else takes over the front office duties. If you're still here, maybe I'll see you then." Her voice made it clear she didn't expect him to still be here by then.

Semiazas traced a finger along her jaw before he turned away. "I'll see you then."

Flipping the black fan idly against his thigh as he went, Semiazas started down the long hallway feeling like a kid just admitted to the free shopping day at the largest toy store in the world.

* * *

A heavy weight pressed Amalya into the mattress and she twisted in an effort to remove the uncomfortable pressure.

"Struggle all you want, bitch. It's more fun that way."

A flash of panic made her surface from her exhaustion more effectively than even a slap to the face would've. The stench of fetid breath paired with a neck-ruffling gravelly voice made Amalya force her eyes open.

Bloodred eyes filled her vision and it took her a moment to look past those to see the pasty-pale face of the demon who currently held her down.

"What do you want?" Her voice sounded small and frail and she mentally railed at herself for showing such weakness in front of a demon.

"I want whoever carries her blood, but for now, I'll take you instead."

Amalya tried to make sense of the words. They were true, but that didn't help her much.

Apparently, this was the one demon that wasn't after her for the bounty Semiazas had placed on she and her sisters. Which was definitely a lucky break but still didn't explain his cryptic words. The demon couldn't mean rape—any demon could sense within seconds that she was a succubus and would willingly take his essence and the energy that would give her.

Which meant he wanted to take something she wouldn't willingly part with.

Fear sliced through her as his grip on her wrists tightened, holding them firm against the bed on either side of her head as he leaned down to snuffle against her neck like an overeager puppy.

At full strength she wouldn't be able to fight off a demon, let alone in her current state where ass-scooting down the stairs had done her in. Frustration churned through her like bitter acid on her tongue.

Sharp pain lanced through her neck and then numbed as the demon licked at the bite wound with a roughened tongue. Amalya cringed away from the contact and swallowed back her panic as a warm trickle of liquid hit her shoulder.

I'm going to bleed to death. This is not how I planned to die.

A feral growl next to her ear made her stiffen, but she held perfectly still and conserved her strength. She would have to take the first good opening that presented itself and use whatever strength she could to escape.

As the demon pulled back to look at her, he snapped his teeth close to her face and laughed when she winced.

She glared up at the demon with the most defiant expression she could muster. "What do you want?"

"Where is the descendant of Caldriel? I taste none of her inside you."

"Caldriel?" The name didn't sound familiar, but demons rarely gave their real names since it allowed anyone with that knowledge a certain amount of power over them. And Caldriel definitely sounded like a demon name.

"Don't play with me, succubus. If you tell me where to find the one I seek, I'll kill you quickly and without pain." He licked his lips, his red eyes darkening. "But if you don't, I'll take my time and only I will enjoy this."

A macabre, hysterical laugh bubbled up through Amalya and she swallowed it back. Talk about horrible options. And even worse, because of her gift, she knew the demon meant every word.

She bit her lip as she searched for a way out.

Jethro and Levi had to be somewhere nearby. She wasn't sure how she'd gotten back upstairs in bed, but she had to believe the two men were still alive and safe. Neither of the men was a match for the demon, and she refused to call them up here only to lead them to their slaughter. Which meant it was up to her to find a way out of this situation without involving either of them.

She forced herself to take a breath and shove away the fear that tried to intrude. She'd been in more dire circumstances before.

Granted, none of them when she was so drained of energy, but she had to believe there was a way through—one that didn't involve anyone besides the demon dying.

She smiled and then winced when the movement made the wound at her neck throb. "I haven't learned that name, but I've met many demons. If you give me more information, I may be able to help you. I—"

He laughed, cutting her off, the evil sound like a slimy caress against her skin. "Helping me is the furthest thing from your mind, bitch." He leaned forward and licked a long wet line up her cheek, his warm tongue reminding her of raw liver.

Bile inched its way up the back of Amalya's throat and she clenched her teeth, battling back the nausea with pure willpower. Throwing up on the demon didn't seem like a good escape strategy.

"I can smell others inside the house. Call them up here. One of them may be able to lead me to Caldriel. And it'll be more fun to kill you while they watch."

She met the demon's red gaze. "No."

His shaggy red brows furrowed as he studied her, his eyes swirling with confusion followed by disappointment. "No?"

"No," she confirmed.

In a move so quick she barely registered it before the pain hit her like a punch to the stomach, the demon let go of her left arm, slashed open her shirt, and sank his long fangs into the flesh just above her left breast.

Searing pain tore through her and Amalya clenched her teeth to keep from crying out. She shoved at the demon with her free left hand, but his bulky form didn't budge. She wished he'd let go of her other hand so she could reach her switchblade, but it was tucked just inside the sheath worked into the right cup of her bra, totally out of her reach.

Hot blood bubbled up from the wound and the sloppy sounds of sucking filled the room. With each pull of the demon's mouth, pain lanced through her as he drank in her energy and life force.

She flailed under him, trying to unseat him even as each movement brought fresh agony stabbing through her. Most of her body was trapped under the sheets and comforter, which limited her options and left her at his mercy.

"Scream," he whispered with his fangs still buried deep inside her flesh. As his lips lifted from her skin, hot blood trickled down her chest and side cooling as it finally dripped onto the comforter.

"No," she gritted out, praying that she passed out before she gave in to the urge to scream.

He laughed, the evil sound scraping along her flesh like sandpaper. "Then let the fun begin."

He yanked his fangs out of her, ripping a chunk of flesh out with it and sending fiery agony shooting through Amalya until spots of white flashed in front of her vision like dozens of tiny lightbulbs.

When the pain receded to a constant dull throb, she realized she was panting as if she'd just run ten miles. Clammy sweat covered her skin and her stomach roiled, threatening revolt.

"Welcome back, sweetheart." His leering smile only lasted a second before he struck forward, clamping his jaws around her wrist until the loud crack of breaking bone and a tidal wave of pain filled Amalya's consciousness.

He worried the wrist like a dog with a play rope and tears filled Amalya's eyes, spilling down her cheeks as wave after wave of agony rolled over her, stealing her breath.

When the burn inside her lungs outstripped the other points of pain, she forced herself to suck in a breath. The sudden influx of oxygen worsened the round of flashes in her vision and added a new dimension of vertigo that made her stomach clench.

She clamped her eyes shut as the soft, smug laughter of the demon taunted her. "A brave one. Just means I'll have to get more creative."

The metallic scent of her own blood filled her nostrils and Amalya whimpered as the demon lifted the damaged remnants of her shirt and nipped painfully at the sensitive skin of her stomach.

She tensed, knowing that if he gutted her, she wouldn't be able to keep herself from screaming. Not only that, but everyone might end up dead.

Forcing her uninjured arm to move, she grabbed the switchblade from her bra, pressed the button, and stabbed the demon. A surprised shout was all she heard before a hard stab of agony seared through her and a wrenching scream of anguish filled the air around her.

*   *   *

Raphael stood stunned, staring down at the man who sat cross-legged on the floor in rumpled, but expensive-looking Italian slacks and a shirt.

Father? Had he heard the man correctly?

To most males, that one word would invoke a frantic mental flip through a Rolodex of women he'd had sex with. In Raphael's case, being an Archangel, he would've known at the time of conception.

And yet . . .

The man who slowly stood in front of him, easily matching his height, had the exact same eyes Raphael saw in the mirror every day. Not to mention, the man had summoned him using blood, which meant, by definition, Raphael's blood ran through his veins.

There the similarities ended, but those along with the blood summons were enough to convince Raphael that somehow despite all odds, this man was his son.

But how?

Raphael slowly stepped closer until they stood toe to toe. He met the man's hazel gaze, opening himself up to peer inside the man's soul.

And nothing happened.

"I'll be damned."

The man laughed. "I find that hard to believe, since if I'm not mistaken, you're an angel."

Only high-level Archangels and a few of the higher-level fallen could soul-gaze. And those of that same blood were the only ones immune to it.

Raphael couldn't help the grudging smile that curved the side of his lips at the calmly stated comment.

"I'm Raphael, an Archangel for God. And however awkward this situation is, given all the evidence before me, I don't believe we've met."

"My name is Obediah Levi Spencer, Duke of Ashford, and you are apparently my biological father."

Raphael looked at the ring the man still held in his palm, and understanding slowly began to dawn. He groaned, picked up the ring, and tapped it to his forehead. "Caldriel." It had been nearly three hundred years since he'd seen her, and now everything that had happened that evening became clear.

Obediah nodded, the detached amused expression on his face totally at odds with the churning emotions Raphael sensed just under the surface. "At least you remember her, that's something."

"Obediah—"

"Levi."

Raphael nodded. "Levi. Maybe we should sit. This may take a while to explain."

Levi waved away the comment. "If you're going to give me the 'mechanics of impregnating a demon' talk, you're a few hundred years too late."

"Not exactly what I had in mind." Raphael sat on the small twin bed, his leathers creaking with the effort. He motioned for Levi to join him and waited while a visible war of impatience raged behind the younger man's eyes.

When Levi remained standing, Raphael shrugged and continued. "You are actually the biological offspring of Caldriel and your father, the Duke of Ashford."

One dark brow rose in a clearly arrogant, mocking gesture. "Even though your own blood summoned you here and I'm very long lived for a half human, half demon, you're trying to tell me Ashford was my father?" Levi snorted and turned to leave.

"Wait." When Levi only slowed, Raphael continued. "I don't deny my blood runs through your veins, but it was Ashford's first."

Levi whirled on him, anger turning his hazel eyes nearly black when a woman's agonized scream rent the air.

10

The anguished sound of Amalya's scream wrenched through Levi as he ran full-out toward the master bedroom.

A blur of movement as Raphael pushed past threw Levi off balance and made him stumble. Levi reached out to steady himself against the wall and regain his footing before he continued his mad dash toward the bedroom. By the time he turned into the bedroom doorway, the sounds of Jethro clamoring up the stairs behind blended with the noise of the pandemonium before him.

Raphael, dressed entirely in black leathers, fought a stocky man that reeked of demon. The rest of the room was mired in the stench of blood and freshly spilled intestines.

Icy fear squeezed Levi's chest as he tried to see past the battle to the bed where he'd left Amalya. But the two combatants' movements were so fast, they seemed a constant blur to Levi.

Raphael and the demon circled and exchanged blows as Levi's fear ratcheted inside him until his ears rang with the overload of adrenaline flooding his body.

Concern for Amalya drove him forward.

He crisscrossed his arms to reach the daggers tucked in either side of his waistband and in one continuous motion slid them out of their sheaths and threw them at the back of the demon's skull.

Both blades found their mark with an audible thunk, and the demon stumbled but didn't fall.

Raphael stepped forward, taking advantage of the demon's inattention, and in a quick motion snapped the demon's neck.

A loud pop echoed through the room, which signaled the demon being sucked back to Hell as its physical form was destroyed.

"Dear God." The anguish in Jethro's voice brought Levi's attention back toward the bed and he had to swallow hard as his brain worked to make sense of what he saw there.

Amalya was covered in blood, her blond hair matted with it. A large gaping wound showed in her neck and above her breast, but the worst was her stomach, which was nothing but so much ragged meat. The only sign she still lived were the short breaths that sounded from her at irregular intervals.

Levi crossed the room in quick strides, but Raphael stepped in front of him blocking his way. "Let me heal her. We don't have much time."

Levi bit back all the denials that sprang to mind and instead clamped his lips closed and stepped back. He wanted to go to her, to touch her, to comfort her, but held those impulses in check and fisted his hands at his sides to let Raphael tend her instead. The inaction went against every fiber of his being, especially when it came to Amalya.

He'd sworn to protect her, and he'd failed.

Self-recriminations flowed through his mind and he clenched his teeth until his jaw ached. A quick glance toward Amalya's still form and he shoved his guilt aside and instead did something he rarely did—prayed.

Raphael advanced toward the bed but stopped short when Jethro pulled out one of his guns, placing himself squarely between Amalya and the large Archangel.

Panic jumped through Levi as Amalya's breathing faltered and slowed. "Jethro, he can help." Levi started forward to reason with the other man, but when Jethro swung the gun toward him, he froze and held his hands up in front of him.

"He's an Archangel. If anyone can save her, it's Raphael." As fear raced through him, he cast about for something to say to convince Jethro to drop the gun. "Please. She may not have much time."

Jethro ignored Levi but met Raphael's gaze for a long moment as tension in the room mounted until Levi thought all was lost. But then, slowly, Jethro lowered the gun until it hung by his side. "If you can save her, do it. Do it now."

Raphael laid a gentle hand on Jethro's shoulder as he passed, but Jethro seemed to barely notice as he turned back to stare at Amalya.

Raphael sat gently next to Amalya's still form on the bed, the mattress dipping under his weight. When he was settled, he held both hands palms down over the gaping wound in Amalya's abdomen and closed his eyes.

Within seconds, a golden glow erupted from his palms and bathed Amalya's entire body in a glow of warm light.

As Levi watched, her skin slowly knitted and closed, the blood fading as if it had never been.

A soft grunt from Jethro who still held the gun limply at his side told Levi Raphael hadn't bothered to mask the evidence of his work from the full human.

When Amalya's stomach was perfectly smooth and unblemished once more, Raphael continued his vigil, sweat breaking out along his brow, his lips set into a hard line of concentration.

Levi watched the scene before him, the silence stretching his nerves until he thought they would snap. But he was thankful now that he'd summoned Raphael, no matter the truth about his parentage. If the Archangel could save Amalya, Levi would deal with his mother's twisted version of the truth about him and his family, later.

A soft moan from Amalya pierced Levi like an accusation. All the self-recriminations resurfaced with a vengeance.

He'd left her alone and she'd somehow been attacked.

Raphael cursed and then gently pulled Amalya into his lap, arranging her so she leaned back against him at an angle, her head cradled by one large arm. "She needs blood . . . mine . . . or she'll die." He nodded toward Jethro. "Put down that gun and come up here on the bed. I need you to hold her arms. She's going to flail, and I need to concentrate on getting her to drink."

"To drink blood?" Jethro demanded.

Raphael turned his heavy gaze on Jethro and the man shuddered as if someone had just touched his soul before he looked away and stepped forward to do as Raphael had asked.

The Archangel's dark gaze turned toward Levi. "I need you to hold her legs. Put all your weight on them. Succubi are strong, especially with the energy kick she's going to get from my blood."

Levi stepped forward and crawled onto the bed, straddling Amalya's legs, ready to bring all his weight to bear when it was needed.

Raphael tucked Amalya's head firmly into the crook of one arm and plucked a dagger from his boot. With a little maneuvering to reach around Amalya's still form, he slashed his wrist deep. Bright blood welled out of the wound and using his free hand to open her mouth, he pressed his wrist to Amalya's lips.

For a long moment, she lay still as blood dripped from the sides of her mouth. Then without warning, she began to fight.

She flailed and bucked, squirming against their hold. Raphael held her head firmly in his grip, forcing his wrist against her lips until she swallowed and then gasped, sucking in a large breath before he pressed his wrist to her mouth again.

Jethro struggled to hold her arms while Levi was forced to use all his body weight and a good amount of leverage to keep her from kicking him off and sending him ass-first onto the floor.

"It's all right, little one," Raphael softly murmured as he held her gently but firmly against his large body while he forced her to swallow again and again.

When every muscle in Levi's body ached, and he was convinced he wouldn't be able to hold Amalya down much longer, Raphael finally wiped her lips and nodded to both men that they could let her go. "Let's take her to the guest room. Fresh sheets and no dead body." He gathered her in his arms and took her down the hall.

Levi jogged ahead of him to pull the covers back and allow Raphael to lay her gently on the bed. Jethro tucked her in like she was a small child, his features pale and drawn.

"It's not over."

Raphael's pronouncement surprised Levi and he had just turned an incredulous stare on the Archangel when Amalya's entire body began to convulse.

He darted toward the bed to hold down her legs as Jethro did the same with her arms to keep her from hurting herself. Her strength increased with each passing second until Raphael had to help.

As the long minutes ticked by, sweat slicked Levi's shirt to his body and threatened to drip into his eyes.

Jethro's curses grew louder as one of Amalya's flailing arms would occasionally catch him in the face.

When her movements began slowly to still, Raphael motioned for Jethro and Levi to move and let him sit beside her. Raphael gently stroked Amalya's cheek with his fingers until her eyes fluttered open and she met his dark gaze.

Amalya stiffened and froze, staring into Raphael's eyes for several long minutes as Levi exchanged concerned glances with Jethro.

Levi softly cleared his throat, impatient to know what was happening. A few long seconds later Raphael glanced away and Amalya relaxed, her eyes fluttering closed.

Jethro rushed forward to the other side of Amalya's bed from where Raphael sat and gently took her hand. "Is she . . ."

"Rest now, little one," Raphael whispered to Amalya as she sighed in her sleep. Raphael glanced up and nodded to Jethro and then slowly stood, his spine making small pops of protest. "She needs rest and then food. She should be fine on energy for a while but probably shouldn't turn it down if either of you are willing."

"I'll stay with her." Jethro's voice was low. "Food is ready downstairs. If you're going to talk, go, so she can sleep."

Levi didn't miss the low thread of anger in Jethro's voice. He didn't need any further accusation to blame himself—he'd already done that from the first second he saw the demon in Amalya's room. He motioned Raphael outside and closed the bedroom door behind them.

Without turning to acknowledge the large Archangel at his back, he walked down the stairs and, for lack of anywhere else to go, made his way into the kitchen and checked the burners under the spaghetti sauce and green beans. Apparently, when Amalya had screamed, Jethro had already finished cooking and had just been keeping things warm.

"Perfect." Raphael leaned over the large pot of spaghetti sauce and sniffed. "I know I could use some food, and it wouldn't hurt you any either." He hunted through the cabinets until he found plates and silverware and set the table for four before taking two plates to the stove to fill them with noodles, sauce, and green beans.

Levi stood frozen in place as his adrenaline ebbed away and he was left with guilt and anger that chewed at his insides like acid. "How did the demon get in?"

When Raphael wouldn't meet his gaze, Levi grabbed the man's arm, nearly knocking one of the plates to the floor. "Tell me."

Raphael sighed and set both full plates of food on the kitchen table before sitting and glancing up at Levi. "You summoned Caldriel before me?"

Levi nodded as foreboding slid through him like an icy caress.

"He was most likely looking for her. Or you," Raphael added almost as an afterthought. "And she probably didn't hide her movements."

"Me?" Levi glanced around the room trying to make sense of Raphael's statement before he turned back toward the Archangel. "Why would he be looking for me?"

"You have the blood of Caldriel in your veins. That alone would make you an enemy of many. I'm surprised you haven't run into that long before now." He gestured to the seat beside him and then took a hot roll from a bowl covered with a linen napkin in the middle of the table.

"I haven't seen my mother in two hundred years." He sat heavily in the chair next to Raphael and stared at the food in front of him as his stomach roiled.

Raphael pursed his lips. "Demons are patient. The best explanation is that he followed the scent of her blood that runs inside you and found a nearly helpless succubus instead of her." He glanced up. "It's not your fault. It's Caldriel's. I don't wish to say something disparaging about your mother, but it's the truth and will keep you from blaming yourself." He picked up his fork and used it to point at Levi. "You and Jethro are going to need all your strength to protect Amalya. You can't afford time for guilt or self-denial. So eat." He nodded toward Levi's plate before digging into his own.

Levi stiffened in his seat, his hand going to his waistband where his daggers usually sat. He'd left them upstairs embedded in the back of the demon host's skull. "How did you know Jethro's name? Or Amalya's for that matter? I never told you either."

Raphael shrugged as if he hadn't noticed Levi's reaction or frantic reach for his weapons. "When I looked into Jethro's soul upstairs that gave me all the information I needed."

Levi frowned as he remembered Jethro had started to argue about Amalya being made to drink Raphael's blood. One quick gaze from Raphael and Jethro had blanched and backed down. "Did you look into my soul as well?" Levi asked feeling violated even without the confirmation.

Raphael swallowed a mouthful of food and laughed. "No. I tried that as soon as you summoned me."

"And?" Levi prompted.

"And . . . nothing." Raphael stood and crossed to the refrigerator where he pulled out a large pitcher of iced tea and brought it to the table along with two glasses he'd found in the cabinets. "You have my blood in you, so you're immune to soul gazing, just like Amalya will now be when she recovers."

As the implications hit him like a gunshot, Levi snapped his gaze to Raphael's.

"You're on the right track. You carry my blood, but Ashford was the one who lay with Caldriel to conceive you."

A sudden kinship with the late duke ran through Levi, even though the old bastard had been a proud and haughty man. "Then how—"

Raphael cut him off with an impatient gesture. "If I tell you, will you eat?"

Levi slowly nodded and picked up his fork and began to eat, if only to hear the story. He slid a large forkful of pasta between his lips but tasted nothing as he met Raphael's gaze to hold him to his promise.

Raphael smirked as he poured them both tea and took a long drink before speaking. "Without going too much into the ancient history of Caldriel, she was able to acquire a long-term human host and has always had a knack for ingratiating herself into any situation she wanted. I'm not sure how she wormed her way into the *haute ton* of British society, but she managed it and Ashford fell madly in love with her."

He took another long drink of tea and set the glass on the table. "Hemophilia ran in Ashford's family like most of those who share blood with the royals. When you were three months old, Caldriel came to me and begged me to save you." Raphael sighed. "Yes, she's a demon, but I think she truly loved your father and she truly loves you. She'd stayed clear of the supernatural politics for quite some time and you had the mark of destiny about you, so I couldn't turn away."

Levi frowned at the "mark of destiny" comment. "So you gave me your blood, just like you did with Amalya upstairs."

Raphael nodded. "Granted, you were so tiny, it didn't take much, but the end result was that when I healed you, all of Ashford's blood was cleaned away and mine ran in its place."

"So in a way, you *are* my father, but so is he."

Raphael nodded. "Exactly." He laid down his fork and met Levi's gaze. "And just as having Caldriel's blood will automatically garner you enemies, so will having mine. Only other Archangels or very high fallen will be able to sense what's inside you. Most others will think you half demon, half human. It's probably best if you don't advertise otherwise."

Levi fell silent as everything he'd learned churned inside his mind trying to fit together in some coherent way. But he was too exhausted to make much good sense of any of it, so he took Raphael's advice and ate.

11

Lilith pulled on her robe with quick, impatient gestures as she tried unsuccessfully to calm her trembling fingers.

"Do you wish me to leave?"

Gabriel's soft question startled Lilith, reminding her the Archangel still sat naked on the edge of the bed.

"No," she said even though she was tempted to say yes. She'd made the decision to exclude Uriel from her sustenance sessions because it had become too hard for her to have him so close and know she would never be able to have him.

The interruption of her time with Gabriel threatened to undermine her resolve, but she couldn't let it. "Please stay."

An urgent knock on the door to her quarters made Lilith scowl. Instead of calling out, she walked across the room and pulled open the door.

Jezebeth stood just outside, her gaze downcast. "My queen. You asked me to alert you to any growing signs of Armageddon in the human world."

Lilith nodded and frowned. The worldwide appearance of shades definitely wasn't a step in the right direction. She wondered what had happened now. "Enter."

Jezebeth hesitated at the threshold. "It was Noah who brought back the information."

Noah, a horror writer in the human realm, had brought Jezebeth back safely just last week. Now Noah served as a messenger and liaison for Lilith, which granted him both immunity from Jezebeth's succubus powers and also the ability to remain with Jezebeth in Lilith's lair.

"Bring him." Lilith glanced behind her, surprised to find Gabriel gone. A wistful sense of loss wound through her. Uriel's poor-timed visit had shattered the bubble of happiness Lilith had created with Gabriel these past several days, and she wasn't sure it could be resurrected. She bit back a sigh and left the door to her quarters standing open as she turned and headed back inside.

By the time she'd curled into her favorite chair, her feet comfortably tucked under her, Noah and Jezebeth stood before her, the door to her quarters firmly closed behind them.

"What did you find?" She caught Noah's gaze and held it.

"Not only are the instances of the shades increasing, as well as the deaths caused by them, but there are parts of the ocean that have begun to bubble."

"Bubble?"

Noah nodded. "I should actually say 'boil'. Even in icy waters, where the bubbles have appeared, any sea life or humans who have ventured too near have been boiled alive."

Lilith frowned and wished Gabriel had stayed to hear this new development. "What's the reaction from the humans?"

"Right now it's being downplayed as an effect of global warming, although certain fringes of the population are beginning to scream about the end of the world. Some say the Mayan's calculations for 2012 were a bit off, the right-wingers say God is angry and punishing the world, and still others say it's the normal evolution of the planet and are unconcerned." Noah shook his head. "There are a lot of scared people out there, and most of the leaders around the world seem to be fighting among themselves to place blame elsewhere."

She nodded. "Just like they handle everything else," she noted absently. "Any word from Amalya, Reba, or Galina?"

Noah and Jezebeth exchanged a quick glance and Lilith frowned. "Tell me."

Jezebeth cleared her throat before speaking. "Sinner's Redemption was burned to the ground earlier today. Most of the workers escaped with only a few injuries. The Madame, Celine, was found pulled in two and dismembered lying outside the smoking remains of the building."

Lilith's grip tightened on the arms of the chair. "Amalya?"

Jezebeth stiffened and she raised her chin. "She's alive. I'd know if she weren't."

Lilith nodded. She would've felt the loss of one of her own as well but was glad to receive confirmation from Jezebeth.

"It's being called another sign of the end times—the prostitutes being punished with fire and damnation." Noah held out a folder. "I've cut out news articles I think you should see and highlighted some that may be signs of Amalya and Reba. I can't find anything on Galina. It's like she's disappeared entirely."

A large wave of exhaustion threatened to engulf Lilith. She took the folder and then waved them away. She needed time to think and to rest. It seemed she could no longer protect those she was responsible for. The world was coming to an end, and she continued to hurt those she loved.

She was afraid to wait and see how this situation could get even worse.

* * *

Uriel tried once more to locate Raphael and cursed when he was unsuccessful. Wherever the damned Archangel was, he was masking his location. He had to be. If Raphael were dead, Uriel would've sensed it, and so would every other high-level angel.

What reason could Raphael have for secrecy?

Uriel had spent the last several hours poring over the journal he'd found at the Badass Café and he needed to share what he'd found. He stood and stretched, walking out through his kitchen and down the hallway to the front door of his two-story brick Victorian.

He had a soft spot for that time in history and had chosen several design elements for his property. He walked out the front door, down the steps and several minutes later, found himself standing just under the weeping willow that Lilith always materialized under when she used to come here a few times a week for her sustenance sessions.

The salty tang of ocean mixed with the astringent scent from the willow left an almost metallic taste on the back of his tongue, and he breathed deep, trying to replace the pungent, musky odor of Lilith's and Gabriel's arousal that still clung to his skin and memory.

He'd known better than to go to Lilith's lair earlier.

As he'd materialized inside her chamber, he'd convinced himself he wanted to tell her he'd found another journal. Instead, just as Semiazas had said, he'd found her in bed with Gabriel.

A vivid memory of the two of them together on top of Lilith's rumpled sheets flashed through his mind and pain sliced through him even as his cock hardened inside his slacks.

He'd tried to lie to himself and say he was surprised, or that he didn't care—he'd only gone on business, after all—but Uriel couldn't abide hypocrisy for long.

Especially his own.

No matter how hard he tried, he couldn't stop thinking about Lilith. Ever since he'd first seen her walk out through the gates of the Garden of Eden all those millennia ago, he'd been drawn to her. Even at the time he hadn't been able to explain the strange connection that always sizzled between them, but he'd risked life and loyalty to intercede on her behalf with the Almighty.

Much to his surprise, it had been granted, and he'd been given responsibility for her well-being. Over the years, he'd remained strong in denying his need to possess her.

Except for that once.

To this day he could recall perfectly how it felt to slide inside Lilith's slick pussy while she arched against him, and helpless sounds of her need spilled from her throat in raspy pants. But even better than that was waking up with her curled against him, her fingers tangled in his chest hair, her hot breath feathering against his skin as she slept.

His heart had ached as he'd watched her, and even as he savored those last moments, he knew he'd have to let her go. He'd been charged with her care but had stretched the rule of no sexual relations with other high-level supernaturals to the very brink. Then in one night, he'd totally broken it.

When he realized his cock was hard and aching and his breath now came in harsh, short pants, he blew out a long breath and frantically searched for calm. The ocean breeze stung his cheeks and ruffled his hair but did nothing to help. He needed to speak to Raphael before he did something crazy and self-destructive.

A harsh bark of a laugh bubbled up from his throat.

For some reason the only time he was in any danger of doing either of those things, the situation always involved Lilith.

Normally if Raphael couldn't be found, Uriel would go and find Gabriel. However, he knew exactly where she was, and as things stood, she would be no help either.

He didn't blame Gabriel or Lilith. The situation had been one of his own making. But living with the outcome was slowly killing him.

A flash of a powerful presence simmered through the air and Uriel snapped his gaze toward his house. The large brick Victorian two-story looked the same as it had when he'd left, but Uriel could tell he had a visitor.

Quick strides took him across the perfectly manicured lawn and up the few steps to the porch. He pushed open the front door and glanced down the entryway finding only the familiar silk paneling, hardwood banister, and the priceless pieces of artwork he'd collected throughout the years.

He concentrated on the tendrils of power and followed them down the hallway through the spacious kitchen and out onto the patio.

The Archangel Michael sat in a deck chair looking out toward the flowing waterfall and lush gardens that made up Uriel's backyard no matter where in the human realm his house appeared.

"Nothing in five hundred years and then you visit me twice in one week. Is this becoming a habit?"

Michael turned and smiled, not bothering to stand. "I sensed your churning emotions and came to ensure you were well."

"Bullshit." Uriel sat and Michael laughed. Uriel's emotions, churning or otherwise, had never seemed to concern Michael before, so he was skeptical of the Archangel's sudden interest.

"Choose to believe what you will." Michael waved away Uriel's thoughts. "Do you deny you were looking for someone to talk to?"

Uriel bit back the urge to tell Michael he'd been looking for Raphael or Gabriel to talk to, not him. What he'd found inside the journals, he would've ended up telling Michael anyway, but since until last week he hadn't seen the Archangel in several centuries, he'd gotten out of the habit of confiding in him—especially not with anything personal.

Uriel glanced up and found Michael patiently watching him. The piercing green eyes tended to unnerve most beings, which Michael usually used to his advantage. But physical appearance alone had little effect on Uriel.

Michael lived a lonely existence as the right hand of their Father. He knew things others didn't and couldn't and therefore carried a heavier burden. By necessity that had set him apart from the rest of them, and every now and then Uriel could see the weariness and pain in Michael's expression before the Archangel ruthlessly hid them behind an utterly calm mask.

Uriel reached into the pocket of his slacks and pulled out a small blue leather journal with gold-embossed pages, ignoring Michael's real question. "Since this latest journal was found, I've been reading and rereading it trying to find any clues to how to slow the onset of Armageddon." He flipped through the pages until he found the one he'd been reading just before he'd transported to Lilith's lair. Memories of the scene he'd stumbled into with Lilith and Gabriel threatened to surface and he swallowed hard as he wrestled to fight them back.

"Uriel."

He glanced up and met Michael's gaze again, but rather than the unnerving gaze he was used to, he saw . . . understanding.

"Do you feel as if they've deserted you?"

Uriel knew exactly who Michael meant but asked anyway. "Raphael and Gabriel?"

Michael nodded. "The three of you have been inseparable since our creation. Nothing ever before this has come between you."

Uriel's fingers tightened on the journal as all his swirling emotions threatened to break through his hard-won control. He swallowed hard before speaking. "I appreciate your concern, Michael, but I'd rather discuss what I found inside the journal."

"As you wish, brother." Michael's overly calm tone and distant gaze made Uriel wince. Michael didn't open up to anyone very often, and Uriel had just slammed the door in his face.

After a tense silence, Michael shifted in his chair. He threaded his fingers together, resting them against his stomach as he leaned back and stretched his long legs in front of him, crossing them at the ankle. "I know we've never been particularly close, but I am always here if you need to speak with me."

Uriel nodded in acknowledgment but not in agreement. As noble as Michael's offer was, he meant what he'd said—this situation was of his own making, and if it estranged him from Raphael and Gabriel as well as Lilith, it was no more than he deserved.

"What did you find?"

Michael was letting him off the hook, and Uriel gratefully took the out he was offered. "Some of the prophecy is in the form of poems, and there are even a few lines in ancient Hebrew."

Michael frowned. "If Semiazas wanted this to find its way into the human consciousness quickly, I would think that it would be written in a more current language."

"I don't think Semiazas wrote these. He doesn't have the expertise to gather all this information."

"Then who?" Michael shrugged.

"I doubt they were assembled by any one person. Whatever ideas and ideologies call to the horsemen would have to be included. Semiazas is very smart, don't get me wrong, but a dedicated scholar he is not." Uriel frowned. The origin of the journals was only a small piece of the current mystery. "Regardless of who assembled them, they're a mishmash of ideas, languages, references, and vague statements. For example, how many people are fluent in ancient Hebrew today?"

"There are those modern-day scholars who can translate enough ancient Hebrew to come close."

"That's exactly what I thought at first, but there are certain words and phrases they continually mistranslate." Uriel opened the journal and pointed to a line that was written in perfect ancient Hebrew, unlike the surrounding text which was a mixture of Latin and old English.

Michael read it out loud, translating into English. "Beware the second of four, the destroyer of worlds, who carries both the blood of temptation and the blood of the angels . . ." His words trailed off and he picked up the journal to study the text. *"Ha-olinim?"*

Uriel nodded, glad to see the concern on Michael's dark features, which meant he understood the implications.

The term, which was used in certain ancient texts literally translated to "the upper ones," or "the Ultimate ones," and always referred to the Archangels. "For as much as you've said the Archangels won't be involved in the final battles, there certainly is some evidence lately pointing to the contrary."

Michael's expression hardened, but other than that, he showed no further reaction. "This could just be a reference to Lucifer, who technically has Archangel blood."

Uriel shook his head, impatience simmering at Michael's direct deception. "You know as well as I do that the term '*Ha-olinim*' wasn't in use until well after the fall and has only ever referred to those of us who remained true to our Father's purpose."

Michael met Uriel's gaze, but said nothing.

"Don't tell me. This is another one of those things you can't share with us." It wasn't a question.

Michael sighed but still managed to retain an air of unaffected calm. "Even I am surprised by certain events, but you know there are things which I can't share and for good reason. Sometimes I would dearly love to share everything with you, my most trusted brothers and sisters, but He has decreed I cannot."

"Decreed? As in actually forbade it?"

Michael's calm gaze continued without a flicker, but he didn't answer the question.

"Fine." Uriel pushed to his feet and began to pace, unable to contain his frustration by sitting still. "You've made it clear where you stand on this, Michael. We'll make due on our own without you."

Michael stood and faced him. "I regret that I can't be more forthcoming, but we have all given our word in certain areas, and I cannot go back on mine without endangering us all."

Uriel stopped and stared at the odd wording of Michael's comment. "In this matter? About Armageddon, you've given your word?"

Michael's lips slowly curved into a slow smile. "It's been good to see you again, my brother. We should not wait so long in between visits next time."

12

Amalya woke to soft whispered chanting.

She wanted to be irritated with whoever it was for waking her, but then she realized as the words trailed off that it had been her. Her throat was sore and dry, her lips chapped from what felt like hours of murmuring in her sleep.

She swallowed hard and then yawned and stretched as if she hadn't moved in too long and she needed to work out her stiff muscles.

"Amalya?"

Relief and urgency was evident in Jethro's voice and she turned her head to find him standing next to the bed watching her carefully as if she might break apart at any moment. He looked rumpled and tired with dark circles under his eyes and a weariness in the way he held himself. His beard had grown several days of stubble and his sandy blond hair stuck up in all directions as if he'd continually run his hands through it.

She smiled. "You look like hell."

He gave a shaky laugh. "You're looking a little rough around the edges yourself, but I can't tell you how glad I am to see you open your eyes and look at me again." He cocked his head to the side and studied her for a long moment. "Do you remember what you were whispering over and over?"

She shook her head, wincing when she found her neck stiff. "No. What was I saying?"

He smiled and waved her question away, his expression too guarded to reflect his true feelings. "There's plenty of time for all of that. I'm just glad you're back."

She frowned up at him and rolled her shoulders tipping her head from side to side on the pillow to work out the kinks. Amalya had known Jethro for a long enough time to understand when he was deliberately avoiding a subject. She also knew from long experience that the best way to get him to discuss it was anything but attacking it head-on. "What did I miss?" Vague memories of swirling night-mares teased at the edges of her memory, but she couldn't bring them into focus.

"How are you feeling?"

She frowned at his blatantly ignoring a question from her a sec-ond time but quickly took stock of herself in case there was some-thing she hadn't previously noticed.

All her fingers and toes moved when she flexed them and she wasn't in any pain. Her muscles were a bit stiff, most likely from being in bed too long, but she was well rested, and other than the tendril of dread that still clung to her from the nightmares and her dry throat, she seemed well.

She pushed up in bed so she leaned against the headboard, only realizing when the cool air inside the room hit her bare breasts that she was naked.

Jethro glanced away giving her privacy as she pulled the comforter up under her arms to cover her breasts but not before the familiar scent of his arousal filled the room. He'd seen her naked before, but just as in the past, an awkward awareness blossomed between them that they both pretended didn't exist.

"Would you like a robe?" He held up a pink terry-cloth robe that looked much too big for her and she shook her head.

"I'd like you to sit down, stop avoiding my gaze, and answer my questions." When he didn't move, she reached out and grabbed his hand, careful not to let the comforter fall and reveal her bare cleavage again.

He finally allowed himself to be pulled down to sit next to her on the bed. He sat stiffly and met her gaze, but his expression remained shielded.

"Jethro." She forced a smile and traced her fingers gently over his thick stubble before she dropped her hand to the comforter and twined her fingers with his. "Tell me what happened."

Jethro swallowed hard, his Adam's apple bobbing with the effort before he took a deep breath and let it out slowly. "I thought I'd . . . we'd," he corrected quickly, "lost you."

Fuzzy images of pain floated just outside her consciousness and as she tried to bring them into focus, they scattered, leaving her with a slight throb behind her temples.

He watched her carefully. "What's the last thing you remember?"

She concentrated and finally remembered falling asleep on the bottom step of the stairs. The explosive sex and the resulting fight with Levi came back with vivid clarity and her cheeks burned. She bit her lip as fast-moving images wavered in and out of her memory of pain, drowning, screaming, and . . . an office.

The last memory made her frown. How did an office fit into all of this? "Maybe you'd better start from how I made it back upstairs earlier and go from there."

Jethro squeezed her hand and a sudden stab of ice pierced her stomach making her suddenly not want to hear anything he had to tell her. She placed their joined hands over her stomach, willing the uncomfortable sensation away and nodded for Jethro to continue.

He told her in quick, concise detail about her run-in with the demon, Raphael's sudden appearance and healing, then ended with his own vigil by her bed for the past two days.

As he spoke, his words filled in gaps in her memory and brought the vague pictures from her nightmares to life, although none of it felt real, even now. Everything Jethro said felt more like something that had happened to someone else or that she'd watched on TV. But with each sentence, the stiffness in Jethro's shoulders lessened, as if he released a heavy burden through telling her.

He kept his fingers joined with hers and several times throughout his narrative he touched her face or stroked the back of her hand, almost as if it helped prove to him that she was alive and well, and she wouldn't disappear before his eyes.

When he finally finished he fell silent, and their gazes met as sexual tension sizzled between them like it never had before.

Surprise stole Amalya's breath and her lips parted as she returned his gaze.

Jethro leaned forward, closing the distance between them, sliding his free hand behind her neck as he gently captured her lips with his. His warmth wrapped around her as he held her firmly against him, his mouth hovering over hers as they looked into each other's eyes for the longest moment.

When he finally closed the slight distance between them, the kiss was sweet, a soft brush of his lips over hers. And again. Then he dipped his tongue inside her mouth and kissed her with gentle but firm expertise.

Amalya kissed him back, waiting for the first flush of passion that should come with such a joining.

His energy, even weaker than normal, thrummed against her in pleasant waves, slowly melting into her skin as it turned into energy.

As she noted the changes in her body that came with the added energy, Amalya couldn't help comparing this kiss to the explosive awareness that had ignited her entire body every time Levi had kissed her.

After a long moment, Jethro pulled away and shook his head. "You're thinking of him."

It was a quiet accusation, and Amalya didn't bother denying it or pretending she didn't know who Jethro meant. Guilt flashed through her, and she wondered why she couldn't respond to Jethro like she did to Levi. They'd been friends for a long time, and the transition from friend to lover would be comfortable and easy . . .

Her thoughts trailed off as she realized how dull that sounded compared with the alternative.

Jethro's hands clenched into fists and he slowly stood. "I wonder if I'd done that years ago if it would've made any difference." He looked down at her for a long moment. "I suppose not. You've known how I feel about you for a long time, Amalya, and you've always taken it for granted." His words were more stiff and formal than Amalya had ever heard them and her heart ached at the hurt she saw in his blue eyes.

"I'm sorry," she whispered finally to his retreating form as he slowly left, closing the door behind him.

*　*　*

Gabriel found Uriel sitting on his back porch, looking out at the waterfall but not really seeing it.

"Michael just left." His flat words held the definite tension of so much left unsaid between them.

A flash of guilt made Gabriel wince, but she knew if Uriel had wanted to talk about Lilith, he would've said so. "Two visits in a week? Maybe the world really is coming to an end."

Uriel laughed, but it sounded hollow. "I said something similar." He held out a small journal, and curious, Gabriel stepped forward and took it. Other than the color, it looked just like the last one Uriel had found through a clue Noah the human had led him to.

"What should I be looking at?" She considered herself fairly well informed but dissecting poems, myths, and snippets of supernatural gossip wasn't something she excelled at, or hoped to practice.

She held out the journal and Uriel opened it to a page near the middle and pointed to a section that was underlined. *"Ha-olinim?"* The words were out before the reaction of shock could hit. "None of us have offspring with a demon. We would've known about it as soon as conception occurred."

"I agree. So why am I convinced that we're missing something?"

"Have you asked Raphael?"

Uriel shook his head, a curt movement. "He's shielding his location."

Gabriel frowned as she reached out with her senses trying to locate Raphael herself. When only a vague buzz, which meant he was still alive, met her senses, she scowled. If he were hurt or in trouble, he wouldn't mask his location, he would've reached out to them immediately. Which meant Uriel was correct, that for some reason, Raphael was shielding his location from them.

But why?

"No luck for you either." It wasn't a question, so Gabriel didn't bother to answer it.

A troubled silence fell between them and Gabriel wondered if she should bring up Lilith. She didn't like having tension between her and Uriel. The fact that he'd asked her to continue to provide sustenance to Lilith in his stead did little to alleviate her sense of guilt and obligation. "She misses you, you know."

Uriel's jaw tightened, but otherwise, he showed no reaction. "She knows where to find me if she needs to speak with me."

When Gabriel took a breath to try again, Uriel cut her off with a pointed glance. "There are larger things at stake here. Let me know when you hear from Raphael. I'm hoping he has insight into the half demon, half angel mentioned in the prophecy."

She nodded, staying put when Uriel rose and walked back into the house, closing the door behind him.

*   *   *

Semiazas materialized on the floor of the Aegean Sea in front of a shin-high wall made of rock that ran for a mile along the sea floor in a perfectly straight line. Sea creatures had made their homes on top and along the sides, obscuring it from prying eyes along with the general sense of aversion that permeated the entire area.

Many humans had explored the area and surmised that this was the site of the ill-fated Atlantis, but no mere single human could unlock the quarantined world. The entire human consciousness had to attract its return. A certain wavelength of ideas and energy brought about by free will and the humans' propensity for information sharing.

Semiazas smiled, small bubbles escaping from between his lips to make their way slowly up to the surface of the sea while his hair waved lazily in the icy depths.

He'd already placed three of the four journals and those ideas were even now speeding around the world thanks to the Internet and social networking sites. This was the perfect time in history to achieve his goals.

The energy from the horsemen pulsed and throbbed just under the sea floor as if they were impatient to be unleashed. They sensed him here, sensed his power and his willingness to see them once again free to roam and mete out their justice unto the world.

Their angry voices merged inside his head as they demanded to be set free.

"Soon. Very soon." He laughed, the sound making an echoing warbling sound under the water as he dematerialized picturing his room where he'd left Sadie up on the surface.

A few seconds later, he rematerialized perfectly dry and comfortable just inside the small room he'd rented here on the island of Santorini.

The woman he'd spent the night with lay on the bed facedown and naked, the sunlight spilling in through the blinds falling across her pale skin in bright slices. Her blond hair spilled across the white sheets and her left leg was slightly bent, leaving her slick, pink pussy open to his hungry view.

She reminded him of Gabriel in certain ways—as long as she didn't open her mouth and ruin the illusion.

Sadie was insatiable in bed. She liked things hard and inventive and never complained about his rough treatment—in fact she seemed to thrive on it.

After his very satisfying afternoon of fucking several whores at Sinner's Redemption and then using Ronald's body to burn down the entire place, he'd come back here and found another woman to spend the night with. He'd fucked her all night in every way imaginable, trying to push her past her limits, make her beg him to stop—not that he would have. But she'd kept up with him, always ready for more.

He wasn't sure if he should be frustrated or impressed that he'd failed in his objective.

She certainly wasn't as much maintenance as Gabriel.

In fact, if he could just fuck this woman and keep her from speaking, Semiazas was able to pretend he was sinking his cock inside Gabriel once more.

It had been such a long time since Gabriel's betrayal. He'd hoped in time that she would see the error of her ways and join him by supporting Lucifer, but instead she clung to the ill-informed view that God still had a plan.

Semiazas laughed quietly. Hadn't any of the Archangels noticed that Michael and Lucifer ran things, not God?

Armageddon would bring about enlightenment. Then Gabriel would see. She would understand what he'd been trying to tell her all along.

His cock swelled inside his trousers as he thought about Gabriel crawling back to him, admitting she'd been wrong and begging him for forgiveness. A quick glance toward the bed showed him the perfect outlet for his appetites and he quickly shrugged out of his clothes and advanced on her.

When the voices of the horsemen still rang inside his head, he shoved them aside. Their time was coming soon, and until then Semiazas was determined to live in the moment.

13

Jethro walked slowly down the stairs as a vast emptiness bottomed out inside the pit of his stomach. Deep down he'd always known Amalya only thought of him as a loyal friend, but stupidly, he'd held out hope that she would grow to love him in time.

She'd never led him on or hinted at anything more, so he had only himself to blame, regardless of what he'd said to her back inside the room. His lack of anger told him just how long he'd been lying to himself and holding out false hope.

At the bottom of the stairs, the smell of the food he'd cooked hit him. He headed into the kitchen, not because he was hungry, but because he had nowhere else to go.

When he entered Levi and Raphael glanced up from their plates.

Levi looked like hell, and a small surge of jealous satisfaction spilled through him at the thought. It might be a very petty reaction, but apparently he wasn't above them at this point.

Raphael, on the other hand, looked like a business executive who dressed like a biker on the weekends with his clean-cut hair, regal bearing, all-black leathers, and shit-kicker boots. Only the wave of power that prickled against Jethro's skin like electricity ruined the illusion of Raphael being only a badass human.

"How is she?" Levi's voice was tight.

"She's awake and feeling better. I suspect she's going to clean up a bit before joining us." A small flash of guilt assaulted him and he looked away, not wanting to meet Levi's gaze. He had no fucking clue what Amalya would do now and was trying hard to convince himself he didn't care. With an internal sigh, he sat at the table and took a roll, breaking off a small chunk of the still-steaming bread as he turned to Raphael. "So, how did you find us, and who the hell are you?"

Raphael smiled, clearly not offended by Jethro's rude greeting.

"I'm the Archangel Raphael, and I'm a friend of Lilith's." He took a large drink of what appeared to be iced tea and after exchanging a glance with Levi turned his full gaze on Jethro.

Jethro winced away. The insides of his mind were still raw and aching from the last time he'd met Raphael's gaze directly; he had no desire for a repeat performance.

Raphael smiled which made him look like a guilty little boy. "I apologize for the soul gaze upstairs. I needed to get to Amalya quickly and gaining your cooperation that way seemed easiest at the time."

"Soul gaze?"

"Archangels have the ability to look inside someone's soul by looking into their eyes and then past them."

Jethro huffed out an amused breath. "So they weren't kidding when they said the eyes are the windows to the soul."

Raphael shrugged. "That saying came from times when humans were open minded to the supernaturals and most of us didn't hide our identities while traveling among you."

Jethro shook his head, sorry he'd said anything. He didn't want a history lesson. Right now he wasn't sure what he wanted. "Thank you for saving Amalya, but if it's all the same to you, I don't think I'll be looking you in the eye any time soon."

Raphael laughed. "You have my word there will be no more soul gazes today, is that good enough?"

After a long moment of deliberation, Jethro slowly raised his gaze. Trusting an Archangel might seem like a no-brainer, but Jethro had learned that everyone lied about something—especially supernaturals. Anyway, at this point, he didn't seem to have much choice. "So Lilith sent you?"

Raphael shook his head. "No. The blood brought me."

Jethro frowned at the wording. "So you're called to anywhere where there's blood?"

Levi laid his fork on his plate. "Are you going to eat that roll or just fondle it?" He pointed toward the roll Jethro still held in his hand. "I, for one, don't care how Raphael got here since he saved Amalya. I think our next question should be if he can help us get past the shades."

Jethro placed the small piece of roll he'd ripped off earlier inside his mouth and forced himself to chew. As the yeasty warm taste exploded inside his mouth, his stomach tightened with hunger and he ignored it. "I would've thought with all the time you two have had together down here, getting us past the shades would've already been a topic of conversation."

Raphael laid his fork across his plate and then pushed it away. "Unfortunately, the shades are out of my control. They will be attracted to energy sources, and Amalya will attract them even more than before with all my blood running through her veins."

Jethro nearly crushed the roll in his fist. "Aren't you an Archangel? Why can't—"

Raphael held up one large hand, cutting Jethro off mid-rant.

"I'm an Archangel, but believe it or not, we have to operate within the rules of the universe too. Every creature needs sustenance of some kind. For you two, it's food and water; for Amalya, it's those as well as sexual energy. For the shades, it's only energy. However, they have started to move toward the cities where there are larger populations of humans."

"So the swarm of shades is gone?" Levi pushed away from the table and paced to the back window.

Jethro thought about looking out a different window when he realized how drained he was and stayed put. He needed food and sleep in any order he could get them, and the situation upstairs with Amalya had drained the last of his reserves, which had run purely on hope and ego.

"I only see one." Relief tinged Levi's voice. "That's definitely a good sign."

Jethro nodded. "We should probably bury the farmer."

"I've already taken care of both him and his wife." Raphael stood and grabbed the plate in front of Jethro before going to the counter and filling it with pasta and green beans.

"Where was his wife?" Jethro exchanged a glance with Levi that showed him the other man hadn't known about this piece of news either.

"She was out in the barn. Both have been returned to dust, their souls moved onto the next plane to start again along with their horses, cow, and two chickens."

"To start again?" Levi echoed the question Jethro had been about to ask.

Raphael grinned. "I don't think now is the proper time to have a discussion on the nature of the universe or the cycle of the soul." He set the plate in front of Jethro and handed him a clean fork. "You need to eat. You'll do nobody any good neglecting your health. Eat, then you two are going to get some sleep."

Jethro thought about arguing, but lethargy was already slipping over him like a heavy blanket. He ate mechanically. The only clue that he'd finished was when his plate was empty and Raphael took it away and ordered him off to sleep. "Amalya," he mumbled, unwilling to leave her unprotected even though things between them were shaky right now.

"I'll watch over her," Levi said automatically.

"No," Raphael countered. "*I'll* watch over her. You two will sleep."

Without remembering how he'd gotten there, Jethro found himself lying on the couch in the living room with a blanket thrown over him. He only had time to frown at the gap in his memory before sleep claimed him.

*   *   *

Amalya stepped out of the master bathroom to find a large man sitting on the bed watching her. An Archangel if the energy pouring off him to prickle against her skin was any indication.

Fuzzy memories of his dark gaze, so much like Levi's, flashed through her mind and she frowned as the full memory remained just out of her reach.

"Greetings, Amalya. I'm Raphael."

She held on to the large towel she'd wrapped around her body when she'd stepped out of the shower—more an insecure reaction in front of a being so powerful than any sense of modesty. "My lord," she said remembering the appropriate greeting for an Archangel as she resolutely stared at his nose rather than his dark eyes.

Raphael's laugh boomed around the room. "There's no need to

fear a soul gaze from any of the Archangels anymore. With my blood running through your veins, you're now immune."

As the truth of his statement radiated against her, the sensation of choking came back to Amalya with unnerving clarity and she raised her hand to her throat.

She remembered the viscous liquid forced down her throat in between quick breaths. Panic surged through her and she glared at Raphael. "You made me drink your blood." She swallowed back the knee-jerk reaction of her stomach heaving at the thought.

He had the grace to look apologetic. "You'd been eviscerated by a demon. If I hadn't healed you and forced that blood down your throat you'd be dead and we'd all be in trouble."

"The demon . . ." As if Raphael's words unlocked another barrage of fuzzy memories, Amalya remembered the heavy sensation of someone pressing down on her and then the agony as her bones broke and her flesh ripped open.

She hadn't realized her legs had buckled until Raphael caught her and gently sat her on the edge of the bed. "Easy now. You've had a rough few days."

Amalya bristled at his kind tone. "Damn it. I'm a strong, independent woman. I've spent more time being coddled over the last few days than I have my entire life. And I'm sick of it."

Raphael's lips twitched but he didn't smile, which was good since it would've only ignited Amalya's temper further.

"I promise I'll let you fall next time." His features remained calm, and even if she hadn't detected the white lie, it was hard to miss the mischief that shone inside his dark eyes.

Stubbornly refusing to be charmed, she held his gaze for several seconds longer, testing out her new immunity to soul gazes. When nothing happened, she smiled. "Let me guess, you got in one last soul gaze right before you gagged me with blood."

Raphael held his hands out palm up at his sides. "Guilty. I had to calm you down enough for you to allow me to heal you."

She sighed. "No wonder my insides ache like someone took a blowtorch to all my internal organs."

"How much do you remember?" He watched her carefully, as if he already knew the answer.

"Snippets really . . ."

Four succubi must stop horsemen to save all.

Amalya gasped as the chant rang inside her mind again. "Four succubi must stop horsemen to save all." She raised her gaze to Raphael's whose expression was stoic. "What does that mean?"

"I think you already know, even if you don't remember the details."

Anger snapped through her and she pushed to her feet and stripped off the towel tossing it to the floor. "Just once I'd love to get a straight answer." She stalked to the closet and pulled it open, hoping to find something to wear because if her few memories of her time with the demon were any indication, her own clothes were a total loss.

"Will this help?"

Amalya turned to find Raphael holding the duffel Jethro had packed for her back at Sinner's Redemption. They'd left it in the truck when they'd made a run for the farmhouse to escape the shades.

She grabbed the duffel from Raphael and bit out, "Thank you" before setting it on the bed and digging out a fresh set of clothes.

Even with her back to him, she felt his gaze, a heavy weight against her skin. It wasn't sexual. Raphael's gaze was more thoughtful and curious.

She sighed. "If you have something to ask me, go ahead. Maybe we can get through two sentences without me snapping at you."

His rich chuckle flowed over her and she shook her head as she stepped into a pair of lace panties and reached for the matching bra. "Just now you reminded me of Lilith."

Amalya whirled around to face him with her bra in her hand. "You've seen Lilith? Lately?"

He nodded.

Excitement and fear shot through her and she blurted out, "Is she well? My sisters?"

"Lilith is well. Jezebeth is well. I have no knowledge of the other two."

Amalya wished she couldn't detect the absolute truth of his statement. She'd like to hold out hope that someone somewhere knew Reba and Galina were well. She sat down hard on the bed as she absorbed the information. "I knew Jezebeth had made it back to the lair. Levi told me. I was hoping for word of Reba or Galina."

"I wish I had more to tell you."

Amalya slipped on her bra and then stood to finish dressing. "Me too."

Four succubi must stop horsemen to save all.

The chant whispered through her mind again and she breathed a sigh of relief. "They're alive. They have to be." She smiled up at Raphael who looked puzzled.

She laughed. "Don't you see? I can't remember why I woke chanting that, but if it takes all four of us to stop the horsemen and save all, then I have to believe they are still alive or we'd somehow know by now."

Raphael shook his head, his stoic expression threatening to dampen her newfound confidence. "I sincerely hope you're right. You know, any other woman would take the appearance of the shades and the boiling seas as signs of the end."

She raised her brows. "This is the first I've heard of boiling seas, but I'm not surprised. If my understanding of Armageddon is any indication, things have to get a lot worse before they can begin to get better."

Now if I can only convince myself!

"Besides, I'm not just a woman. I'm a succubus." She pulled on jeans and a tank top and then dug into the bottom of the duffel for socks and the extra pair of running sneakers Jethro had packed. "What did you mean," she asked nonchalantly, "when you said if I died, we'd all be in trouble?"

She turned to sit down on the bed and pull on her socks and shoes, careful not to look up at Raphael, although the sudden flux in his powerful energy as it buzzed against her skin told her she'd hit a nerve.

"Did I say that?"

The false question hit her immediately. Raphael knew very well he had said that exactly.

She finished tying her shoes and stood, meeting his gaze, daring him to dissemble again. "You know, don't you." It wasn't a question and it hung between them as tension crackled and built. "You already know what my chant means, and you aren't going to tell me."

Raphael met her gaze calmly a long time before answering. "We've all made vows and promises we must keep. Events will play out as they must without my interference."

"Does it ever make you crazy?"

From the confusion that flashed across his handsome features she'd surprised him. "What do you mean?"

"You know, having to follow all the rules when Lucifer's side doesn't. Having to take the high road when you think that maybe sometimes a nudge or two from you could ensure that God's side comes out on top?"

He grinned, suddenly looking like the mischievous little boy. "Absolutely." He glanced around the room and Amalya frowned at the sudden change. He'd looked directly at her during the entire conversation, so why was his gaze searching the room now?

"Amalya, have you ever been to Oregon?"

Confused by the sudden switch in topic she frowned trying to figure out where this had come from. "I think so, but I was probably just passing through and it was long ago before modern times. Why?"

He shrugged. "There's a really beautiful place there called Graveyard Rim Cliff. In ancient times it was a pagan holy place. In more recent times it has become property of the Catholic Church, which has fenced it in and made it more of an outdoor mausoleum to all the people buried there."

"I don't think I've ever heard of it." She resisted the urge to ask him why he'd suddenly chosen to tell her about it.

"In ancient times people would go there when they wanted to travel to see the gods. They would slit their wrists, and as their blood drained out into the earth, it was thought that a portal to the other side would open and the gods could choose to let that person enter the otherworld if they were worthy. I think the church took pity on all those they considered godless sinners and buried them there where they would always be remembered."

A chill trickled down Amalya's spine. It sounded like a horrible, creepy place. "I take it you've been there. Does it have some special significance I'm missing?"

Raphael smiled a bit too brightly. "I've been there quite a bit. It's very peaceful for the most part."

She laughed. "Except when people are bleeding out and calling for help from the other side?"

"Exactly." He shrugged. "The interesting part is that all those pagans thought they were calling out to gods, but it was usually one of the Archangels who heard them. It's pretty loud lately with all the shades there. Apparently, it also sits on a natural energy vortex, so thousands of them have congregated there."

Amalya shuddered. "Thanks for the tip. No upcoming trips to Oregon in my future. Nearly dying twice is my quota for a lifetime if I can help it."

Raphael smiled down at her, laying a gentle hand on her shoulder. "I'm glad I was here to prevent the second and also glad Levi and Jethro were able to bring you back from the first."

She cocked her head to the side as she studied him. "Wasn't saving me the kind of interference you're not supposed to engage in?"

"I am the healer among my kind. It's what I do. How could I see a woman in so much pain without rendering aid?"

"Even when that woman is a succubus?" she countered.

He smiled. "Especially in that case."

14

Amalya pulled the blanket Jethro had kicked off back over him before she climbed the stairs to an office on the opposite side of the house from the master bedroom. She'd hidden inside the guest bedroom like a coward until Raphael had come to tell her that both men were asleep.

After that it had taken another several hours for her to convince Raphael to leave. He'd helped her to the extent he was able but had promised to keep an eye out for Reba or Galina. Then just before he left, he'd fortified the house against further demon attacks and gave her some unasked-for personal advice.

She smiled to herself and shook her head. Men, no matter what species, always thought they knew best. Unfortunately, this one might actually be right.

Amalya quietly opened the door to the office and, thanks to succubi having excellent night vision, immediately made out Levi's large form on an oversized couch that sat against the back wall.

She padded across the floor to where he lay facing her. The

blanket had slipped down around his waist to reveal a broad expanse of bare chest that she remembered well from their meeting at Sinner's Redemption. His dark hair fell over his brow and she smiled at the urge to brush it back or to trace his long sideburns with her finger.

Instead, she crossed her arms as she studied him with a quiet sigh.

Since she'd met him he'd lied to her by omission, manipulated her, and even talked over her straight to Jethro.

He'd also protected her and saved her life. Although, to be fair, she'd known immediately about the lie of omission and hadn't called him on it. So some of the blame fell on her own shoulders.

From everything she could tell, he was a good man, loyal, honorable, and determined.

He still intrigued her. Despite the world falling apart around them, she found herself wanting to know more about him.

Raphael's advice had been about appreciating the small things. The small perfect moments in time that made all the others worthwhile. She'd never thought about life in quite those terms, which surprised her with as long as she'd lived. But succubi, just like humans, often became creatures of habit.

Before she could talk herself out of it, she kicked off her shoes and stripped off the rest of her clothes, dropping them on the floor in a pile. With a smile, she lifted the blanket that covered him and slid in front of Levi, tucking herself back against him spoon-style.

He murmured in his sleep as one strong arm slid around her middle pulling her tight against him before he stilled. The musky male scent of him surrounded her and the heat of his body radiated against her back making her sigh against the comfortable sensation.

Amalya smiled and let herself relax.

It had been a long time since she'd fallen asleep in someone's arms. In her profession, distance was something to be kept at all costs. Especially when she needed sexual energy to thrive and survive, she couldn't remain too dependent on just one person to provide it.

Or so she'd always thought.

But the idea of letting herself open up and care for someone fully besides her sisters was both terrifying and tantalizing. She'd befriended Jethro, but he'd been right, she'd never let him close. There had always been a wall of distance that she'd kept between them, and no amount of time would've changed that.

But somehow Levi had skirted all her protections and he'd gotten too close before she was able to erect a strong enough wall between them. She grinned into the dark. The lack of barriers between them probably explained why the man could make her so crazy.

She took Levi's hand and tucked it more securely around her middle as she let her eyes slip closed.

No matter what happened tomorrow, she'd face it. It was worth it for this one perfect moment.

Damned if Raphael wasn't right.

*   *   *

As soon as Raphael left the farmhouse, he made his way to Uriel's property. He'd felt the repeated telepathic nudges that told him first Uriel and then Gabriel had been looking for him. But he wasn't sure how much of what he'd told Amalya was true. Would Michael and even their Father consider healing Amalya interference?

He hadn't yet been summoned by Michael, and he hadn't spoken directly to his Father in some time. So he had to assume that he'd skirted any standing orders Michael had given them, however vague they had been.

Sometimes Archangels had to function blindly, just like humans.

He materialized on Uriel's porch and rang the bell.

Seconds later, Uriel pulled open the door. "Are you well?"

The concern that laced Uriel's voice threatened to send guilt slicing through Raphael, but he reminded himself how many times both Uriel and even Gabriel had gone off on their own. "I'm well. I was doing some healing."

An awkward silence fell between them and Raphael knew Uriel sensed there was more he hadn't said. It wasn't as if Raphael was trying to hide anything, but he didn't believe in coincidence. There had to be a reason that out of all days, two days ago he had been summoned to meet Levi and be there in time to save Amalya.

As much as he hated to admit it, this very situation helped him to understand Michael's dilemma of not being able to share everything.

"I've found another journal," Uriel said finally as he stepped back and waved Raphael forward. He turned to head deeper into the house. "It mentions something odd that I wanted to run by you. Neither Michael nor Gabriel had any idea what it could refer to."

Curious, Raphael followed Uriel out to the back porch, the soothing sound of the waterfall in the background making him feel welcome as it always did. He sat without being asked and waited for Uriel to do the same.

Uriel laid a blue leather journal on the table between them. This one was the same size as the previous journal, worn around the edges with gold-tipped pages. A long green leaf marked a page near the center and Raphael reached out to open the journal to that page.

He laid the leaf aside and began to read. When he reached the word *Ha-olinim* his blood ran cold. "Beware the second of four, the destroyer of worlds, who carries both the blood of temptation and the blood of the angels . . ." He let his words trail off as the possibilities percolated inside his mind.

It might be a reference to Amalya, who now carried his blood in her, but Raphael didn't think so. His instincts told him it alluded to Levi. He would definitely have a part to play in the end times. But the question remained . . . which side needed to beware of him?

Since he'd shared a soul gaze with Amalya before he'd shared his blood, he'd been able to see Levi through her eyes. The man wasn't capable of doing great evil. But it wouldn't be the first time evil had used an innocent man as its pawn in the larger scope of events.

"I can tell by your expression you know who this refers to."

Raphael met Uriel's gaze and nodded. "I'm not sure what part he will play, but he's already involved. He's currently protecting the succubus Amalya."

"Amalya?" Uriel frowned. "Sinner's Redemption. That's where he found her, isn't it."

Raphael nodded, confused with the sudden turn in the conversation. "Why?"

"We need to go and speak with Lilith."

* * *

Uriel and Raphael were ushered inside Lilith's throne room to find Gabriel already there.

There was no telltale musk of arousal hanging in the air, but Uriel still had the potent scent burned into his memory along with the sight of the two of them twined together on Lilith's bed. Jealousy curled through him and he wrestled it back and clamped it down mercilessly.

A small crease appeared between Lilith's brows as she looked between Uriel and Raphael. "What's happened?"

Tension caught and held as she met Uriel's gaze, and almost absentmindedly Uriel noted how Gabriel and Raphael shifted uncomfortably as long seconds ticked by.

Gabriel stood abruptly. "Raphael, why don't you fill me in while Uriel and Lilith talk?"

Uriel turned to ask them to stay, but they were already out the door by the time he found any words. When he turned back, Lilith looked as stunned as him with their sudden departure.

"Please, sit." Lilith's small smile was forced and Uriel resisted the urge to make up some reason to flee. Instead, he sank into the chair she offered.

"I don't like this tension between us, Uriel." The words were blurted out more than stated.

It was the most honest they'd been with each other in a long time and Uriel blew out a relieved breath that she'd broken the stalemate between them. "I don't like it either. I'm sorry I brought us to this." He waited for all the familiar arguments they'd had in the past, but none came.

"We need to find a way to coexist without losing all semblance of the relationship we've had." She swallowed hard and studied her hands in her lap. "I know we can never have—" She waved away what she'd been about to say. "Anyway, I don't want to dread being left in the same room with you, Uriel. We care for each other. There has to be a way for us to make a friendship of some type work."

He nodded and reached out to take her hand in his. The fine-boned fingers were warm to his touch and he feathered his fingers over her knuckles as he'd done a thousand times in the past. "I agree." He forced himself to meet her gaze. "I miss you."

A small, sad smile curved her lips. "I miss you too."

Silence fell again, but this time it was much less uncomfortable. Finally, Lilith squeezed Uriel's hand and glanced up. "Why did you come to see me today? I know it wasn't originally to talk."

Lilith was right. He'd been a coward, and if Raphael and Gabriel hadn't taken the choice from him, he would've avoided this talk with Lilith for as long as possible. All because he couldn't find a way to reconcile his desires and his duty. He didn't blame Lilith—she'd been completely honest about what she wanted from the start. He'd been the one to sleep with her, then tried to redraw the line of separation between them. Even as he'd pushed her away, he'd felt like he was betraying something deep inside him.

What a hypocrite he was. And even knowing that, he had no idea how to change things.

He sighed and met her gaze. "What do you know about Obediah Levi Spencer, Duke of Ashford?"

Lilith's lips pressed into a firm line and the crease between her brows returned. "He is Amalya's protector."

"What deal did you make with him?"

Her expression remained wary, but Uriel knew she wouldn't deny him the information. "He wanted information on his parentage in return for escorting Amalya safely back here."

Raphael had filled Uriel in on Levi's parentage before they made it to Lilith's lair. "If I'm not mistaken, he's already in possession of that information."

Lilith raised one brow in question. He knew she prided herself on finding and bartering rare information. If Levi had found out through another source, Lilith would want to know who had told him and why.

Uriel quickly told her about Levi and Raphael's meeting and what he'd found inside the journal.

"I suppose it was Raphael's story to tell," she said with a thoughtful expression. "Don't worry, I'll find something of equal value to pay Levi with. I have a knack for deal making." She smiled and Uriel was gratified to see something of the old Lilith in the expression.

"He is somehow integral in the end times. I'd like to keep him close if I can. If he comes to you for any other deals, I'd be interested in buying that debt from you."

She glanced at him from under her lashes, the mischievous Lilith flashing through quickly. "Buying it from me? With what?"

Uriel grinned. "Yes, buying. We can discuss details later."

Lilith's artful expression fell away to reveal the real being beneath. She looked down at their joined hands and then up into his gaze. "No. This is one debt I'll happily pass along to you. I'm grateful for all you've ever done for me. And most of all I'm grateful to have not lost your . . . friendship forever."

Uriel noticed the slight hesitation before the word "friendship," but he wasn't so sure he knew how to define what they had either.

Lilith smiled. "Don't worry. I'm a master at getting humans indebted to me. You'll have Levi's debt. I promise."

He leaned over and brushed a kiss across her brow before standing. "Thank you," he murmured before he turned to walk away.

15

The fresh, warm scent of sunshine and woman filled Levi's senses as he slowly surfaced from sleep. He was relaxed and comfortable, his face resting on a pillow of silken hair, the front of his body pressed against familiar soft curves. His arm was around Amalya's waist holding her close, and her hand rested over his as if to ensure he didn't move or pull away.

From her deep, even breathing, she was still asleep, and Levi enjoyed the comfortable moment to just savor their closeness before the world encroached on them again.

He spread his fingers over her perfectly smooth stomach, forcibly erasing the gory image of how she'd looked after the demon had gotten hold of her. Raphael had saved her, and Levi would feel forever in his debt.

Amalya stirred in her sleep, shifting against him and reminding his body there was a very desirable naked woman in front of him.

His cock grew and lengthened against her ass and he had to resist the urge to lay a line of gentle kisses along her neck and shoulders.

He shifted to try to find a more comfortable position where the silky skin of Amalya's back and lovely bottom wouldn't brush against his erection with her every breath.

She thwarted his efforts when she stretched in front of him, arching back and reaching back under the covers to lay her hand on his bare hip. "Mmm. Morning." Her voice was filled with sleep and pure female satisfaction.

"Good morning." He swallowed hard, not sure where to go from here. The last time they'd spoken, back before the demon attack, they'd fought horribly and he'd stormed out. He wasn't sure if he'd been forgiven or if this was some sort of diabolical female test.

She turned over, wriggling against his aching cock unmercifully on the narrow couch. When she settled herself comfortably, his cock lay pressed against her stomach, her full breasts flush against his chest and her feet tangled with his. "You look well rested this morning," she said with a slow smile.

"As do you," he ventured as he searched her face for clues about how to proceed. "In fact you look quite mischievous this morning."

She laughed, tracing her fingers over the stubble along his jaw. "You don't need to be afraid of me, Levi. I'm sorry for the other day. I don't react well when people keep things from me."

"I suppose I don't either. I'll endeavor to do better in the future."

"Good." Her slow smile lit her face and his chest ached from how beautiful the woman in his arms was. "Is Levi short for something? It's a unique name."

"My full name is Obediah Levi Spencer, Duke of Ashford."

She laughed. "Your Grace. That's why Jethro kept calling you that. Do you still hold the title?"

"Technically, yes. But I haven't been a practicing duke for a long time."

"That explains a lot, you know." She traced her fingertips over his lips and Levi sucked in a breath as a spear of hot arousal shot straight to his groin. "I'm sure that's where you get the haughty arrogance." She smiled to soften the comment. "But when you're not busy being overbearing and bossy, you're actually very sweet."

"Sweet?" he asked with disbelief. He'd been called many things through the years, but sweet had never been one of them.

Ignoring his reaction, Amalya wriggled tighter against him. "How about we start again? After all, Raphael did remind me to enjoy the little things and not let all the good parts of life slip by me." She smiled up at him. "What do you think . . . Your Grace?" she murmured before brushing her lips over his.

The sudden softness and warmth made his entire body tighten. He opened for her, excitement swirling through him as she dipped her tongue inside his mouth, stroking and enticing until he growled low in his throat and pulled her tight against him.

Her seeking fingers teased and stroked as did her talented mouth while she arched against him until he was panting and breathless.

When he would've rolled them over and covered her with his body, she preempted him by sitting up and shifting him over to lie on his back on the couch so she could straddle him. The wet heat of her pussy pulsed against his cock teasing and beckoning while she ground against him, thrusting her tongue inside his mouth as if showing him what she would soon let him do to her.

When he thought he would go mad from all the erotic sensations careening through his system, she finally shifted and reached between their bodies to guide the tip of his cock to her opening.

She traced him up and down her slit, the hot slickness of her arousal coating him, the exquisite sensations ripping a long moan from his throat. "Amalya," he said through gritted teeth.

She didn't answer, but instead sank down on him fully, impaling herself with a ragged gasp and began to move, her body slick and smooth as it accepted him.

She anchored her hands on either side of his head as she rode him, her blue gaze burning into his. An unnamed connection slowly formed between them and grew stronger, tighter as he stared into her eyes while pleasure built between them.

This was much different than last time. Amalya was here. Present. She wasn't purely using him to gain energy. She wanted him for him, and it showed. The difference was clearly stated in her every movement, and it sent possessive warmth swirling through him.

Mine! he wanted to say.

Her blond hair spilled around them in a sensuous waterfall that caressed his arms and chest with each movement. The tips of her ripe breasts bobbed teasingly just in front of him. He rested his hands on her hips, enjoying the play of her muscles under his fingertips as she rode him. She looked like a Greek goddess come to life, her long hair moving around her as ecstasy lit her face.

When she shuddered against him and her skin took on a shimmering glow, he frowned up at her.

She slowed, drawing out her movements as if savoring the delicious friction between them. "Your pre-come. When it comes into contact with my body, I absorb it and it feels like a mini-orgasm."

He smiled as understanding dawned and he tightened his grip on her hips, widening his thighs and thrusting up inside her until his swollen tip came into tight contact with her cervix.

Amalya gasped and tipped her hips to take him even deeper.

The sensation of being buried fully inside her tightened his balls against his body and he had to suck in several breaths to stave off the familiar tingling deep inside his pelvis.

When Amalya gasped again and the golden glow rippled across her skin, he smiled as he realized what had happened.

Her breathing had become raspy and her movements more urgent as she continued to let him guide her. The walls of her pussy tightened around him as arousal swirled higher inside him.

Amalya stiffened on top of him and cried out, her eyes dark with passion, her skin flushed with exertion. Levi had never seen her look so lovely.

While she continued to recover from her orgasm, he pulled her down on top of him and rolled her over so he covered her.

Amalya sighed as she slid her fingers into the hair at the back of his neck and pulled him down for a kiss.

Levi went willingly, meeting her in a searing kiss as he slowed the rhythm between them, sliding inside her with long, slow movements before pulling back and sliding inside her once more.

Time spun out slowly between them as he banked the fires of his own arousal and concentrated on which movements pulled small sighs or gasps from Amalya. The hard tips of her breasts teased against the hairs on his chest as he moved and she dug her nails into his back as she arched beneath him.

Only when she began to tighten around him again did Levi loosen the hold on his own control and allow the delicious friction that built between them to beckon him toward his own release.

"Yes," she murmured against his lips. "Come inside me, Levi. Let me feel you and see you."

He pulled back to watch her face as he continued to move inside her. The wonder that shone in her eyes awed him. Had a woman ever looked so lovely spread beneath him, her blond hair spilling over the pillow, passion darkening her eyes, and the scent of her body filling his senses?

She moved with him staring into her eyes as her muscles convulsed around him as she came.

A few more thrusts in the tight heat of her body slammed his own orgasm through him, stealing his breath and making him cry out as he continued to thrust, unwilling to stop until they'd both experienced every last ounce of pleasure to be had between them.

Amalya cried out again as he spilled inside her, and this time the golden glow that feathered across her skin tingled against him in a teasing rush.

Movement from the doorway had Levi glancing up to meet Jethro's angry glare.

"We need to get moving. Something's coming."

Guilt stabbed Amalya deep as she met Jethro's angry gaze.

She knew him well enough to see the pain beneath the anger, but she quickly reminded herself that she'd done nothing wrong. She'd never promised herself to Jethro and she hadn't invited him up here this morning.

When Jethro turned and walked away, his heavy footsteps echoing down the stairs, Amalya sighed.

"Are you all right?" Levi brushed her hair back away from her face as protective concern glittered inside her gaze.

She nodded but didn't meet his gaze as he pulled out of her and sat up. "He's been a friend for a long time. I never wanted to hurt him."

Levi nodded, his jaw tight. "Can I assume you didn't come up here to fall asleep with me only to make him jealous?"

His voice sounded flat, but Amalya didn't need to be supernatural to sense the bristling male pride in that statement. She smiled and leaned over to brush a kiss across his lips before she tipped up his chin to make him meet her gaze. "You can." She held his dark gaze for a long moment to make sure he'd understood her before she grabbed her clothes and headed down the hall to the bathroom.

His warm gaze sent shivers of awareness over her naked skin as she left the room with a smile.

No matter what the "something" turned out to be that Jethro knew was coming, Amalya was glad she'd taken Raphael's advice last night. Her body had the well-used ache that came in the aftermath of good sex, not to mention the warm thrum of energy from not only the ingested power but a few really wonderful orgasms too.

It had been centuries since a man had curled her toes just with a really good kiss. Levi could do that and much more, so there was no surprise that the total body orgasms he gave her were more than noteworthy.

She cleaned up and dressed quickly, jogging downstairs, thankful for her total return of energy. What would it be like to wake up every morning feeling like this? She forced the smile from her face as she suspended that train of thought.

Just because she and Levi had made up and had some amazing sex didn't mean he wanted any type of relationship beyond this trip back to Lilith's lair. Besides, even if he did, she still belonged to Lilith and there would be a price to pay for anything beyond that.

Her slightly darker mood took her through the doorway into the kitchen where she found Levi and Jethro looking out the window, a tense silence thick in the air between them.

"What's going on?"

Jethro stiffened but didn't move to face her. "There are dark clouds coming from the east. I think it might be the bounty demons. It's the same thing that happened before they made it to Sinner's Redemption."

Memories from that day flooded back, including her last view of Celine being pulled back and forth between the two bounty demons. Worry clenched her gut. She hoped all the others had gotten away safely.

She shook her head reminding herself she needed to concentrate on the here and now. If the bounty demons were coming, they couldn't afford to waste any time. "Let's go."

Jethro turned and Amalya braced herself to meet his gaze. But where she'd expected to see anger or hurt, she only saw distance. Not that she blamed him, the situation was uncomfortable and she couldn't do anything to change it or fix it. But knowing he felt the necessity of putting up barriers between them squeezed her heart painfully.

He took her hand and placed something in her palm before closing her fingers over it. She recognized the familiar weight of her switchblade and smiled up at him as she pressed the button and watched the clean blade spring forward with a snick.

"I didn't want you to leave it behind."

Emotions threatened to close her throat and she swallowed hard and managed to nod before Jethro turned away.

"We still don't know how we're going to get across one of the portals." Levi's voice stopped Jethro and he turned back.

"We may just have to choose the closest one and fight our way through."

Levi made a derisive sound. "And what would you rate our chances? All the portals are heavily guarded. We need to find another way."

Amalya walked to the window letting their continuing argument wash over her. Something niggled at the edge of her mind. Some type of solution to this problem. She agreed with Levi—the portals would only see all three of them dead or, even worse, in Semiazas's hands. But there was something else . . .

She raked her gaze over the cotton farm, tracing the destruction they'd left with the truck and then glancing up toward the gathering dark clouds. Movement near the truck caught her attention and she glanced back to see a lone shade hovering over the cab of the truck. "Too bad the shades can't take us. They don't need a portal to get to the other side."

Shades were neither of this world nor of any other, therefore boundaries did not apply to them. If they could find a way to use that—to lure the shades to them and then hang on as they moved through the realms . . . It sounded crazy, even in her own head, and yet Raphael's story about Graveyard Point Rim came back to her and she smiled. No interference, huh? She supposed telling her a story didn't count as direct interference, especially since she had to choose to use the information or not.

She turned back to the two bickering men and held up her hands. "Enough!"

When they both fell silent, glaring at her with all the anger they'd built between them, she resisted the urge to roll her eyes.

"I know how to get us across. Let's go. We can talk on the way."

She braced for more argument, but both men surprised her by falling silent and heading toward the door.

16

Levi cursed as they tried again to make the truck's engine turn over. The shades had sucked the battery dry—something they should've foreseen and hadn't. The farmer had a pickup truck and even a tractor next to the house, but they'd already tried those as well with no results.

He stepped out of the truck and faced Amalya and Jethro. "Take her and get her to safety," he said directly to Jethro. "Get her as far away as you can and I'll find you when I'm done."

Amalya stepped forward to stand toe to toe with him. "No way you're dictating what I should do or where I should go. The three of us need to stick together if we're going to make it."

"Amalya, I don't want you to get hurt." He looked into her lovely face all flushed with anger and fire and wanted to hold her and keep her safe forever.

Instead, she poked him in the chest with her finger. "Don't you dare treat me like some fragile porcelain doll. I'm not one of your servants you can order around."

A snort from Jethro made Levi glare at the man over Amalya's head, which had absolutely no effect on either of them.

He tried to keep the frustration from his voice when he asked her, "Then what do you suggest?" Didn't she see there were very limited options here?

"I suggest you use your brains instead of your testosterone." She turned to Jethro to glare him into silent submission as well.

Levi kept a tight rein on his temper, resisting the urge to shake Amalya into understanding that his was the only option available to them.

She fisted her hands on her hips and glared up at him. "There's a generator in the mudroom that we can use to charge the battery."

"What about jumper cables? We need some way to get the energy into the battery," Jethro offered.

"Celine always kept jumper cables in all the vehicles for Sinner's Redemption," Amalya said over her shoulder.

Shock slapped at Levi. Why hadn't he thought of that? He'd known about the generator and so had Jethro.

Damned if the woman wasn't right. He'd been thinking with his testosterone, thinking a fight would solve everything. He gathered all his bruised male pride and forced himself to nod. "Good idea."

After a long moment where she was most likely receiving the overwhelming truth of his statement she smiled. "Good. I'll steer, you guys push."

After several teeth-jarring minutes of Levi and Jethro pushing the truck forward over the up-and-down bumps that marked the cotton field, the truck was parked hood-first against the back door of the farmhouse and Jethro and Levi were working together, male bonding over the best way to get the power from the generator into the truck battery.

Amalya wandered back inside the kitchen and searched through the cabinets. The dark clouds were getting closer and lower to the ground with every passing minute and she knew they needed to be ready to escape as soon as they could.

She continued to look for anything that could help them on their upcoming adventures and as an afterthought ran out to the barn to rifle through the farmer's supplies.

Guilt edged through her as she helped herself to several items that she packed carefully into the bed of the truck. The two men were too involved with the generator to notice, and she was back sitting in the cab of the truck by the time Levi motioned for her to try the ignition.

When she did, it turned over on the second try and she slapped the steering wheel and laughed. "Yes." Neither man would meet her gaze but seemed wholly engrossed in studying either the engine or the generator. She shrugged. It was a small price to pay to let them retain their male pride.

They let it run for several minutes to charge up the battery and then Levi unhooked the jumper cables and wound them on his forearm as he neared the open driver's door.

"Shift over. I'll drive," he said as he slipped the jumper cables behind the seat.

Amalya raised one brow and glared at him. "I'm perfectly capable of driving, and since you two have pointed out that you're better in a fight, that will leave your hands free in case the need arises."

Levi clenched his jaw and she could tell he was battling against his normal instinct to order her to do as he wished. Instead, he walked around to the passenger's side and motioned for Jethro to get in first.

"I fight with guns, remember? I can do that better riding shotgun than straddling the hump in the middle."

Levi's expression darkened, but he nodded in one jerky movement and slid into the middle until his thigh pressed against Amalya's, his feet both resting on the passenger's side so he didn't block Amalya's ability to shift.

Just as the neck-ruffling sensation of demon reached them, Jethro jumped in and rolled down the window, checking his ammunition as Amalya backed the truck away from the farmhouse and peeled out toward the main road.

Amalya glanced up into the rearview mirror and cursed. The two demons were running behind the truck, their supernatural speed gaining on them.

She upshifted, pressing the accelerator until the truck was at its top speed.

The demons slowly receded in the rearview mirror, but Amalya knew they would eventually catch up.

"We have to get to Oregon. Fast."

*   *   *

Using a crowbar, Jethro broke the lock on the eight-foot-high metal fence that surrounded the entire graveyard and separated it from the sharp cliffs on all three sides. To the right and left were rocky slopes too steep for easy walking and at the far end of the graveyard, just past the tiny church that had stood for centuries, was a steep drop-off to the Pacific Ocean.

The only way in was through this gate and the small courtyard beyond.

When he swung the gate wide, it protested with a high-pitched screeching that made Jethro wince and clamp his teeth together. He motioned Amalya and Levi past him into the courtyard that held only three unmarked thigh-high stone graves.

Amalya pulled out her switchblade and sliced her palm with a hiss against the pain. She trailed her bleeding hand over the wrought-iron bars that made up the fence of the courtyard.

Jethro shook his head and turned back to pulling the supplies inside.

"Are you sure this is the best way to do this?" Levi helped Jethro drag their boxes of supplies inside the gate and then pulled it closed. "We can figure out a better way."

Rather than yell over the sound of the creaking gate, Jethro waited until it was closed and then pulled out several locks of various kinds from the boxes and secured the gate.

Locks and gates might not hold back the demons, but hopefully they would slow the damned things down, which was all he wanted. He didn't expect to live through this, so he planned to enjoy pissing off and poofing back to Hell as many demons as he could before he died—and probably ended up joining them there.

Wouldn't that be an ironic bitch of fate.

"We don't have time to figure out another plan and you know it." He handed more locks and the crowbar to Levi and hefted two of the boxes of supplies before he walked deeper into the courtyard past the first stone casket, then the second. With a grunt, he lowered the boxes on top of the second casket and then continued on past the third until he reached the back courtyard gate that gave way to the rest of the graveyard.

Silently, Levi shoved the locks into Jethro's hands and, using the crowbar, popped the ancient lock that currently held the gate closed.

He straightened and met Levi's gaze. "Protect her." It was a stern warning, and when Levi nodded solemnly Jethro knew the man would use his last breath to keep that silent promise. "I'll hold them off for as long as I can. Go."

Jethro turned his back on Levi, intent on walking away and avoiding any drawn-out good-byes, but he nearly ran over Amalya who stood waiting right behind him.

A thousand emotions churned through him, each one more painful than the last and he couldn't bring himself to say anything. After all, what could he say that hadn't already been said? And that she wouldn't know for a lie immediately.

Instead, he reached out and slowly rubbed a strand of her blond hair between his fingers, memorizing the silky feel to take him into his last moments of life.

"I'll see you on the other side, Jethro." She stood on her tiptoes and brushed a kiss across his cheek that made moisture and heat burn at the backs of his eyes. He blinked hard to keep from embarrassing himself in front of both her and Levi, and then she was gone, disappearing through the back courtyard gate with Levi right behind her.

As it should be, he reminded himself sternly.

Levi made Amalya happy and could at least offer her some chance of matching her life span.

Biting back all the sarcastic replies to his internal thoughts, he methodically relocked the gate with six locks of various types and strengths before returning to his supplies. He would spend the end of his life in this small space, so he might as well get comfortable and set up.

He shrugged away the morbid thought and lifted the two large plastic jugs of holy water from one of the boxes. Unscrewing the tops, he walked the interior perimeter of the gate, splashing the holy water on the ground, the locks, and on the black iron bars of the fence, murmuring a prayer and essentially blessing the site the best he could with little to no experience.

With that complete, he tossed the jugs back into the boxes and lined up several refills of jacketed hollow points for his twin Glocks as well as a dozen bottles of whiskey.

"A damned waste of good whiskey," he muttered as he uncorked the first bottle and took a healthy swig. The comforting burn of the alcohol seared down his throat as he held up the bottle in a mock toast to the oncoming demons. "Come and get me, you bastards."

He grinned as anticipation spiraled through him. He welcomed a fight. All the running over the past few days had gone against everything he'd always believed in. He'd spent his life attacking situations head-on.

All except Amalya, his conscience reminded him.

He shook his head. If he were honest with himself, he had known early on that she didn't return his feelings. In a totally out of character and cowardly move, he'd resigned himself to be content with being her protector.

With a curse, he wrestled his thoughts back to the present.

He took another long drink of whiskey before he uncorked the rest of the bottles. Methodically, he stuffed rags into the neck of each one and then wedged the corks back inside to hold the rags in place. That complete, he fished a lighter out of his pocket and set it on the weathered stone grave next to the bottles so he'd be ready when the time came to light his homemade Molotov cocktails.

He'd never actually used anything like these. Back during his short stint in the army, he'd used grenades and some missiles, but there was something uniquely male and exciting about blowing things up using something handcrafted that appealed to him.

All the rest of his supplies he laid out within easy reach until they were needed.

The line of demons and other beings eager to cash in on the bounty on Amalya had just begun to appear over the ridge. They looked like a motley assortment of people who might be found at a crowded mall in any city. Apparently, demons liked to blend in since Jethro didn't see any supermodels or other famous faces in the crowd, although he wouldn't have been surprised to see some, which would've helped to explain some of the more bizarre behavior that set exhibited.

He swept his gaze in a wide arc, noting that from his position on top of the hill, if this didn't work, he would be dead soon anyway. The thought was oddly comforting. He cursed himself for being a damned sappy fool to prefer death by demons over enduring watching Amalya grow closer to Levi. Even though she and the damned Brit fought constantly, Jethro could clearly see the bond and the affection growing and expanding between them.

Sounds from the demons grew louder as they moved in closer and he glanced up to check their progress. They were still far enough away that none of them had noticed him. There were no easy escape routes once he was surrounded, and they had to pass him to make their way toward where Amalya and Jethro would make their stand.

He didn't for one minute really believe Amalya's crazy plan would work, but as always, he could deny her nothing, so here he stood, ready to fight an army of demons just to buy her and Levi time to die as they chose.

A quick glance behind him allowed him to judge Amalya and Levi's progress deeper into the cemetery. He could no longer see them past the assortment of mausoleums and gravestones, but if the moving column of fog was any indication, they were nearing the back of the property and pulling as many shades to them as possible.

He tipped his head from side to side, working out some lingering stress and reminding himself that at least he'd get in some great target practice before he died. He chuckled at his own joke, even though it wasn't particularly funny.

A few stray shades that hadn't joined the large bank of fog edged close, the icy slimy sensation that they left behind on his skin making him shudder. Jethro picked up a spray bottle he'd brought filled with salt water and sprayed it toward the opaque figures. They instantly shied away. "Go find Amalya and Levi. They've got lots of tasty energy to spare, and you're going to miss out if you hang out here with me."

Something nudged him from behind and he whirled to find another shade edging away from him. He grinned. "These clothes were soaked in salt water and then dried. I told you. Go find them and come back for me in a while." He pointed toward Amalya and Levi's probable position as the noise of the oncoming crowd increased.

Jethro cradled his twin Glocks, one in each hand, enjoying their weight as he waited and watched.

He knew the exact moment the first demon spotted him. A demon who looked like he inhabited an accountant, complete with an off–the-rack three-piece suit and gaudy tie, snarled and jogged forward leaving the crowd behind.

Jethro smiled and let him come. Might as well have a test case.

When the demon rushed forward and touched the large iron gate, it recoiled and jumped back as smoke rose from its hands a split second before the stench of charred flesh reached Jethro.

"I'll be damned, that holy water actually worked. Or maybe it's just the consecrated ground." He laughed, the joyous sound echoing down the hill, which made several other demons snap their gazes in his direction.

The test case demon didn't waste any time in edging the length of the fence and testing it for weakness, but Jethro lost track of him as the throng of demons rushed forward with the same results as the first.

As the rushing crowd behind them pressed in, they were shoved against the iron bars to smoke and char, their bodies twitching until loud pops filled the air as they were sucked back to Hell.

Enjoying the show of self-mutilation, Jethro turned in a slow circle, grinning as he watched the cursing, spitting hordes hasten their departure back to Hell.

A sudden charge in the air prickled the hairs at the back of Jethro's neck and swept over him in a rush that left him gasping for air. He glanced around searching for anything that would resemble the electricity produced by a downed power line running through the graveyard.

The wall of bodies pressed against the fence not only made the entire area stink of burning hair, cloth, and flesh, but it also restricted his vision of what might be the cause of the new phenomenon.

Jethro raised the Glocks and took aim, squeezing the triggers several times and hitting several demons between or through the eyes.

Not bad for moving, squirming targets.

Large holes blossomed in foreheads and eye sockets and several loud pops sounded as the demons were sucked back to Hell and the bodies, now lifeless shells, slumped to the ground to be trampled by the wave of those still possessed behind them.

As the first line of bodies fell, Jethro caught sight of three large demons easily seven feet tall and nearly half that wide—which meant the iron gate was only one foot taller. "Fuck." A fresh surge of adrenaline spurted through his system, leaving him a bit light headed. "They brought out the big guns. Lucky me."

Two of them looked like the bounty demons they'd escaped from back at Sinner's Redemption and then the outpost store. The third looked like a cross between a wrestler on steroids and the Terminator. Its skin flashed silver and copper in the sunlight. It carried a long curved scythe in one hand; the other hand ended in a set of wicked-looking animal claws.

No doubt these three were the source of the sudden charge in the air, and Jethro had his doubts as to the effects of the holy water on keeping them at bay. Not that any of that changed his plan, which simply put was to send as many demons back to Hell as he could before he died.

He shrugged to relax his shoulders and began picking off several more demons, reloading as needed and reserving ammunition for those who had gotten creative and used the bodies of the dead to stack against the gate and crawl on top of them as if they were fleshy ladders.

The air filled with shouts, pops, and such loud sizzling sounds that Jethro briefly wished he'd brought earplugs.

When the lumbering bounty demons neared, they spread out to cover the entire length of the front gate.

"You're ready to play, are you?"

Jethro grinned and holstered his Glocks as he picked up the first of the Molotov cocktails. He flicked the lighter, which brought the flame to life, and then held it under the rag allowing it time to catch fire. He watched the rag darken for a few seconds, making sure it was well lit, before he jogged forward a few steps and lobbed it up and over the fence.

When it cleared the top of the fence he cheered and then quickly ducked behind the first stone grave just in time for the resulting explosion and fireball.

High screeching accompanied several loud pops and he covered his head as glass shards and a few still burning remnants rained down on him. He brushed them away and glanced up over the grave to evaluate the damage.

A hole in the wall of demons and the fiery remains of the fallen were quickly erased when others took their place.

Time to up the ante.

Jethro lit two more and threw them up and over the wall in quick succession, ducking in time to avoid the worst of the fallout but still managing to catch a few shards of glass in his arms and on his back. The wounds burned into him and he did his best to ignore them, flexing his arms to ensure he could still fight and move.

A loud roar rent the air and battered Jethro's eardrums until he clapped his hands over his ears to lessen the pain. When after a few seconds, his ears adjusted and he was able to drop his hands. He glanced up over the grave in time to see the pestilence demon screaming as fire licked at the constantly moving black mass that made up its mottled outer skin. The thing flailed and the roar became a high-pitched squeal as if someone had stabbed a herd of pigs. As it gesticulated its arms wildly, it bumped into other demons, catching their clothing on fire and starting a scene of chaos on the other side of the gate.

The sounds of wrenching metal from the far right side of the gate made Jethro whirl to find the Terminator bounty demon slowly bending open the bars of the iron fence, the other demons pressing forward, trying to squeeze into the hole the larger demon was soon to create.

"Damn." Jethro picked up the other Molotov cocktails lighting them and tossing them as fast as he could to cover the length of the fence.

He tried to duck for the worst of the explosions, but several more burning shards caught his arms, legs, and back, making him wince and stumble.

When some of the smoke cleared, he saw that half of the Terminator's face had melted away and one arm hung uselessly at its side, but the famine demon still looked intact.

"Time for plan B."

He laid his Glocks gently on the stone casket in front of him and began shucking out of his clothes, dropping them beside him until he stood naked, the cool breeze stinging against his fresh injuries.

"All right shades, time to do your stuff," he muttered as he picked up his Glocks and began killing the demons one at a time. He aimed a few shots toward the famine bounty demon, but when they bounced off harmlessly, he returned all his efforts to the lesser demons, trying to ignore the fact that underneath the possession, there was still a human trapped inside those bodies.

When the first clammy slap of sensation slid through his shoulder, Jethro had to brace himself against the urge to shy away from the contact. "Come and get it. Lots of energy right here for the taking," he said to the shades as he reloaded his Glocks and took aim again.

More of the freezing touches followed the first until he felt as if his soul had been dipped in ice water. As his energy slowly ebbed away, his reaction times suffered, as did his aim. More arms, legs, and torsos took the brunt of the jacketed hollow points, and a few shots even ricocheted off the insides of the iron fence.

Jethro laughed at the idea of being killed with one of his own ricochet shots and robbing both the demons and the shades of their chance with him.

But then his vision began to waver, and it took all his willpower to reload his Glocks and slowly pull the triggers, hoping the shot discharged close to something vital in the crowd of demons.

The loud wrenching sound of bending metal sounded almost surreal as it trickled through his fading consciousness, and he found himself on his knees, not remembering how he'd gotten there.

He gritted his teeth as the fluttering cold touches continued and with all his remaining willpower raised his arms and emptied both cartridges of ammo into the crowd of demons.

As he felt the last flicker of his life force leave his body, he whispered, "Amalya . . ."

17

Amalya ran, dodging around graves, crumbling mausoleums and sliding on the grass and gravel underfoot when she took a turn too sharp. Her chest burned and there was hot pressure behind her eyes. She didn't try to deceive herself that those sensations had anything to do with her current mad dash or the scene she planned in a few short minutes.

She'd already been brought to the brink of death by the shades once before and knew there was nothing to fear. It was Jethro she worried for. Levi was just beside her and would be right beside her no matter what happened. But Jethro would be all alone.

She knew she couldn't protect him, any more than she could return the emotions that he'd always had toward her. But it felt cruel somehow to leave him there, no matter how logical the plan had sounded when they'd all discussed it.

Levi grabbed her hand, threading his fingers through hers and pulling her forward. "Don't look behind you, just keep running."

She grabbed tight to his hand and increased her speed but couldn't help tossing a quick glance over her shoulder.

A huge wall of undulating fog rose up behind them so tall that it blocked out the sky.

Her blood chilled inside her veins, and as adrenaline spiked through her she ran faster until she was dragging Levi with her to keep up. She'd banked on the shades following her, but they had to make it to the cliff's edge to allow enough time for Jethro to distract the demons.

Gunshots sounded at the front gate and her steps faltered as an urge to protect Jethro rose up so hard and fast that she was turning around before she realized she intended to.

Levi caught her and tossed her over his shoulder, running full-out until her stomach bounced painfully against his hard shoulder with every step.

Explosions rocked the ground beneath them and Levi fought not to stumble as he gripped her tighter to his shoulder. More gunshots and more explosions followed at different intervals, and Amalya's hands squeezed into fists as she tried to imagine what Jethro was dealing with back at the courtyard.

She pushed up, bracing herself from the impact enough so she could look behind them. What she found surprised her.

The wall of fog wasn't a wall at all. Amalya could make out individual shapes of opaque humans with very distinct features, and they looked . . . hungry . . .

As if they sensed her scrutiny, a deep, bass buzzing began, and for a moment, Amalya thought there might be an earthquake, but as the sound increased until she could feel it deep in her belly she realized it was coming from the shades.

They weren't happy, and she wondered if they'd had time for everything they'd planned during their lives.

Levi dropped her to her feet so fast that she stumbled and it took her a few long seconds to catch her footing. By the time she glanced up, Levi was sloshing a messy circle around them with the holy water.

Amalya tracked his progress as she began to shuck off her clothes as the first of the shades found her, sliding through her body in an icy, clammy rush that made her skin crawl. She resisted the urge to wince away from them as she kicked off her shoes and nudged them just outside of the wet holy-water circle.

When she turned toward Levi he stood barefoot and naked from the waist up. He slid off his trousers and boxers in one smooth motion and laid them on top of her jeans and shirt in the middle of the circle.

He hugged her to him and captured her in a searing kiss, the warmth of his body buoying her against the soul-deep cold the shades left behind.

As Levi's tongue dipped inside her mouth, Amalya swayed on her feet, unsure if it was an effect of the shades or from Levi's kiss. Levi caught her and gently lowered her to the ground as he slid onto his side and pulled her down on top of him.

"Levi, what are you doing?"

Even as her vision wavered she laughed at the evil glee in his dark eyes. "If they want energy, let's give them energy, shall we, love?"

Before she could answer him, Levi had lifted her and impaled her on his cock.

A long moan broke from her throat as he filled her in one swift stroke.

Rather than pushing up and riding him, she laid on top of him, closing her lips over his and enjoying the sensation of having him buried deep inside while she kissed him.

The contrast between the slimy ice cold that was the shades stealing her energy and the searing heat that she and Levi created between them intensified the moment, and she said a silent thanks that she could spend her last few seconds of life this way.

And if this didn't work, she giggled at the thought of whoever would find a dead couple in a graveyard buck naked and still joined together.

Amalya gave herself up to the differing sensations and immersed herself in Levi—his musky, male scent, the taste of him that reminded her of warmed whiskey, and the reverent, almost desperate way he touched her.

As black spots danced in front of her vision and her full weight slumped forward onto Levi, his chest rumbled underneath her and she could just make out the words, "See you on the other side, love."

* * *

"She did it." Raphael grinned at Lilith who stood with him watching the scene at Graveyard Rim Cliffs. "I wasn't sure she got my reference, but here they are."

"My succubi are very smart. They have to be to survive." Lilith glanced up at him from under her eyelashes. "You came very close to interfering, Raphael. You must be more careful."

Raphael adopted his best innocent expression. "I only told her a story about a place I'd visited in Oregon." He shrugged.

Lilith raised up on her tiptoes to brush a kiss across his cheek. "I'm grateful and always shall be."

Heat seared into Raphael's neck and cheeks, and he managed to mumble, "You're welcome."

* * *

Jethro blinked and then winced away from the bright sunlight that streamed down through the swaying branches of the tree above him.

Branches? What the hell?

His demon battle in the open-air courtyard had taken place under a cloudless sky. There had been no trees to block the sun, let alone the tangy ocean breeze that currently ruffled his hair and teased against his bare skin. The front of the graveyard had been too far from the cliff to even hear the crashing of the waves.

Rather than the courtyard's hard gravel and packed dirt, his back and shoulders were now brushed by springy grass, and he shielded his face with his hand to look around him.

A verdant expanse gave way to a beach with pristine white sand and waves slowly caressing the beach. He turned his head the other way and saw a Victorian brick two-story mansion that was both stately and mysterious. "This is Heaven?" He laughed as he pushed up on his elbows. "It certainly doesn't look like Hell."

"This is only an in-between area, but your next decisions will decide where you'd like to spend your time."

The sultry voice moved over him like a physical caress and his cock hardened, swelling against his belly as he turned to find a woman standing at his feet. She was a stunning dark beauty with long hair that flowed over her shoulders and an hourglass body that in comparison would've made Marilyn Monroe look like a ten-year-old boy.

Jethro slowly stood, glad he could even move after the episode with the shades. He didn't bother with false modesty. She'd already seen everything on him there was to see, and Jethro had never been ashamed of his body. "Who are you?"

Her musical laugh stole over him and a spurt of pure, hot arousal shot through him making liquid seep from the tip of his cock. "I'm Lilith."

"Wait." He made a chopping motion in the air in front of him and looked Lilith up and down again, seeing her in the fresh light of everything he'd ever heard about her from Amalya. "Lilith, Queen of the Succubi?"

"And Incubi," she added lightly, her voice infused with a sexual playfulness that both invited and teased.

Even though his body was on high alert to her proximity, his mind was still back at the cemetery. "Where are Amalya and Levi?"

"Their fates are decided separately from your own, human." She shrugged, which did wonderful things to her breasts currently encased in a form-fitting black dress that seemed to be held up only by one small tie in the front.

He internally cursed for letting himself be distracted. "Their fates are decided separately, which means?" For lack of anything better to do with them, he fisted his hands at his sides and slowly turned as she circled him, keeping her in sight at all times.

"Which means that I have an offer to make and then you'll have a decision before you."

He was instantly on guard. He knew full well, even if it was only from hearsay, that nothing in the supernatural world came free and that behind every deal were a million nuances of meaning. "What's your offer?" he asked slowly.

She laughed. "So suspicious." She tipped her head to one side and studied him. "But then I suppose Amalya has told you much about our world in your time together." She blatantly looked him up and down as if evaluating a piece of livestock for auction. When her heated gaze reached his swollen cock, her lips curved into a knowing smile and she licked her bottom lip. "Although I don't think you've ever enjoyed her favors or provided her energy, other than through the most innocent means." Her gaze snapped to his and he ground his teeth at the playful spark he saw there. "Am I correct?"

Her insinuation that he'd never slept with Amalya wasn't lost on him. She was baiting him and he wasn't sure why. "What's the offer?" he asked again pointedly.

"Before I offer, I want to make sure you understand that Amalya will never be yours."

Even though Jethro already knew that, hearing it from Lilith caused a sharp pain inside his gut. "I thought you had an offer," he pressed, gritting his teeth against showing any reaction to her pointed jab.

"So I do." She shrugged as if it made no difference to her either way. "Here's how things stand, human. Your life-energy has been taken by the shades back on earth. Because of your help to me and mine, your body with the soul intact has been pulled here to this in-between place." She gestured around her at the utopian land-scape. "However, you cannot stay here, and your other choices are limited."

"Limited how?"

"You could go on to Heaven. Because of your self-sacrifice for both Levi and Amalya, you have definitely earned a place. You could still choose to go to Hell as many have done over the centuries be-cause they feared what they would find in Heaven or secretly thought they weren't worthy. In either of those cases, your body would be returned to the earthly plane where you died and your soul would continue on to the destination of your choice." Her inflection clearly told him there was another choice.

"Or?"

"Or you can do something for me." Her dark eyes shone with amusement and he wondered how many millions of men, or women for that matter, had looked into these same eyes and made a deal that would keep them out of Heaven or Hell for just a little longer.

"What would you need from me? I'm only a human, remember?"

She grinned and ran one long finger down his chest, leaving

behind a rush of dark shivers in their wake. "I recently became aware that the protector I sent for one of Amalya's sisters has been killed. I need someone to take his place."

"And do essentially what Levi did?"

She nodded and held up what appeared to be a sterling silver earring that held the same design as the amulet Levi wore. "Something like that."

He didn't have Amalya's gift of telling truth from lies, but he knew immediately that Lilith hadn't told him the entire truth. "Why don't you spell out exactly what it's like so I can get an idea of what I would be agreeing to?"

Lilith nodded once as if approving his cautious manner. She pursed her lips as if choosing her words carefully. "Let's just say Reba is something of a handful, even among succubi."

Jethro raised one eyebrow, waiting for her to continue.

"If she doesn't feel you are her equal, she'll refuse to come with you." She shrugged. "She's stubborn and outspoken and won't respect you for one second if you ask instead of take."

Jethro grinned, a sense of challenge churning through him. Amalya would never be his, he'd accepted that. But he was being offered another chance to make a life for himself, or so it sounded. And if his heart wasn't involved like it had been with Amalya, dealing with a headstrong succubus wouldn't be all that difficult. "And if I successfully retrieve her and return her to you?"

The smug smile that curved her lips sent irritation churning through him. "Then your life will be spared and you can continue to live out whatever mortal days you have left."

"No."

A look of surprise flashed across Lilith's features. "No?"

"If I bring her back to you, I want an extended lifetime and immunity from the effects of both succubi and incubi."

A furrow appeared between Lilith's brows and she raised her chin in an imperious gesture that Jethro was sure she used often. "What makes you think I can provide you with such things?"

"Amalya mentioned you sometimes adopt humans into your fold. I don't want to be adopted, but I'd like the perks of such an arrangement in exchange for this service."

"You are already receiving your mortal life in exchange for the service. Why would I grant you something more?"

Jethro smiled. Lilith hadn't outright refused, which only strengthened his hunch. "Because you're out of options on who to send after this little hellion, or you wouldn't be asking me—a dead man."

She narrowed her eyes, her dark gaze snapping with displeasure as she studied him. "I could find someone else. I only offered this opportunity to you because of your kindness toward Amalya."

Jethro shrugged. "All right then. Please wish Amalya well for me when you see her." He turned away and headed toward the Victorian mansion. He'd only gone a few steps when he heard her huff of frustration behind him.

"On one condition."

He stopped the smile that threatened to curve his lips as triumph spiraled through him. His back still to Lilith, he stopped but didn't turn to face her.

"No one can know the details of our agreement."

Confusion made him turn. "Why?"

"Why isn't a concern of yours. Do we have an agreement?"

Jethro closed the distance between them and held out his hand. "When do I begin?"

As Lilith shook his hand, power shot through him as if he'd stuck a fork inside an electric socket.

Pain sheared through him as his breath was sucked out and he fell to his knees. Convulsions wracked his body and he wondered if Lilith had betrayed him or if this was the normal route to conversion. A laugh tried to escape at this very calm thought trickling through his brain while his body went haywire, but since his lungs still screamed for breath, it never emerged.

Lilith stepped forward, her touch gentle against his left ear a split second before a sharp pain lanced through his lobe. As blackness closed in around him, Lilith's quiet answer reached him.

"You begin now."

*   *   *

"Lilith." Levi bowed deeply as Lilith entered the quarters he'd been assigned to within her lair.

Lilith smiled and held out her hand.

He took it and easily fell back into his Regency-era habits of feigned seduction and flattery. After all, intrigue and politics in the *haute ton* weren't that different from the cutthroat inner workings of the supernatural power hierarchy. Granted, the supernaturals were a bit more deadly.

He raised Lilith's hand, lightly brushing his lips over the backs of her fingers while maintaining eye contact.

When she smiled and her dark eyes sparkled with pleasure, he knew he'd played the scene correctly.

"Already up and around, I see. You're an extremely fast healer."

He nodded once in acknowledgment. "Yes, my lady. One of the perks of not being entirely human."

She quirked one eyebrow and he immediately realized she knew. "I knew your father, you know."

Levi remained silent, not sure which "father" she referred to. He covered his discomfort by motioning her to a nearby chair and sitting in the one just opposite her.

Her smoky laugh echoed around the room as she settled herself, kicking off her shoes and tucking her feet under her. The dichotomy between the seasoned and desirable seductress and the action of sitting like a little girl disconcerted Levi. The action made Lilith appear more approachable . . . and human, although he knew better.

"Your father petitioned me for an audience once."

Levi stiffened in his chair. The only one of his two fathers who would need to petition to see Lilith was the Duke of Ashford.

Her lips curved. "Since I see you're smart enough not to ask and end up owing me something for the answer, I'll tell you anyway. After all, the information from our original agreement is useless to you now."

Levi burned to know how she was so well informed, but for the very reason she stated above, he was reluctant to ask. Instead he nodded, which still acknowledged she'd spoken but remained ambiguous and would keep him from getting himself into any type of implied agreement with Lilith, which was always a danger.

She sighed and leaned her elbow on the arm of the chair before resting her chin in her palm. "Smart, careful, attractive, and only remotely human. It's no wonder."

"No wonder?" he asked breaking his own rule of just a moment ago.

Lilith waved away his question. "We'll get to that soon, but don't ruin your good record of restraint just for that. Why don't I give you leave to ask anything without price for the next ten minutes? You're too good at the game playing to make it much fun to trap you." She glanced up at him from under her lashes, enjoyment at drawing out his curiosity sparkling in her eyes.

"Any questions for ten minutes without price of any type?" he asked trying to ensure this wasn't just a more elaborately laid trap.

She nodded. "I do not guarantee to answer, only that no price will be extracted for your asking."

"Or for your answer if you choose to provide me with such information of your own free will?"

She laughed, a carefree sound he doubted she allowed herself often. "You are good. Very, very good."

"And?"

She smiled. "And no price will be extracted for you asking *or* for any answers that I provide of my own free will."

"May I ask one last stipulation?" He deliberately asked it as a question since they'd already agreed there would be no charge for him asking or her answering.

"One," she agreed.

"That only truthful answers are provided during that ten minutes?"

"Agreed."

He was tempted to put more detail around her answer, but he was already skirting the boundaries of pushing his luck as it was. "Then, my lovely Lilith, I thank you for any information you are generous enough to provide to me."

She laughed again and leaned forward as if she was a confidante imparting a juicy secret.

"Your father wanted a son who would carry on his legacy for longer than a single lifetime. He petitioned my help to bring that about."

Levi frowned. This definitely wasn't anything that he'd expected. He'd been convinced Ashford hadn't known anything about the supernatural world. Instead of sharing his surprise, he said, "I had no idea something like that was within your power. No disrespect intended."

"None taken. That is well beyond my power. And yet I'm very good at instigating and setting events in motion." She smiled. "In order to survive and thrive as long as I have, I've had to learn to gain the things I need with all the gifts at my disposal."

"What help were you able to give him?"

"Caldriel had always longed to live among the humans, to make a place for herself within them. I procured entry into polite society for her and made sure she was thrown together often with Ashford. Nature took its course from there."

"Nature?"

"Believe it or not, they fell in love. Just old-fashioned nature at work."

"And what about Raphael's involvement?"

"That, I admit, had nothing to do with me. I didn't know of it until recently when Raphael himself told me."

A flash of intuition hit and he narrowed his eyes at the stunning succubus across from him. "Raphael asked you to share this information with me, didn't he? To tell me what really happened."

She only smiled in response.

He couldn't help but laugh at her audacity. "You would've let me barter payment for something you'd already agreed to do for him for free?"

She pursed her lips, clearly enjoying the banter between them. "I have my reasons. But I also knew it would most likely come to nothing. Those biddies who ruled society back in your day were amateurs, but you've long outlived them all and have had to hone your skills. Although I admit, I do enjoy having a worthy opponent. It's been a long time."

Levi shook his head. He tried to muster anger toward Lilith for her manipulations, but he understood the need to survive, and her information so far had shed new light on who he thought he was. He'd always believed Caldriel had targeted his father specifically, had used the man just to establish herself in the human realm.

He'd never allowed himself to see it before, but in hindsight that wouldn't have been much different than the marriage mart that was common practice in those days. But finding out they'd met at social functions and had fallen in love threw an entirely new light on things.

His mother was still a manipulative bitch, and a demon, but maybe he hadn't given her as much credit as she deserved.

That was a sobering thought considering the only contact he'd had with her over the past few hundred years was summoning her recently and demanding help or answers.

God, he really was the arrogant ass Amalya had pegged him for. Thoughts of her made him realize that Lilith's sudden information about his past had sidetracked him. He'd meant to find out when he could see Amalya as soon as Lilith came to see him. "How is Amalya?"

"I go to see her next. From what her sister Jezebeth has told me, she's still asleep. Nearly dying three times in so many days has taken its toll."

He wanted to see her, to sit by her side until her lovely eyes fluttered open and her welcoming smile curved across her lips. But she hadn't seen her sister in seven hundred years. He wasn't sure Jezebeth would welcome his intrusion, and he wasn't sure he had the official right to even ask for a visit . . . yet.

All the information he'd just learned from Lilith made it imperative for him to visit his mother and Ashford House. He had to come to terms with his old life before he could start anew.

"What are your plans now that you've met the terms of our agreement?"

"It looks like I need to find myself." *And put things right in several cases*, he added silently. He started to ask what terms would be needed for him to continue in Amalya's life but stopped as he checked his wristwatch. His ten minutes were up, and that question, and the associated bargaining he would tackle when he returned.

18

"Amalya?"

Jezebeth's voice broke through the heavy sleep that held Amalya and as excitement slid through her, she forced open her eyes.

Her sister's lovely chocolate brown eyes were the first things she saw. "Jezebeth?"

When her sister pulled her up into a bone-crushing hug, Amalya laughed into the silky mass of her sister's hair and hugged her back. "I thought I'd never see you again. Any of you."

With a final squeeze, Jez pulled back, leaving Amalya sitting up. Jez gripped Amalya's upper arms as if afraid Amalya would disappear if she let go. "I had begun to think I'd be the only one who made it back." Tears glistened in Jez's eyes and she swallowed hard.

Amalya took a long moment to study her sister. Physically, she looked the same. Long chestnut brown hair that flowed down to her ass, lovely features, and a dimple that winked in her left cheek when she smiled. Concern traced her expression, but there was something else, a contentment about her sister that Amalya had never sensed before. She remembered hearing that the horror writer, Noah Halston, had accompanied Jez back to Lilith's lair. Perhaps feelings had grown between the two of them?

For her sister's sake, she hoped so.

"Any word on Reba or Galina?"

Jez's lips hardened into a line. "The escort Lilith sent for Reba was found dead, but from everything we can find out, it doesn't sound like he ever made contact with Reba."

Worry churned inside Amalya's belly, and she shoved it away. "If any of the four of us are likely to survive on our own, it would be Reba. What about Galina?"

"No word at all. It's like she fell off the entire supernatural radar about five hundred years ago."

"Is she . . ." Amalya couldn't bring herself to say the word "dead."

Jezebeth moved her grip to Amalya's hands and shook her head. "No. She's alive."

"But how do we know if she hasn't been heard from—"

"Lilith has heard from one of the Archangels that even though no one can locate her, Galina is still alive. Somewhere."

The worry inside Amalya's gut lessened slightly at the news. After all, if anyone would know, the Archangels would, although why they would confide the information to Lilith, she didn't know.

She glanced around, finally realizing she was back inside her old quarters inside Lilith's lair. It had been seven hundred years since she'd last left this room, and she was surprised to find it unchanged. Compared to her sumptuous room at Sinner's Redemption this was larger but definitely a step down. Amalya missed all the women she'd worked with over the years, and even a few of her regular customers, but looking at her surroundings, she wouldn't choose to go back. She belonged here with her sisters and with Lilith. An insider at long last rather than an outsider looking in longingly and pretending she didn't want to belong.

There was only one thing missing. Or one person, actually.

"Where's Levi?" She bolted out of bed, ignoring the cool air that hit her naked skin as she stumbled onto the smooth stone floor covered intermittently with throw rugs. A wave of light-headedness made her sway and she closed her eyes against the nausea that roiled inside her stomach.

"Amalya!" Jez caught her as she nearly fell and gently guided Amalya back to sit on the edge of the bed. "Take it easy, you nearly died. Three times in the span of a few days. It's going to take some time to recover."

Amalya closed her eyes and sucked in several deep breaths, welcoming the slow relief that added oxygen brought. When she was sure she wouldn't faint or slide off the end of the bed without help, she slowly opened her eyes and glanced up at her sister. "Where's Levi? Is he all right?"

Jez picked up a robe off a nearby chair and wrapped it around Amalya, her expression carefully neutral as she knelt in front of Amalya and took her hand. "He's alive. Lilith is with him."

Amalya stiffened and tightened her grip on Jez's hand. "What does Lilith want with him?"

"I don't know."

Amalya tried to stand, but Jez held her in place. "Don't forget, he knew Lilith before you even met him, so they most likely have unfinished business."

Amalya gritted her teeth against the vivid images of Levi and Lilith together that flowed through her mind. Most of the time unfinished business with Lilith meant a payment for services rendered—usually in the form of sex. She wasn't naïve enough to assume Levi's deal with the queen would be any different.

Besides, no matter what emotions she might have developed for Levi, Amalya knew she still belonged to Lilith, and without Lilith's permission, she might never see Levi again.

Panic fluttered inside her stomach starting as a group of butterflies and growing into a full-blown colony of bats. She swallowed hard and tried to suck in several breaths to keep the sudden reaction at bay.

She'd let herself believe Levi cared for her, and the thought of him in Lilith's bed ripped at her. Jealousy burned through her like acid and she fell back on the bed, her legs dangling off the side as her overpowering emotions threatened to overwhelm her.

Three sharp knocks on her door pulled Amalya's attention back to the present and she struggled to sit up and thread her arms through the armholes of the robe Jez had wrapped around her shoulders. She managed to stand long enough to wrap the thin material around her before she sat down heavily. Even the thin shield of cloth would help her feel more in control at this point. "Come in."

The door opened and Lilith stood in the doorway just as beautiful as Amalya remembered. She started to slide off the bed to bow before Lilith when the queen stayed her with a quick gesture.

"I appreciate the sentiment, but since we'd also have to pick you up off the floor, maybe that can wait until later." Lilith walked inside Amalya's room and motioned for Jez to leave.

Jez cast a quick glance toward Amalya who forced a smile. They were both Lilith's creatures, and even if Amalya wished Jez would stay, neither of them dared override Lilith's directive.

Jez slipped quietly from the room and the door made a quiet snick as it closed behind her.

Lilith approached Amalya and held out her hand, which Amalya immediately accepted. "Welcome home."

"Thank you, my queen."

When Lilith sat next to Amalya on the bed, the bed dipping slightly under her weight, foreboding curled through Amalya and she snapped her gaze to Lilith's. Lilith had always been caring in her own way for those under her, but she'd never been one to comfort or coddle.

If her sisters were all alive, then that meant . . .

No! Denial curled through her and she swallowed hard to keep her swirling emotions from escaping in front of Lilith. "Levi?" The one word was all she could manage before her throat closed with tamped down emotions.

"I thanked him for returning you and he left."

"Left?" Pain and panic filled her, tightening her chest and threatening to crash over her in overwhelming waves. She fisted her hands to try to keep them under control. "Without saying good-bye?" The words came out like an accusation and Amalya winced at her own carelessness.

The queen cared for her subjects but wasn't known for her patience with disrespect. So Amalya was surprised when Lilith nodded. "Before you think I disallowed it, Levi left of his own free will."

Amalya stiffened. "Did he receive his payment?" Thankfully her words came out sounding flat and emotionless, although she mentally cursed herself for asking the question at all.

Lilith laughed, the smoky sound filling Amalya's senses as if it were a separate living entity. "He did not. His payment was no longer needed by the time he fulfilled his side of the bargain."

Amalya burned to ask for further details but knew better than to test the queen's patience.

Lilith reached up to her neck to pull a black cord attached to a red amulet with intricate markings off over her head. "The only one who can stop Semiazas is Lucifer. You and your sisters must approach Lucifer and ask for his protection. I wish I could do this for you, but I cannot. All I can do is give you this amulet. Wear it at all times until you and your sisters approach Lucifer and it will give you both some measure of protection and entry into his lair." Lilith ran her thumb over the mysterious markings before laying the necklace in Amalya's palm and closing her fingers over it. She stood and turned to go. "I'll send Jezebeth back to you. Rest and we'll speak again when you have recovered."

"Did Levi say where he was going when he left?" Amalya hated both that she'd been unable to keep from asking the question and that her voice sounded so wounded.

Lilith turned back only enough to glance at Amalya over her shoulder. "He only said he was off to find himself."

Amalya stared up at Lilith feeling as though she'd just been sucker punched. They'd just survived demons, dying, and a slew of other encounters, and Levi was off to fucking find himself?

Was this some late supernatural midlife crisis?

Anger slid through her veins bringing with it solid determination. She was at least thankful this new emotion had chased back all the others that had threatened to make her a crying, swooning idiot.

As soon as the door shut behind Lilith, Amalya stood, testing her balance, and when she could stand with only a tiny wobble she set her jaw. "You arrogant, selfish bastard. Just wait till I find you."

* * *

Levi materialized just outside the gates to Ashford House and stumbled as the unfamiliar sensation left his stomach wrenching and twisting as vertigo slashed through him.

He sucked in large breaths as he tried to calm his stomach and convince it not to empty the contents of the meager breakfast he'd had back at Lilith's lair.

If dematerialization and rematerialization felt like that every time, he wasn't sure how the supernaturals stood it on a regular basis. He swore to himself he would avoid a repeat experience at all costs. But he was glad Lilith had made the offer to help him transport anywhere he'd like. It did save time, if not his dignity.

"Your Grace?" A tentative voice from just beside him startled Levi and he glanced up to see a pretty thirtyish woman wearing a business suit, her short bob cut framing a pixie face. She gasped when she saw his face but then regained her composure. "Are you well?"

Levi nodded and swallowed hard as he forced himself to straighten. It wasn't done for a duke to be seen with any kind of weakness outside his own chambers. He sighed at how easily the rules of this society came back to him. "Yes, very well. Thank you."

"You should come inside the gates before you attract the attention of the shades, Your Grace." She gestured toward the fog that had begun to coalesce in the middle of the road that ran in front of Ashford House.

Levi shuddered as he remembered his recent experiences with the shades. He definitely didn't relish a third time, especially since he'd run out of free passes to the other side. "Probably a good idea." He gestured for her to precede him.

She eyed him warily as they approached the gates together and the guards quickly waved them both through. Apparently, even though he hadn't been here in the last two hundred years, his mother had ensured the entire staff knew him. He couldn't really complain since it made getting inside that much easier.

As the gates clanged closed behind him, he noticed a buildup of shiny crystals clinging to the black wrought iron bars and stepped forward to trace his finger over the bumpy surface.

Salt.

"Pardon me, Your Grace, but if you'll stand clear, we need to chase back the shades before they try to cross through the gates."

Levi stepped back and two of the guards armed with power sprayers stood side by side, aiming the nozzles of the sprayers toward the shades.

When the strong spray of water hit the gauzy figures, they shied away, undulating as if displeased, but kept their distance.

"Kosher salt and holy water?"

"No sir. The duchess ordered only kosher salt to spray the shades and also to be sprinkled along every edge of the property except her private entrance."

Levi nearly laughed. Of course she wouldn't lock herself in or out of the grounds by allowing the use of holy water. "How are the shades kept from breaching her private entrance?"

"There's a guard there at all times, Your Grace. I'm not privy to their techniques to guard that gate, however."

Levi smiled and nodded. He wondered how many of the staff knew his mother was a demon, and if they cared. Most likely they'd be loyal to Lucifer himself if he held a proper title. Levi shook his head at the traditions he'd grown up with seen in a new and different light. "Good job. Carry on," he told the guards who practically beamed with pride at the small compliment. That fact alone assured Levi that his mother treated the staff as she always had. She paid them extremely well for their loyalty and their service, but the only further compliment they would ever receive was their continued employment.

Levi bit back the surge of guilt as he realized he'd treated them all much the same during his tenure living here as the duke. Amalya's description of him as an arrogant ass was proving itself a bit too apt for his comfort.

He strode across the expansive front garden missing Amalya. Sadness and longing squeezed his heart and he quickened his steps, eager to be done with this errand and get back to her.

Levi glanced up at the imposing gray brick facade of Ashford House as thousands of memories assaulted him both welcome and not. Somehow the house seemed less imposing and suffocating than when he'd left so long ago. He wondered if that was purely from so much time having passed or from all the new truths he'd learned about his life.

Either way, he was here and needed to figure out who he was and who he wanted to be going forward. His mother wouldn't be happy that he hadn't come home to fall in with her plans, but he hoped she could shed some light on the truths he'd heard about his past.

He navigated the several steps up to the front porch, rang the bell, and waited, wondering what type of reception he would receive. After all, he hadn't stood in this spot for two hundred years.

If his mother used human staff, he'd be long forgotten by now—although knowing his mother she'd found a way around that.

Maintaining appearances was too important to her.

When the large double doors opened, the ancient-looking butler showed only a split second of surprise before his face returned to an inscrutable mask. "Your Grace." He opened the door wide allowing Levi to step inside.

Levi smiled as his assumptions about his mother proved true.

He tried not to crane his neck to take in all the changes that modernization had brought to Ashford House. Many of the priceless antiques and statues still stood in the same places he remembered from his time here, but there were new treasures as well.

At least his mother had impeccable taste.

"Is my mother at home?"

"The duchess is in the drawing room with some guests, Your Grace." The man was definitely human and stood stiff, staring straight ahead and not examining his long-lost employer. At least not openly. Some things here never changed.

Levi started forward and then stopped. "What's your name?"

"Your mother calls me Jenkins, Your Grace."

Levi laughed and turned back to face the man. From the time he was a small boy all their butlers had been called Jenkins, purely because his mother didn't want to have to bother to remember their names. That particular practice was a definite throwback to the heyday of noble families here in England. "What's your actual name?"

"Ian Simms, Your Grace."

"Do you prefer Ian or Simms?"

A horrified expression crossed the butler's staid expression. Levi wasn't sure if the man was worried about facing his mother's wrath or the impropriety of the long-lost Duke of Ashford using his first name.

"How about we split the difference and go with Simms?"

When the man's wrinkled face relaxed, Levi nodded, the matter settled. "All right, Simms. Are my old rooms still mine? Or has my mother redistributed them for her use?"

The man stiffened as if the question had been an insult to his skills. "Of course your rooms are still yours and reserved solely for your use, Your Grace. Your wardrobe has been periodically updated so all would be ready for you if you ever had need of them."

"Perfect." He grinned. "Please don't tell my mother I'm here. I'd like to freshen up a bit, change, and then surprise her."

Simms looked dubious, as if torn between loyalty to the woman he had to deal with on a daily basis, and the man who actually owned the house and grounds and held the official title.

"I'll tell her I ordered your silence." He grinned when Simms frowned. "Don't worry, Simms. She'll be thrilled I did something so worthy of a duke as bullying a servant."

He took the steps of the grand staircase two at a time, a habit he'd never quite broken and one that he was sure his mother still hated. Apparently, it wasn't regal enough for a duke. Which, of course, gave him even less incentive to break the habit.

A quick right turn at the top of the staircase and he followed the hall to the end where he found the large door to the ducal suite.

He opened the door to his room and was surprised to find it almost exactly as he'd left it. The bedspread and wallpaper had been updated to a more modern pattern, but the same royal blue color scheme he remembered ran throughout and the same pictures sat on the bedside cabinet and chest of drawers as the last time he'd left this room.

He walked inside slowly, trying to ignore the sensation that he was trespassing. The room around him was both familiar and foreign—a relic from times gone by. He picked up a picture that sat on the cabinet next to the bed and studied it. It was a drawing of a woman.

"Amalya."

He sucked in a breath of surprise as memories flooded back and he sat down hard on the bed as he continued to stare at her image.

He'd drawn this picture from memory. She'd captured his imagination even though he'd only seen her once, and he'd spent several months looking for her before he'd left Ashford House for good.

Why hadn't he remembered her when he'd seen her at Sinner's Redemption? He shook his head with a small laugh. Did Lilith somehow know of their tenuous connection? Was that why he was assigned to Amalya instead of one of the other three sisters?

All those years ago, Amalya had been leaving a storefront and he'd been drawn by her grace and assurance as she crossed the street and was handed into an unmarked carriage. The memory was so vivid he could remember exactly what she'd worn, the smell of meat pies in the air from a passing vendor, and even the quick flash of her pale ankle he'd seen as she stepped up into the carriage and disappeared from view.

She was lovely, her hair elaborately twisted on top of her head in the style of the day, her expression teasing and welcoming just as it had been when they'd made love just before the graveyard and the shades.

He very much wanted Amalya to be a part of his future, and apparently without him knowing it, she was also a tiny piece of his past.

He set the picture back where he'd found it, and ignoring the other mementos that lay neatly placed around the room, he went to the wardrobe, happy to find fully modern clothes rather than those he'd left behind so long ago. Just next to the wardrobe was a door that had been added since he'd been here last. A quick investigation revealed a modern loo complete with a shower.

"Thank you, Mother. This is one change I wholeheartedly approve of."

Levi stripped quickly, glad to leave the remnants of his ruined suit and shoes for the valet to deal with. Something told him his mother had kept a valet employed just for him all these years. The poor man was either ecstatic with his lack of any real duties or bored beyond belief.

Levi showered quickly, availing himself of the razor and shaving cream he found tucked into the recesses in the custom marble walls of the shower. When he finished, he pulled fresh silk boxers from the chest of drawers, choosing not to dwell on how his mother knew what type of undergarments he now wore. After all, when he'd lived here last, men had worn smallclothes.

After pulling on socks, he chose a navy pin-striped suit from the wardrobe and dressed quickly, thankful men's attire no longer included a starched neckcloth. When he was finished, he studied his image in the full-length mirror and decided he was presentable enough to keep from mortifying his mother and her company.

Not that he'd ever worried much about that, but if he hoped to get her to talk to him, he needed to make some concessions—especially since once she found out he still refused to bow to her wishes, she would loose her anger and he would lose his chance to find out anything from her.

He stopped to tuck Amalya's picture inside his breast pocket and then stooped to pull open the bottom drawer of the bedside cabinet. He pulled the drawer all the way out and set it aside, ignoring the assortment of letters and other things he'd deemed worthy of keeping so long ago. Once the drawer was removed, he opened the compartment below and reached inside. When his fingers closed over a small box, he smiled, pulled it out, and slipped it inside his pocket. If his mother had found it, the box wouldn't have remained here all these years.

He quickly put the drawer to rights before he stood, straightened his jacket, and left the room for the last time.

He made his way downstairs and tossed a smile toward Simms who hovered nearby in case he was needed.

The man looked distinctly worried, and Levi hoped for the older man's sake that Levi's coming run-in with his mother didn't negatively affect the man's employment. Levi might technically own everything around him, including the bank accounts that paid all the salaries, but his mother was the real puppet master, and the staff apparently knew that as well as he.

He turned the knob to the drawing room and stepped inside as four female faces turned toward him.

His mother sat in a high-backed chair holding court with the three ladies who vied for space on an antique settee that he remembered to be distinctly uncomfortable.

"Obediah." His mother smiled and rose expectantly as if they greeted each other daily and he had just happened to continually miss everyone else's visits for the past two centuries.

He crossed the room and took her hand as he brushed a quick kiss across her cheek. "Mother." He turned his attention to the ladies. "Ladies." He nodded and they stared in return. They had the best gossip scoop in years—they had actually sighted the elusive Duke of Ashford. Mentally grinding his teeth at their expressions of ill-concealed glee, he forced a smile. "I apologize for the interruption, but I'm afraid I need to borrow my mother for a while on urgent business."

The three women rose in unison, clearly eager to escape and begin to spread the news.

"No problem at all, Your Grace," the middle one said. She was a tall, attractive woman of around thirty with a distinctly calculating gleam in her eye. "Perhaps we will see you at the charity event tomorrow?" She pursed her lips and gave him what looked to be a very well-practiced "fuck me" look.

"I regret that business will keep me from attending, but I do hope you enjoy it." Mentally dismissing them, he turned to his mother. "Shall we?" he asked holding out his arm in what probably appeared a very antiquated gesture.

His mother smiled up at him, clearly pleased with his performance of titillating the masses. When she took his arm, he quickly guided her out of the drawing room and down the hall into the breakfast room. Simms would ensure the guests found their way out.

This room too had been updated and now melded the beauty of the past with the elegance and convenience of the present. Although he still hated the long, formal dining table that took up most of the center of the room. He remembered as a small boy sitting on one far side, his mother on the other. He'd always wondered if the entire British Empire would crumble if he sat somewhere else but at the head of the table but hadn't ever braved society's wrath enough to find out.

There had never been warmth and caring within these walls. Levi had grown up with duty and appearances and wealth.

The familiar sensation of the loneliness that had engulfed him frequently as a child threatened to rise up and swamp him and he shoved it back with pure willpower. He was now a grown man, old enough to choose his own life rather than only reject one as he'd done so long ago when he left.

"You've returned." His mother beamed up at him and brushed an imaginary piece of lint from his lapel. "I knew you would."

"Why didn't you tell me the truth about you and my father?"

His mother stilled, her blank mask falling into place, which was enough to tell him she knew exactly what he meant. "There was nothing to tell that you didn't already know." Her voice was flat, her tone clearly indicating the subject was closed—another thing he frequently ignored that continually drove her mad.

"How about that you and Ashford actually loved each other, at least at first? Or how about the fact that he not only knew about the supernatural realm, but he also wanted a son who would live longer than a mortal lifetime?" He clenched his fists to keep from reaching out and shaking his mother. "Or what about the fact that Ashford was actually my biological father? Not the one who gave his blood to allow me to live but the one whose sperm contributed to my existence?" He stepped closer so they were toe to toe as all the pent-up anger and betrayal he'd suppressed since he was a child threatened to explode. "Did it never occur to you that those facts might have been good things to tell your son sometime over his long lifetime?"

His mother raised her chin in a familiar defiant gesture as she stood straight, glaring at him as she had done so often throughout the years. "I don't know where you heard such rubbish, but all that matters now is that you're finally home."

Tense silence sizzled between them and Levi bit back a laugh. He didn't know why he should be surprised. It wasn't as if he'd expected his mother to tearfully apologize and finally fill him in on all the details of his life now that he'd broached the subject. Or had he?

He'd come here on a fool's errand and would walk away with less closure than he'd come with. He should've known better from the start. Through clenched teeth he said, "No. I came to make peace with my old life, and hopefully with you." He met her gaze squarely as her eyes flashed actual fire. "But I suppose neither of those is very likely at this point."

"Do you mean to tell me you've come all this way just to tell me you won't be returning?" His mother's voice dripped with icy disdain.

When Levi remained silent, he thought he saw a quick flash of pain in her gaze before she covered it with her normal expression of smug indignation. "Then you needn't have bothered returning at all. I've made my way just fine without you or Ashford for a very long time and will continue to do so."

A black hole of emptiness opened inside him threatening to swallow him whole. "What will you do if the rumors are true, Mother? What if Armageddon is on its way and everything around you is reduced to dust?" He gestured at the expensive room around them. "You've abandoned your place in the demonic realm to cultivate your place in the human one, but you can't follow them into Heaven, only Hell."

Hate glittered in her eyes as she glared at him. "Get out. I should never have saved your life. I'd already provided Ashford you as an heir. Beyond that was his problem." Each word was bitten out as if they tasted sour on her tongue.

Pure willpower allowed Levi to calmly step back and say, "Good-bye, Mother" as he walked out of the breakfast room toward the front door.

He stopped when he saw Simms in the hallway. "Why don't you bring my mother some tea liberally laced with whatever it is she's drinking this century? I think she's going to need it."

19

Amalya left the portal in Lilith's lair, and rather than following it through to the human realm directly where a legion of demons were most likely waiting, she edged along the far wall until she came to a long, dark tunnel.

A quick walk down those stone steps and the clammy cold of being deep in an underground cavern clung to her skin and reminded her she was under tons of rock.

Well, since this wasn't the human realm, she really had no way to know exactly what was above her, but her growing and previously unknown claustrophobia wouldn't listen. Her breathing came in short pants and her heart raced as she quickened her steps to escape this oppressive place that much sooner.

She'd never had any problem with claustrophobia before, but she admitted it could be because she hadn't allowed herself to entirely recover before setting out after Levi, sneaking out like a grounded teenager.

But she refused to entertain thoughts of turning back.

She had to find Levi, and then . . .

She still wasn't sure what she would do when she found him, but there was still time to figure that out.

In the meantime she needed to pay attention and pick her steps carefully. Minutes dragged out and still more darkened tunnel lay ahead of her. Committed to her path, the farther she walked, the more focused she became. The goal of finding Levi became her motivation to place each foot in front of the other as the prick of betrayal churned into outright anger and indignation.

He'd portrayed himself as someone solid she could depend on. Someone who cared for her and was worthy of her trust.

And then he'd walked away without a word.

Bastard!

She took a deep breath to calm her swirling emotions and glanced up. A tiny speck of light flickered off in the distance in front of her.

The promise of relief beckoned and she resisted the urge to jog forward since she'd most likely fall and break her neck on the damp, slimy rocks.

As she progressed, the light grew and the atmosphere around her became warmer and drier. She let out a long breath as relief pounded through her when she stepped out under a large whispering willow and onto an expansive green lawn.

The ocean sounded in the distance and the taste of salty air sat heavy on her tongue. A large Victorian mansion sat off in the distance, and at any other time, she would've longed to explore. All the succubi had heard stories about Uriel's property, but none to her knowledge had ever gotten to visit or see inside, except Lilith.

However, since she hadn't been invited and she was using Uriel's property to sneak back into the human realm, it definitely wasn't a good time to stop for sightseeing.

She'd overheard several of Lilith's human male pets talking about this side way out of the lair and back to the human realm. She hadn't thought any more about it until they'd mentioned that this week Uriel's lair overlapped the human realm somewhere within the United Kingdom.

Every seven days, the lair would be accessible to a different place within the human realm, and only those with permission to enter could even see the property. But since she was leaving and not entering from the human realm, she was banking on the fact that no permission would be required.

She hoped.

With a quick glance around to ensure she was alone, she skirted the edge of the property, walking along the beach until she saw a fuzzy distortion about twenty feet out. "I hope there aren't any sharks," she muttered as she stepped into the cold ocean and gasped as the first icy wave soaked through her tennis shoes and splashed her ankles. "Damn you, Levi. You'll pay for this."

She walked forward, a few tentative steps at a time, sucking in a breath each time another wave soaked her more thoroughly than the last. By the time her feet left the ground and she was forced to swim, she was only a few feet from the distortion that hung in the air.

Fighting a wave that tried to pull her back toward shore, she muscled her way past the veil and yelped as she fell forward.

Her cheek smacked into green grass quickly followed by the rest of her body. The impact whooshed the air out of her lungs and she lay dazed for a long moment taking stock and ensuring she could still move.

For the first time since her emotions had overwhelmed her back at the lair, she thought maybe this hadn't been the best idea. Especially since she hadn't yet fully recovered, and Jezebeth would be furious when she realized Amalya had left without telling her.

She winced as she envisioned the hurt and anger in her sister's expression and then shoved the mental picture aside. The quicker she found Levi and returned to the lair, the better.

Amalya slowly sat up, relieved when nothing hurt other than her pride and her cheek. She'd most likely have a bruise to show for her ungraceful fall, but how could she have known that exiting Uriel's lair inside the ocean would not mean she would enter the human realm still inside one?

Her clothes were sopping wet and she cursed as she slowly stood and wrung them out the best she could. The cold wind sliced through her and she winced as she realized how ill planned her entire trip had been.

There was nothing to be done about it now but to move forward.

She squared her shoulders and glanced around. She seemed to be on a manicured lawn of some type, and since she hadn't been arrested yet, hopefully it was public land. At least she'd thought to bring some money. She could always barter for more if she ran low, although the idea of having sex with someone other than Levi definitely didn't hold appeal even if it would help to restore her energy.

She stopped and frowned. When had her preference for Levi become so pronounced that she would turn down sustenance from others?

One problem at a time, she reminded herself as she picked a direction and started forward, her shoes squishing with each step. Now she had to find Ashford House and confront the stubborn man on his own turf. She'd worry about how to get back to Lilith's lair later.

Halfway across the manicured lawn something cold and slimy slapped across her arm.

Amalya whirled to find a group of shades arching back from her, an angry buzz reverberating through the air. When she realized they weren't coming any closer, she laughed. "Okay, I take it back. The dip in the ocean might not have been such a bad thing." She had no desire to nearly die a fourth time in the span of a few days. Besides the obvious downsides, Jezebeth and Levi would never let her live it down and neither would Jethro if he was still speaking to her.

A thread of sadness swirled through her at how things stood between her and Jethro. She truly cared for him and missed his friendship. Lilith had assured her Jethro had made it safely to the other side and was on an errand for her to repay that debt. Hopefully when he returned from wherever he'd been sent, they could talk.

The noise of traffic caught her attention and she left the shades to head toward the sounds. As she crested a hill, she saw a main road below her and carefully made her way down the hillside until she found herself on the sidewalk that ran along the main road.

She hoped she could find a taxi. She would gladly part with some of her cash if it meant a ride straight to Ashford House and Levi.

Nearly twenty long minutes later she found a taxi parked by the side of the road and she leaned in the front passenger's window. "I'm looking for a ride to Ashford House." She'd passed through London a few hundred years earlier, but it had merely been a travel stop on her way to France and Spain where she'd spent much of that period in history. She could've ridden right past Ashford House back then and not have any idea that's what she was looking for today.

"Hop in, darlin'. I can drop you at the gates, but you won't be getting very far looking like that. It's quite a posh place."

Amalya dug inside the pocket of her jeans and bit back a curse as she pulled out a fifty-dollar bill. "I only have American dollars, is that all right? You can have the entire fifty if you can get me there." She held up the bill and he smiled.

"Ashford House is just a few streets over. I'm sure even with exchange rates I can deal with some extra quid jangling in my pockets."

Within minutes he'd dropped her off in front of the imposing gates of Ashford House and she'd sent the driver on his way with the fifty-dollar bill. Several shades tried to accost her but were repelled by her still-damp clothes and the salt that still clung to her skin from her impromptu dunk in the ocean.

She approached the gatehouse and smiled up at the first guard who immediately raked an appreciative gaze up and down her body. Amalya wasn't surprised. Even though her clothes were no longer sopping wet, they were still damp and very much plastered to her body. The musky scent of his arousal on the air made Amalya smile and she greedily inhaled it as her skin ached—the succubus version of a stomach growl.

She personally might not be interested in having sex with anyone but Levi, but her body wanted its needs met regardless of the details.

"What can I do for you, love?" he asked her with a quick smile, the endearment reminding her of Levi.

"I'm here to see the Duke of Ashford. Can you please tell him Amalya is here to see him?"

He glanced at her indulgently. "Do you have an appointment?"

She smiled and looked at him from under her lashes. "I realize I look a little bedraggled, but I had to jump into the ocean to avoid a group of shades. I'm really very late for an appointment with the duke. He's expecting me." Which wasn't a complete lie. She had been in the ocean and it had helped her avoid a group of shades. What he assumed from the rest was entirely up to him.

"Let me check, Miss . . ." Now that she'd given him the impression she was an important appointment for the duke, he expected a last name.

"Lilith," she said using the name of the queen as she'd done for centuries whenever a last name was required.

He nodded and she turned away while he called the main house to see if Levi would admit her or not.

Within seconds he was back and treating her as if she'd suddenly proved herself queen rather than just an expected guest at Ashford House. "Right this way, miss." He opened the gate and ushered her through. He left his post and escorted her up to the front doors where he rang the bell.

The wide front doors opened and an ancient-looking butler met her with a deferential nod. "Do come in." When he'd closed the door behind her he gave no indication he even noticed her bedraggled state. Instead, he motioned toward a long hallway that started just past the bottom of the grand stairway. "Right this way, please."

She glanced around the large front entryway of Ashford House wondering about Levi when he was a boy growing up here. He hadn't spoken much about his childhood, but while the place was historic and very beautiful, it was still cold and formal. No wonder Levi had grown up with all the defense mechanisms he had.

After the butler quietly cleared his throat, she realized she'd been standing and staring about her. "Sorry," she mumbled, and followed the butler down the hall.

He opened a door on the right and ushered her through. "The duchess will receive you shortly, ma'am."

Duchess?

* * *

Caldriel waited until she heard Obediah's parting remark to someone named Simms before she let loose her temper. Anger burned through her in a searing rush until an explosion of energy mushroomed out from her rattling walls, smashing figurines and vases, and skewing furniture as she screamed.

As searing heat flowed through her steaming off her fingertips, she bit back her rage before it conjured forth her fire and ended up burning down Ashford House around her.

Being a fire demon had its perks, but not many she could use while trying to blend into society as a well-bred human. It would probably feel amazing to just let loose and vent her anger right now, but it would definitely set back her plans, which made it an unacceptable option.

As the rest of her expended energy left and the room slowly quieted, Caldriel ground her teeth to contain the rest of her ire and straightened her dress.

She'd given Obediah every opportunity, had saved his dukedom for him all these years, and yet he still chose to walk away.

Being a practical woman, she didn't bother to try to convince herself that she'd done it all selflessly. She'd wanted her place in the upper crust of British society and she'd gotten it. But Ashford had been only a human and had died long ago. She'd shared his hope that his son would live a long and prosperous life as the duke, but she'd also hoped for the added benefit that she could enjoy the perks of such a life by her son's side.

Here he had everything—money, status, power. He would never be alone or want for anything. But instead, he walked away and made his own fortune and life separate from those he'd been born with.

Why? What could have enticed him from her side a second time?

Something very akin to jealousy burned through her along with the very natural urge to destroy whatever it was that had stolen her son away from her and her well-laid plans.

When Obediah had walked into the drawing room dressed impeccably and using polite manners, hope had blossomed that he'd seen the light and was ready to take his place. He'd obviously survived the meeting with Raphael, and since the Archangel had yet to show up on her doorstep, she had to assume things had turned out well.

Other than Obediah learning all the backstory about his life and hers.

What did all that matter? She had to admit that as a demon, her perspective on parentage might be skewed, but how someone came into existence was surely less important than the mark they ended up making on their own.

A soft knock sounded against the door and Caldriel startled. She had no illusions this time that it might be Obediah. His leaving made it quite clear where he stood. "Yes," she snapped, and waited with a raised eyebrow for Jenkins to open the door.

"Madam, there's an Amalya Lilith at the front gate to see the duke." He stared straight ahead and made no reaction to the obvious destruction that had taken place inside the room.

Lilith. The word lodged inside her mind and she cocked her head to the side as she studied it.

When Obediah had summoned her, he'd been inside a farmhouse with a human male and a succubus. And now a woman came calling for him with a last name that matched the Queen of the Succubi and Incubi?

Much too coincidental to be ignored.

The jealousy that had curled inside her gut roared to life licking its fangs in anticipation. Maybe she'd find a way to release some of her pent-up anger this afternoon after all.

She allowed a slow smile to curve her lips as she stared at Jenkins. "Show her into the second drawing room." She gestured around her at the skewed furniture, smashed porcelain, and scorched curtains and floor where she stood. "This one needs straightening."

20

Levi neared the distortion in the air that marked the edge of Uriel's property and stopped short. Lilith had told him if he ever needed to come back, he could find Uriel's lair by using the amulet she'd bade him to keep for now. The same amulet that had given him immunity to Amalya's succubus nature.

She'd been right about finding the property. He'd just focused on finding it and ended up here. The fact that it was on the outskirts of London surprised him. He'd expected to have to travel halfway across the world since the property moved every week.

Not that he was complaining.

He had left Ashford House more confused and angry than ever. All he wanted now was to get back to Amalya and make sure she was all right. He would have to try to make sense of his life later.

But he'd have to find time to sort it all quickly. He owed it to Amalya to know himself before he muddied the waters with proposing any type of long-term relationship between them.

Amalya deserved better than that.

Hell, she probably deserved Jethro who would be a loyal and devoted puppy at her feet until the day he died. Anger curled inside his stomach at the thought of Jethro with Amalya, but he shoved the disturbing images aside, surprised that thoughts along those lines still taunted him.

It wasn't as if he hadn't tried to settle his life. Logically Levi knew his mother was hurt. She had never been good at giving up her grudges, and forgiveness wasn't big on her skills list either. Apparently, she'd now added guilt and victimhood to her list of tools. Not that she needed any more to find what buttons to push to anger him and push him away.

And anger him, she had. The bloody woman could drive a priest to murder.

He stopped short as he realized he was talking about his demon mother, which totally ruined his comparison. He'd walked away from her twenty minutes ago and she was still taunting him like a sharp pebble in his shoe—relentlessly annoying and persistent.

He saw a wavy distortion hanging in the air in front of him bisecting the park and cutting through the middle of a large Elfin Oak. It reminded him of oil floating on water, fluid spirals of subtle color morphing into shiny metallic versions of themselves before disappearing and making the seer think they'd imagined them.

This had to be the place.

Taking a deep breath, Levi hitched his travel pack higher on his shoulder and stepped through the distortion.

When the first wave of icy water hit him, Levi sputtered and sucked in a lungful of seawater.

After a quick moment of disorientation, he surfaced, shook the water from his eyes, and glanced around, treading water against the strong, icy waves.

Who the fuck had put ocean where solid ground had been just a step ago?

He bit back his anger and impatience and tried to get his bearings. Couldn't anything in the supernatural world be simple?

Just over his left shoulder he spied the shore. It wasn't too far off. He swam toward it, allowing the powerful waves to help propel him forward.

When he reached solid ground, he tossed his soaked travel pack higher on the shore and then rested on all fours, taking a minute to catch his breath as the gentle breeze cut through his wet skin sending gooseflesh marching over him.

He forced himself to his feet, rinsing the sand from his hands before grabbing his travel pack and walking up the beach toward the brick Victorian mansion he saw in the distance. Lilith hadn't specified how to find her lair once he'd made it to Uriel's property, and Levi cursed the fact that he hadn't thought to ask. He'd had his fill of dealing with supernaturals lately, even if he was more part of them than he was human.

Levi was curious as to how the mechanics of an entire property appearing in a different earthly locale every week worked, but for now he needed to concentrate on other things.

A quick glance around assured him no one else was in sight and he set off at a brisk pace, allowing his anger and eagerness to see Amalya to push him forward.

He made it as far as the front steps of the mansion before he ran face-first into the intimidating Archangel who appeared from nowhere. He stumbled back and scowled, unused to having to tip his chin to look up at anyone. At six foot five, Levi was usually the tallest man in the room. But Uriel had at least two inches on him, which only added to Levi's discomfort at having just been caught trespassing on the Archangel's property.

"Levi, isn't it?" Uriel asked almost absently. "What message has Lilith sent you with?"

Levi stopped short and met Uriel's gaze. "Message?"

"Lilith didn't send you? Then what are you doing here?" The "on my property" was left unspoken but was clearly understood between them.

"Lilith left me with her necklace," he said as he pulled the sterling silver necklace chain out of his shirt so Uriel could see it. "And told me if I ever needed to return to her lair, I could get there through your property. I apologize if I've intruded." He noticed the churning anger that still laced his voice, but it was too late now to temper his words.

Uriel reached out to touch the round disk that hung on the chain. He ran his thumb over the Hebrew characters that meant "Temptation," and something like pain flashed across his features before he raised his gaze to Levi's. He kept eye contact for several long seconds before the Archangel's eyes widened and he gently dropped the necklace so it hung around Levi's neck once more.

Levi watched Uriel's expression as the Archangel realized that a soul gaze wouldn't work on him. Rather than anger or frustration as Levi had expected, Uriel's expression turned thoughtful.

"Who are your parents, Levi?"

Levi frowned. "You mean you don't know?" The words were out before he could think better of saying them. Apparently, he'd given the Archangels too much credit. He'd thought they knew every human and how they interconnected with everyone else. But now he supposed there was some type of supernatural computer somewhere that kept track of all those things instead. Talk about ruining the mystery!

Uriel smiled. "I must rely on information I pick up from people's minds as well as soul gazes. Although you probably won't be surprised to hear soul gazes don't work on you. Which makes me very curious about your parentage." He cocked his head to the side studying Levi as if he'd just become very interesting. "I have means of finding out, but it's usually much easier to ask."

Levi snorted. "Do you want the official version or the long version?" Sarcasm dripped from his voice, so he was surprised when Uriel's answer was calm and even.

"The pertinent recap will do."

"My mother is Caldriel, a demon." He watched Uriel for a reaction, and when he received none he mentally shrugged and continued. "My father by conception is Thomas Levi Spencer, the Duke of Ashford."

"Father by conception implies there is another."

Levi had to give Uriel points for being quick. "I nearly died as a baby and my mother begged healing from a supernatural." Raphael had warned Levi to keep that relationship private from those who might use it to his disadvantage, so he kept his explanation very general.

"And by healing, you mean he gave you enough blood so barely any human trace remains within you."

Since it wasn't a question, Levi didn't bother to answer. After all, he couldn't deny the Archangel blood running through his veins. Being half demon wouldn't explain his resistance to a soul gaze to someone like Uriel. The Archangel was too perceptive even without all the relevant details.

Uriel studied Levi for a long moment and then a slow smile curved his lips. "As impossible as it sounds, you have his eyes. You've met him, I take it?" Levi knew immediately they were speaking of Raphael.

He nodded. "We've met."

"Is that why you're running?"

Levi bristled at the soft question, his anger flaring back. "I'm not running from anything."

"Aren't you?" Uriel met his gaze squarely. "You've obviously not come to terms yet with being part demon, and part Archangel. Are you afraid that makes you someone different from who you already are? From the man you've made yourself all these years?"

Levi wasn't sure what to respond, so he remained silent, especially since the Archangel had just succinctly cut through to what had been bothering him. It was like suddenly finding himself on quicksand after years of trusting where he stepped would be solid ground.

Uriel continued to study him as if all the answers to life were written on Levi's forehead. "And there's more. You have the look of a man who is walking away when he knows he should stay."

This last observation surprised him and Levi frowned. "I'm not walking away from anything. My mother and my responsibilities there can be sorted out later."

Uriel gave a derisive laugh. "I'm not speaking of your past but your future."

"And you know this how? Soul gazes don't work on me, remember?"

Uriel waved away the comment. "Call it experience from watching humans since they were created. What you're doing is called running away."

Anger flashed through Levi. He didn't care if this was one of God's Archangels. The damned man didn't know what he was talking about. How could he? He was a pure Archangel, his paternity and where he came from were very clear.

Not to mention that Levi had no right to ask Amalya to be with him until he knew who he was. What could he truly offer her at this point? Even if he came to some arrangement with Lilith so he could be with her, what kind of life would they have? "You don't understand."

The first hint of impatience creased Uriel's expression and power flowed off of him in waves. "Don't I? You've been given possibilities and yet you throw every one of them away. You've spent your entire life railing against the unfairness of living longer, healing faster, not being quite human—which is something thousands of others would kill for."

Uriel's animated gestures showed more than anything how angry he was. "You wasted an entire mortal life wallowing in self-pity instead of living life to the fullest with what you'd been given. And now you've been given even more, and you're ready to throw that away as well. There will always be challenges and hurdles to be overcome, but that's no excuse to run from what you've been given."

Uriel's words stabbed deep and adrenaline fueled with anger curled through Levi. "It sounds like you're very familiar with wallowing in self-pity." It was a total shot in the dark, but when Uriel's hands clenched into fists, Levi laughed. Apparently, the Archangel had definite chinks in his own armor.

"Are you going to strike me down for disagreeing with you? You're one of God's enforcers, aren't you?" He held his arms wide in open challenge. "What are you waiting for? Smite me for my blasphemy."

Tension crackled between them for a long moment and then Uriel broke it with a small huff that might have been a laugh. "If you're waiting for me to kill you and give you the easy, coward's way out of this, you're going to be waiting a very long time." The Archangel took one step back, the tension lessening with that one action. "We all must deal with the life we're given to the best of our ability. And the sad fact is, we can usually see another's path more clearly than our own."

The condescending lecturer's tone snapped Levi's restraint on his temper and he swung forward, aiming a right hook toward Uriel's jaw. When his fist connected with a surface harder than granite, pain radiated through his fingers and wrist, and then down his arm.

He stumbled forward.

Uriel stepped back, allowing Levi to fall on his knees onto the grass.

Levi just caught himself from kissing the grass by bracing his uninjured hand on the ground.

He cradled his broken fingers, wrist, and arm close to his body, sucking in large breaths to combat the rising nausea and dizziness that came as a reaction to the sudden pain and stupidity.

Uriel knelt next to him but didn't touch him.

Levi cast a wary glance toward the Archangel. Not that he'd expected Uriel to heal him after he'd just taken a swing at him, but he couldn't be sure what purpose this close stance could have.

"Some advice, Levi. Take all that anger and passion and instead use that energy for love and acceptance. Be brave enough to do whatever it takes to make yourself and those around you happy."

Levi frowned through the pain. The words were spoken in a way that implied Uriel wasn't that brave. He opened his mouth to ask, but Uriel cut him off.

"Life, even one as long as yours, is fleeting and must be savored. Don't waste it." Before Levi could think of anything to say in response, Uriel touched Levi's temple and the world spun for a long moment.

In the next breath, Levi found himself in the same position he had been, only rather than grass underneath his knees and uninjured hand, it was cold, polished marble. His clothes were now completely dry, although they still felt stiff and uncomfortable from the encounter with the salt water. As the vertigo disappeared, a pair of white tennis shoes edged into his line of sight.

Levi tilted his head back and looked up at a dark-haired succubus he'd never met before. She stood with her hands on her jean-clad hips and a scowl on her beautiful heart-shaped face.

"I'm Jezebeth, Amalya's sister. You must be the jackass she calls Levi."

"Excuse me?" His voice was tight with pain, but he forced himself to slowly stand. Amalya had spoken of her sisters, but he wasn't sure why he was currently on the receiving end of a very cold shoulder from this one. After all, he'd brought Amalya back safely, hadn't he?

She raked a dismissive gaze over him. "Can you walk, or do I need to find someone to carry your sorry ass?"

He huffed out a short laugh, not sure what to make of the little spitfire. He had no problem seeing this headstrong beauty being related to Amalya, but he wasn't sure where the hostility came from. "Excuse me?"

"You already said that. All the pain endorphins steal your cutting British wit?" She rolled her eyes skyward. "Come on then. I'll get someone to look at your arm."

He thought he caught the mumbled words "before I break it again" as she walked away from him.

"What seems to be your problem?" he called toward her, retreating back as he cradled his injured arm close to his body.

"You are," she said as she rounded on him. "Amalya woke up to find out you'd left without even a word. She's still weak but recovering, no thanks to you, you selfish prick."

He met her brown, unforgiving gaze and resisted the urge to wince under her intense scrutiny. After all, he *had* left Amalya without speaking to her. Looking back he now realized he'd rationalized that the sisters would want to spend time together so he could wallow in self-pity, as Uriel had so succinctly said it.

Perhaps he was a selfish prick. "Is she all right?" he finally managed.

"Define 'all right,'" she countered before she turned and walked off down the hall leaving him to follow or not.

Levi followed, stopping now and then to catch his breath when the movement aggravated the multiple breaks up and down his arm. What the hell had he been thinking trying to deck an Archangel? No wonder women liked to prattle on about male stupidity, because men like him proved the axiom daily.

He thought about heading directly toward Amalya's quarters, but he agreed with Jezebeth on one thing, he needed to get his arm looked at. Finding Amalya only to pass out when he tried to hold her wasn't a good plan. And that was if she even let him near her. Amalya's temper may not be as explosive and creatively descriptive as Jezebeth's, but it was still very formidable, as he well remembered.

Jezebeth led him down a long hallway and into a room at the end where two incubi who reminded him of boy band singers manned what looked like an infirmary of some sort. "This is Levi and he's apparently broken some bones." She chucked her thumb over her shoulder toward him.

When identical smirks graced both incubi's faces, Jezebeth scowled. "I didn't break them. But that doesn't mean I'm not considering giving him a matching set." She glared at both men until they dropped their gazes. When they did, she turned for the door without looking at Levi.

"Set the breaks and don't bother being gentle. Once he's recovered enough to get around, let Lilith know he's back. But under no circumstances is he to see Amalya until you hear differently from either myself or Lilith." She started to leave and then turned back. "Got that?"

"You won't stop me from seeing her." The angry words were out before he could think better of saying them. Making a further enemy out of Jezebeth wasn't a good approach.

"Try it and you'll find yourself back in the human realm without a pass faster than you can call me a *bloody bitch*," she said in a pretty close imitation of his own clipped British accent.

She left, slamming the door behind her, and he had to restrain himself from bolting up and going after her. Even if he hadn't done something stupid and gotten himself badly injured, there were political waters to be navigated here. And to complicate matters even more—stubborn females were involved.

21

Misgivings curled through Amalya as she stood damp and cold inside a fancy drawing room decorated with priceless antiques. She'd never asked Levi if he had a duchess, but apparently there was a full-fledged one about to come through that door.

A quick spurt of cowardice made her want to bolt before she had to face the woman who shared Levi's title, and his bed. But anger, betrayal, and jealousy rooted her to the spot and demanded answers.

Amalya had been the other woman countless times throughout her life—especially after she began working in brothels. Both men and women would come in for experiences they weren't getting or were afraid to ask for at home. But in all those instances, she'd known up front and there hadn't been any emotional attachment between her and the client.

Things with Levi had gone way past that.

He'd slipped past her protective walls and seen the real her—and accepted her as she was. Or so she'd thought before he'd walked out without a word.

She sensed a change in the air even before the doorknob slowly turned and the door slid inward.

Demon.

Not particularly high in the pecking order judging from its power signature but demon nonetheless.

Amalya glanced around to evaluate her escape options. There was a window along the far wall, but she'd have to pass the door to reach it. She snatched the switchblade out of her bra and quickly transferred it to the pocket of her jeans, keeping her fingers closed around it as she stepped back to put distance between herself and whoever was about to come through the door.

An impeccably dressed woman about Amalya's own height entered the room, carefully closing the drawing room door behind her. Physically she looked to be in her late twenties with sea green eyes and rich brown hair worn in a fashionable style.

Amalya immediately knew the woman before her was a demon and had no illusions that the duchess, if that's who now stood before her, recognized Amalya as a succubus.

"You must be Amalya. I apologize for keeping you waiting." She raked a dismissive gaze up and down Amalya leaving no doubt as to her impressions.

"Is Levi here?" Amalya tried to keep her expression polite while she tried to figure out what was going on.

"I'm afraid Levi has stepped out."

A half-truth.

"But I did want to meet you."

Full truth this time.

She crossed the room to Amalya and gestured to two comfortable-looking chairs placed near the fireplace. "You look cold. Why don't we sit and have a little talk. I'll ring for some tea."

Amalya stiffened. There was a price on her head in the demon realm. Now that she realized Levi wasn't here, exhaustion seeped through her, weighing her down like a bellyful of lead and she wished she'd never left Lilith's lair this morning.

The demon pulled a long braided silk cord that hung in the corner of the room and then snapped her fingers so a crackling fire roared to life just behind the fireplace grate. "Please sit."

A fire demon. Even low-level fire demons could be dangerous, for that one gift she'd just witnessed.

Amalya slowly backed away toward the door. "I'm sorry for intruding. I'll come back when Levi is here."

"He and his father, Thomas, fought constantly. Did you know that?" The clipped cultured words reminded Amalya of Levi, even as shock at their meaning slapped at her. Why would the demon choose to share that with her?

The demon laughed. "I'll take that as a no. Obediah has always been a very private man." She sat in one of the chairs she'd gestured to a moment ago, crossing her legs at the ankle, her posture impeccable and graceful. "Please, sit. I really just want some time to speak with you."

Truth.

That combined with the yearning sadness lacing the demon's voice made Amalya cross the room and sink down into the other chair. The warmth from the fire reached out like a welcome caress, chasing the chill from her skin and loosening some of the cold deep in her gut.

The sound of the door opening made Amalya bolt to her feet, cursing herself for believing a demon. She tightened her fingers around her switchblade and turned to watch the same butler who had opened the front doors carrying a tray so laden with food she was surprised it didn't topple him.

Amalya stepped back, watching him carefully while he laid everything on the table just next to the chairs where the demon still sat.

Her stomach rumbled at the array of small sandwiches, scones, and tea, but she refused to let down her guard. This could still be a trap.

It had definitely not been wise to leave Lilith's lair before recovering fully.

"Thank you, Jenkins." The demon waved the man away and began pouring two cups of tea. When the butler disappeared and shut the door behind him, Amalya waited for her fight-or-flight response to kick in, but when none came the knots in her belly slowly unwound.

"Please, my dear. It's only tea. It's perfectly safe, and as I said, I'd like to speak with you."

More truth.

Amalya couldn't deny her own gift's answers, but she knew she needed to stay wary. Besides, the temptation of finding out more about Levi's past beckoned like forbidden fruit—a fitting comparison with both a succubus and a demon in the room.

She slowly sat and reluctantly unwrapped her fingers from her switchblade before she removed her hand from her pocket.

The demon smiled and handed Amalya a cup of tea perched on a dainty china saucer. "Please help yourself. It's nice now and then to not stand on ceremony. Usually I have to worry about the smallest faux pas showing up in the morning gossip columns." She sighed, and for the first time Amalya saw the weariness of the millennia in her eyes. "The intricacies of the supernatural world puts the humans' backbiting efforts to shame, but at least in situations like this, we can be who we are."

Amalya had often felt like that herself. Only another being who had watched most of human existence go by could understand. But that didn't mean she was ready to let her guard down entirely. She waited until the demon added cream and sugar to her own tea and then took a drink before she did the same. As a succubus, she was immune to most human poisons, but with a demon, Amalya knew she needed to be on guard—truthful statements or not.

The tea was rich and dark and Amalya wanted to relax back in the chair and sink into the comfort it offered as its warmth spilled through her. Added to the warming effects of the fire, she'd almost begun to feel normal again.

"Let's not waste time on small talk, shall we? Officially, I'm Cate or Catherine Spencer, the Dowager Duchess of Ashford."

Dowager duchess. Amalya bit back a sigh of relief. The woman in front of her was Levi's . . .

"Yes, I'm Obediah's mother. And as I'm sure you already know, I'm a fire demon." She gestured toward the fireplace. "I am called Caldriel." She smiled, but the expression never reached her green eyes.

Amalya stiffened in her seat. "Why would a demon of any type give me her real name?" Names had power, especially among the denizens of Heaven and Hell. That's why so many beings used false names.

Amalya was glad the same thing didn't apply equally to succubi and incubi, although it did with Lilith. That was how so many unwary mortals found themselves in servitude to the queen after accidentally summoning her and being tempted into agreements with her. Amalya still wondered what deal Levi had made with Lilith. Lilith had said it was for information that Levi no longer needed, but what could be so important that he'd risk his life to learn it?

Caldriel set down her teacup. "Let's be honest. I know there's a price on your head and that you have very little reason to trust me. With you having the power of my true name, we're on more even footing and we can sit and talk."

Truth.

Amalya studied the woman across from her. Her words were true, and besides, Caldriel could've summoned Semiazas while Amalya had waited for Levi. There was no reason to stall her—for the sake of his revenge, Semiazas would've dropped everything and materialized here in an instant. "What did you mean when you said Levi stepped out? He's not coming back, is he?"

Pain flashed through Caldriel's green eyes. "No."

Truth.

"But he was here? Earlier?"

"Yes. He came to see me. We fought, as usual, and he left. Most likely for good."

Even if Amalya hadn't felt the quick surge of truth to tell her Caldriel's words were true, the stark expression and pain in the woman's eyes was enough.

"Most likely to return to you."

Caldriel's simple pointed words sucker punched Amalya in the gut and she swallowed hard, not sure how to react. Could it be true? If she had just stayed at Lilith's lair and finished recovering, Levi would've returned to her? She resisted the urge to laugh at herself and the unreasonable anger that had driven her to come after him.

"Do you love him?" Caldriel's green gaze had turned intense, burning through Amalya, peeling back all her layers of protection until she felt naked in front of the woman's gaze.

Her first instinct was to say no outright. After all, she hadn't known Levi for long, and they were constantly fighting about something. "I care for him . . ." she began, and then trailed off as memories of her time with Levi flashed in front of her. Not just the parts where they'd saved each others' lives, but the little smiles, the teasing laughs, and even the small gestures of encouragement that existed between the two of them and no one else.

Did that mean she loved him? She shook her head even as her gut answered a resounding yes. "No, I can't . . ." She glanced up at Caldriel to find the woman watching her. "There's Lilith . . . and Jethro—" She broke off, her thoughts swirling as she tried to make sense of this new and conflicting information.

The voice deep inside her remained insistent until she allowed herself to entertain the possibility. As soon as that last wall of denial had fallen, she knew.

Dear God, she'd gone and fallen in love with Levi.

That stubborn, pigheaded, chauvinistic, bossy, witty, smart, protective, sexy, wonderful man who made her feel like she was capable of anything she put her mind to. The man who challenged her to be the best person she could be. The one she'd followed straight into the mouth of danger without a second thought because she couldn't stand the thought of being without him.

She shook her head in wonder as the newness of the realization warred with shock and surprise that she hadn't figured it out sooner. Amalya raised her gaze to Caldriel's. "But we fight all the time."

Caldriel sighed and a small, sad smile curved her lips. "That's how it was with me and Thomas. Levi's father," she supplied when Amalya's brows furrowed. "He was so stubborn and outspoken it made me crazy. It didn't matter that he was only a human and that I could live through a bullet wound and lift a carriage by myself. He still treated me as if I were the most precious, fragile thing in the world." She shook her head, her gaze misted with memory. "I thought

I could carve a place for myself in human society and then move on when that human died to the next. But Thomas got inside my skin, past my defenses, and I couldn't help falling in love with him."

Her gaze cleared and she looked straight at Amalya. "He knew what I was, and he didn't love me *despite* it, he just loved me."

Caldriel's words resonated inside Amalya and they shared a look of complete understanding.

Caldriel set her tea aside. "I know Obediah hates me."

When Amalya opened her mouth to object, Caldriel waved away her words before they could be spoken. "I've behaved very badly. Selfishly. His ire is no more than I deserve at this point. But he's my son, and despite the fact of what I am, I love him and I care what happens to him."

"Does he know?" The words were out before Amalya could think better of them, but rather than offense or pain, a look of puzzlement flashed across Caldriel's features.

"That's a good question. I'm not sure I've ever told him that. I've been too busy trying to convince him to do my bidding." She laughed, but the sound was bitter. "I'd always thought the experience of becoming pregnant and having a child was overrated until I experienced it firsthand. I loved my son and raised him to be smart, independent, and most of all, a survivor. But I always took it for granted that Obediah would want the same things I did. I realize now that those very traits I instilled in him, drove a wedge between us when I tried to manipulate him."

A twinge of regret sliced through Amalya. Succubi and incubi couldn't reproduce. God periodically gifted Lilith with new fully formed succubi, but Amalya would never be able to have Levi's child. "I think if I were gifted with a son, I'd want to make sure he heard those words as often as possible." Her words sounded wistful and she forced a smile. "It's never too late to tell him."

Caldriel laughed. "It's about bloody time I showed him, but my pride rebels against even that." She waved away her own words. "When you came here looking for him, I was angry. You'd taken him away from me, lured him, tempted him."

Amalya's protective walls surged to life and she stiffened, waiting for the betrayal that still might come.

"But then I realized after speaking to you that I'm very glad Obediah has at least one woman he will accept love from. You should take your own advice and tell him."

Amalya squirmed under Caldriel's intense scrutiny, but damned if the demon wasn't right. She'd be a coward not to confront Levi and at least be honest, no matter what the outcome. She set her tea aside and slowly stood. "It was nice to meet you." She was surprised to find that statement true as she held out her hand and Caldriel rose and took it.

"Jenkins will see you out." When Amalya relaxed her hand to pull away, Caldriel didn't release her grip. "Take care of him."

"I will," she promised, and silently added, *Whether or not he lets me.*

22

Amalya made her way to the front doors without bothering to find
Jenkins. The poor man probably had enough to do without walking her down a hallway and opening a door. Besides, too much of
what she had learned still churned through her mind, leaving her
off balance.

As she reached the front foyer, the large front doors beckoned
like the promise of freedom as an overwhelming urge to find Levi
burned through her.

Amalya stopped suddenly on the polished marble tile as icy tendrils of premonition tickled down her spine.

She stiffened as every sense came to full alert and told her to run.

The doorknob turned and the door swung inward before she
could obey the command.

Too late! her fear screamed through her.

A familiar tall figure blocked the way.

"Semiazas."

The word fell from her lips in a hissed whisper. She instinctively backed away, reaching inside her pocket to close her fingers over the comforting hardness of the switchblade. She yanked it from her pocket, pressing down the button until the blade slid out with a soft snick. She brandished it between them feeling silly when he only smiled down at her.

He stood wearing a suit that was straight out of Regency days complete with starched neckcloth and kidskin breeches that clung to his muscular thighs and tucked into dark boots. His dark hair curled over his high collar and his piercing blue eyes pinned her in place. He would be handsome except for the hate-twisted smile that curved his full lips and the hard coldness in his blue eyes.

"Hello, Amalya. It's been too long." He advanced so quickly she had barely registered the motion before he grabbed her hand that held the switchblade and forced her backward. She glanced left and right but knew, short of a miracle, there was no way she could run from Semiazas. He'd found her, and on the power scale he was a dragon and she was a kitten.

Amalya waited for fear or resignation, but instead all she found was anger and indignation. She refused to cower and beg in front of this demon who had scattered her family and forced her to live in fear and look over her shoulder for the past seven hundred years.

Amalya stood her ground, raising her chin to glare up at Semiazas. "It hasn't been nearly long enough if you ask me." She raked a gaze over his costume and raised an eyebrow as if he didn't still have her hand and only weapon in a death grip. "A little overdramatic isn't it?"

He smiled down at her, a combination of amusement and a leer as interest sparked in the depths of his blue eyes. "There's no such thing as overdramatic." He twisted her wrist in a quick flick and a sharp sting lanced against her throat.

Amalya gasped and brought her free hand up to touch the small warm trickle of blood that had welled where Semiazas had cut her. She set her teeth together against the wave of anger that tried to swamp her.

Semiazas held her gaze as he leaned down and sensuously licked the blood from the blade of the switchblade.

Revulsion shuddered through her and she tried to wriggle her hand out of his iron grip, but he only laughed and yanked her against him. "Don't tell me you have an issue with ingesting a little blood, my beauty, it smells and tastes like you've used several liters as an upgrade since I last saw you." He wrapped his free arm around her waist holding her against him while he held her hand with the switchblade out to the side so he could bury his nose against her neck. The prickling sensation of Semiazas's hot breath against the sensitive skin of her neck made her gag. She tasted the sharp tang of bile on the back of her tongue as she bit back the urge to whimper.

Blood. Archangel blood.

Semiazas smelled it inside her pumping through her veins and she'd forgotten all about it.

That much power flowing through her had to have an effect of some type, and the power that usually beat against her in biting waves whenever she'd been in the same room with Semiazas was now only a low hum. She hadn't noticed it when she'd first opened the door because her fear was too busy sending her the fight-or-flight signal to run.

The new blood obviously hadn't made her strong enough to break Semiazas's grip, but she hoped she lived long enough to find out what benefit Raphael's gift to her *did* have.

Semiazas held her tight while he looked up over her shoulder. "Thank you for your service, Caldriel. It will be remembered and rewarded."

Betrayal stabbed deep, tightening Amalya's chest until she thought her heart would stop.

After everything they'd said between them, Caldriel had summoned Semiazas.

* * *

The two incubi cut away one arm of Levi's dress shirt and set his broken bones—three fingers, a wrist bone, and his ulna—following Jezebeth's advice to the letter about not being gentle.

He'd gritted his teeth and remained silent since he knew the bones needed to be set before they began to heal and had to be re-broken. Jezebeth herself might volunteer for that duty if their previous meeting was any indication.

One of the blessings and curses that came with longevity was quicker than human healing. In fact, within a few days he wouldn't even need the sling that he made himself out of some cloth he'd found in one of the cabinets.

He carefully stood and crossed the room to fish through the cabinets, praying to find any type of pain medication. When he found a large bottle of Vicodin he muttered, "Thank God," then popped open the bottle and swallowed four without water.

He sank back onto an uncomfortable cot set up in the corner and closed his eyes to wait for the drugs to kick in.

They would slow his reactions slightly for the next hour or so, but he threw off the effects of medication too fast for them to do more than that. For that very reason he'd been surprised to find any pain-killers here. Perhaps succubi and incubi had better luck with drugs than he did with his oddly mixed heritage.

The door burst open and slammed back against the cave wall with a booming echo.

Levi bolted to his feet, ignoring the flash of pain that radiated down his arm from the sudden movement.

Jezebeth's stricken expression froze Levi in place.

"Where is she?" Something had happened to Amalya. He couldn't say how he knew, but he did. Something deep inside him told him she needed him, and he didn't have long to get there, wherever there was.

"She's gone." The desolation in Jezebeth's voice sliced through him like an accusation. "Do you know where she would go?"

That was part of Jezebeth's frustration, he realized. She hadn't seen Amalya for seven hundred years before yesterday, and it pained her to have to ask him for information that she, as Amalya's sister, should've known. He met her gaze. "No. Her entire goal was to make it safely here to Lilith and her sisters."

Jezebeth's expression softened slightly as if she were grateful for even that small piece of connection to her sister.

Levi cast about for something she might have said or done to help them figure out where she might go. Or if there was some way to track her if she hadn't gone willingly . . . His thoughts tumbled over and over as a trickle of hope expanded inside him like a spark of warmth in a blizzard. When Lilith had made the deal with him to escort Amalya, she'd mentioned amulets that she would give each sister once they returned. Levi struggled to remember what their purpose was, praying it would offer some protection or at the very least act like a beacon they could follow. "Has she already received the amulet from Lilith?" he asked.

A furrow appeared between Jezebeth's brows as she stared at him. "The one that will allow her into Lucifer's lair? Yes. Why?"

"Lilith should be able to track it."

When she glared at him skeptically, he held up a hand to forestall her objections. "Because of their purpose, the maker had to be supernatural, correct?"

She nodded, impatience snapping in her gaze.

"The medallion Lilith gave the companions kept me safe so Amalya didn't drain me. What if the amulets she gave you contain the energy of the maker?"

Several emotions flowed across Jezebeth's face, including realization, surprise, and then hope.

"Uriel," she whispered. The word hung in the air between them for a long moment before she turned and ran down the hall.

Levi started after her and both incubi moved to stop him.

He quickly rammed his left elbow into the first man's face, the telltale crack of the incubus's nose breaking ringing around them in a macabre echo. The force of the blow traveled down his arm making its way to the other side of his body to painfully jar his still healing bones. He sucked in a breath, his only concession to the pain.

He used his momentum to duck low and head butt the second incubus in the gut, knocking him back to fall against the unforgiving stone floor where he lay still.

Not bothering to wait to see if either of them would rally, Levi bolted after Jezebeth, holding his injured arm away from his body the best he could while maintaining a breakneck speed. He dodged around succubi, incubi, and humans who periodically blocked his path, hoping his intuition that Jezebeth would go straight to Lilith was correct.

When he reached the door to Lilith's lair it stood open and he pushed inside, hoping he hadn't guessed wrong. Garnering the queen's displeasure was never a good survival strategy.

He mentally breathed a sigh of relief when he saw Jezebeth already there speaking with Lilith in agitated tones. They both looked up at his intrusion.

"I'll go after her," he blurted through panted breaths.

Jezebeth's gaze narrowed while Lilith stood and crossed the room to stand in front of him, her expression neutral. "Jezebeth has already asked to go."

Levi searched for some argument to convince Lilith. True, he didn't have any real right to go after her. Jezebeth was her sister, but he loved Amalya. She was his.

His thoughts faltered as he realized what he'd just thought and replayed it inside his head. "I love her . . ."

He didn't realize he'd spoken aloud until Lilith raised one dark brow and Jezebeth sucked in a quick breath.

Technically, Amalya was Lilith's creature, just the way a dog or cat belonged to a human. Amalya had no leave to have a relationship with him or even return his love without permission from the queen. He knew all this. He prided himself on effortlessly navigating the complex political waters of both the human and supernatural realms. And yet he'd just given Lilith an excuse to keep him from Amalya permanently if she wished.

"You may go . . . for a price to be named later." Lilith's words hung in the air between them.

Levi was tempted to barter, to clarify, to negotiate some terms up front. But Amalya was out in the human realm alone and in trouble and it was his fault. He couldn't say how he knew, but he trusted his gut instincts enough to know he would willingly bet his life on that assumption. Which he probably was, making such an open-ended deal with Lilith. "Agreed. I need to speak with Uriel."

Surprise flashed across her features before her lips curved into a slow, sensual smile. "So be it. Jezebeth will accompany you to find Amalya."

"She's in just as much danger inside the human realm as Amalya," he protested.

Lilith cut him off with a sharp look. "Her protector will be angry with my decision, but he's currently on a fact-finding mission for me and we don't have time to discuss it. Jezebeth goes."

He stopped short when he realized Lilith had said that Noah, a human, would be angry with her for her decision? Levi wondered what type of arrangement Noah had made that allowed him that much leeway with Lilith. He frowned and started to protest again when a wave of familiar energy prickled against his back. It reminded him of walking out of an air-conditioned building into the hot sunshine. He slowly turned to find Uriel watching them expectantly, his expression guarded.

Uncomfortable tension crackled between Lilith and Uriel, and Levi resisted the urge to step back out of their line of sight.

"My lord Uriel." Jezebeth rushed forward to stand in front of the Archangel, breaking the heavy pause that had blanketed the room.

Uriel's lips quirked, but the humor never made it to his eyes. "You never remember to call me 'my lord.' I must've been summoned for something very dire indeed."

"Amalya is gone. We need to track her using the amulet you gave her."

Uriel's face smoothed of all expression. "I'm unable to directly interfere with you or your sisters."

Jezebeth nodded impatiently. "I know. But . . ." She faltered as she seemed to search for a good argument to convince Uriel.

"Please," Levi interjected. "I've decided I need to run to instead of from." At his direct reference to their conversation after Levi had broken his bones trying to knock Uriel on his ass, Uriel studied him for a long moment.

Silence stretched between them until slowly Uriel nodded. "Run quickly. Time grows short."

Jezebeth's brow furrowed as she looked back and forth between them. "I don't care where we're running. We need to find her."

Uriel placed a hand on Jezebeth's shoulder. "I can't interfere with the four of you, but I can help someone who has decided to take my advice." He glanced up from Jezebeth to meet Levi's gaze.

Uriel reached inside his pocket and pulled out an amulet similar to the one Levi currently wore, the one that gave him immunity from the effects of Amalya's succubus nature. This amulet was red, had different markings, and the energy radiating from the metal was much different than his, even though Levi recognized the similar workmanship of both items. "This amulet will be drawn to its twin that resides within the human realm. I regret that I cannot bring you back, but I'm sure you'll find a way." Uriel gave Levi a long, meaningful glance that Levi wished he knew how to interpret.

Levi started to reach out with his left hand and winced as pain shot up and down his arm.

Uriel took Levi's left hand and placed the amulet in his palm, closing his fingers over the warmed metal. "Energy runs through all things. Like calls like."

The cryptic words hung in the air for only a second before Jezebeth spoke, her tone brisk and impatient. "We're wasting time. She's out there alone."

Levi understood that three of Jezebeth's sisters were out there under similar circumstances, which probably only added to her fears. But Amalya had been safely sleeping in her room just a scant handful of hours ago. He shared Jezebeth's frustration and sense of urgency.

She took the amulet out of his hand and stood on her tiptoes to loop it around Levi's neck. It fell just over his badly rumpled shirt. She faced him with a determined expression hardening her features.

He blinked and suddenly Uriel stood in front of him. "What—" He swung his gaze to the side to see Uriel standing there also. Confusion swirled through him as he looked back and forth between the two Uriels.

An impatient sound came from the one just in front of him. "Amalya can sense truth. I can shape-shift. Figured this form might give us an advantage. Let's go, we don't have time for this."

He stared hard at the person standing in front of him that he now knew to be Jezebeth but could find no difference between her and the real Uriel, except Jezebeth couldn't duplicate the powerful energy that flowed in waves off the Archangel.

The Jezebeth-Uriel made another snort of impatience and grabbed his hand, threading large masculine fingers through his in a very feminine gesture. Levi stiffened at the oddity of the situation but forced himself to stay still as he looked up across the two inches that separated them in height.

"Concentrate on the amulet and finding the other one. It was given to you, it won't work for me," she snapped as if he were a daft student.

Levi frowned and closed his eyes concentrating on the thrumming energy from the new amulet around his neck. Once he was comfortable with it he reached out with his senses, searching for its twin.

He was surprised to find one just across from him—most likely around Jezebeth's neck. He reminded himself he shouldn't be surprised, since each succubus was to receive one once they returned to Lilith's lair. Although apparently hers wouldn't work the same way.

He reached out farther, his awareness slipping beyond these rooms and reaching out into the human realm as if pulled by a magnet.

A small gasp escaped him as he felt a connection with the other amulet.

A wrenching sense of vertigo ripped his stomach across the miles a split second behind the rest of his body—or at least it felt like that. He opened his eyes shocked to find himself standing in the ballroom of Ashford House.

The smell of demon and blood was thick on the air, and both he and Jezebeth, still in her Uriel form, whirled to face the other occupants of the room.

Amalya lay limp on the same antique settee where Levi had stolen his first kiss, her arm flung out toward him. Her shirt and bra were ripped open baring her breasts, and her neck, breasts, and torso were covered in dozens of cuts that still oozed blood. Her face and skin were pale, her eyes closed.

A familiar figure leaned over Amalya—

Levi shook his head, an instinctive denial to what his mind told him he saw.

Caldriel slowly straightened and turned to face him, cementing this odd reality. "Obediah," she said as she stared at him.

Betrayal and anger slashed through him as he stared at his mother in cold disbelief. "What have you done?"

Jezebeth started forward and Caldriel's brows furrowed, most likely as she tried to make sense of the dichotomy of Uriel's form, but with the energy of a succubus.

"What are you?" she demanded, a trace of worry finally cracking her defiant veneer.

While her attention was distracted by Jezebeth's borrowed Uriel form, Levi walked forward slowly as he slid his silver dagger out of the sheath in the waistband of his trousers. He now wished he hadn't taken the Vicodin. Not only would his reactions be slower, but he would have to fight left handed if it came to that. And fight he would to save Amalya, even if it meant killing Caldriel.

"I'm pissed off, that's what I am," Jezebeth answered in Uriel's voice. "What have you done?"

Caldriel's gaze snapped to Levi as she finally noticed him closing in. Her gaze pinned him in place and she stood unmoving, her expression sad. "She's right. I should've told you. But actions still speak more loudly."

She knelt slowly and grabbed something near her feet, straightening as she brandished it in front of her. It took him a minute to see past all the blood covering the blade, but when he did his anger flashed anew.

Amalya's switchblade. The one he'd watched Jethro lay into her open palm not too long ago.

He looked at his mother as horror bloomed through him.

He'd never deluded himself that his mother was a saint. She was a demon, after all. But she'd apparently hidden many things from him in her quest to keep him as the duke so she could maintain appearances and the lifestyle she'd built. But he'd mistakenly thought her time among the human realm had mellowed her, tempered her.

He'd obviously been very wrong. And now Amalya had paid the price.

She'd come here looking for him, he realized as guilt stabbed deep. He'd left Lilith's lair without a word to her, and his stubborn, independent Amalya had followed him, knowing him well enough to know where he would've gone.

This entire situation was his fault. If he'd just talked to her before running away as Uriel had accused him, she would still be safe in her rooms back at Lilith's lair rather than lying limp in a house that embodied his past.

Amalya's arm moved catching his attention, and he bit back a sigh of relief that she was still alive. Instead, he kept his attention on his mother, trying to figure the best way to get both Amalya and Jezebeth safely out of here. "You've also just made it quite clear where your loyalties lie . . . Mother."

A quick gasp from Jezebeth reminded Levi that his relationship with Caldriel wasn't commonly known. If they survived this, there would be fallout from that. But that was a worry for another time.

"Obediah—" Caldriel began.

"Welcome to the party, Levi, and thank you for bringing me another of the four." The smooth voice sent icy fingers of dread racing down Levi's spine and out of his peripheral vision he saw Jezebeth-Uriel stiffen.

"Semiazas." Uriel's voice with Jezebeth's now familiar inflections struck Levi as odd, but all he wanted at this moment was to run to Amalya's side and spirit her back to safety. Instead, he turned so he could keep everyone in sight.

Semiazas's appearance surprised him. He supposed he'd expected someone more . . . sinister. Instead, he was dressed in a Renaissance gentlemen's riding costume, and the only clue to his true identity the shrewd icy expression in his blue eyes.

"Isn't this cozy," the demon said as he sauntered forward. "I like you much better in your own form, Jezebeth. Uriel's never been quite my type."

Jezebeth stepped away, keeping distance between them, her fearsome Uriel form still managing to look vulnerable in the face of the demon she'd hidden from for seven centuries.

"Ashford," Semiazas said, using the name of his dukedom, as was common among English peers. "You do realize there's a bounty on Jezebeth's head here, don't you? I'll be happy to pay it to you. Anything in particular you'd like? Your mother has already earned the one for Amalya."

Levi's anger burned and he tightened his grip on the dagger in his hand. He could clearly imagine plunging it deep into both Semiazas's heart and then Caldriel's. But those actions wouldn't save Amalya or Jezebeth.

Energy runs through all things. Like calls like.

Uriel's cryptic words echoed through Levi's mind, and as their meaning finally became clear, he allowed a smile to curve his lips. He placed the blade of the dagger in his right hand and ignoring the pain, he closed his right fingers around it, welcoming the stinging bite of the sharp blade as it sank into his skin.

He pulled the dagger free, slicing deep until he could smell his own blood thick and heady.

Caldriel's slow smile confused him and made him doubt for a split second, but a quick glance at Amalya decided his actions. Levi took a deep breath and yelled at the top of his lungs, "By your blood that runs through our veins, I summon you."

Nothing happened for a long pregnant pause and Semiazas began to laugh. "I'd say you're on your own, Ashford. Apparently, your blood isn't worth all that much."

Jezebeth met his gaze and held up a hand as she pointedly looked at his dagger. He had more, so he tossed her the one in his hand, which she caught easily despite his awkward left-handed toss. Just as she adopted a fighting stance and faced Semiazas's amused expression, the familiar static electricity that heralded the onset of the summoning crackled through the room raising all the hairs on Levi's body and sending energy swirling through the room in a breath-stealing rush much more intense than it had been the last time.

An earsplitting boom crashed through the room as Raphael appeared wearing his black leathers, his face a mask of anger and retribution as he turned in a slow circle taking in the entire scene.

"You've no right to interfere here, Raphael," Semiazas's voice boomed through the room. "I'm not to interfere with the succubus, but I have blood debts owed to me from everyone in this room except you and one other."

Semiazas sneered. "I noticed you'd shared a bit of yourself with

Amalya. That will only make her a better plaything for me." He shrugged. "Faster healing, more endurance, and more of an energy burst each time I drain her."

"My blood debts take precedence over your revenge, and I'll fight for those in this room who owe me. You'll have to wait for another time."

"Choose your battles wisely, Raphael. The only reason I let all of you live last time we met was nostalgia for Gabriel."

Raphael laughed as he reached out to pull Jezebeth behind him. A very odd scene since she was still in Uriel's large form. "Nostalgia had very little to do with it as both you and I know."

Semiazas slowly smiled, the expression sending dread curling through Levi. "Kill her."

Caldriel nodded and met Levi's gaze for a long moment.

Levi could kill her but not before she plunged the switchblade through Amalya's heart.

"Mother, no. Please." His voice was pleading.

"I'm sorry," she whispered as she lifted the long silver blade and quickly sliced open her own throat.

It took a long few seconds for Levi's mind to make sense of what he saw, and when he finally did he rushed forward catching his mother's light form as she crumpled to the ground.

23

"No!" As *Caldriel* crumpled and Levi caught her limp form, Amalya found the strength to push herself up to sit. She'd finally figured out what benefit all of Raphael's blood had afforded her. Semiazas had drained nearly half her blood, torturing her for nearly an hour, but she continued to heal. She was low on energy, but even now she knew she shouldn't be able to sit up, let alone speak.

Everyone in the room seemed to freeze as they realized who had spoken.

"I really must thank you for your gift to the succubus, Raphael," Semiazas growled. "As I said, it will make her much more interesting for the next million years or so until I get tired of her."

"No." Amalya slowly pushed to a stand, pulling her dress closed to cover her bare breasts.

"No?" Semiazas laughed. "My dear, what can you do about it?"

Raphael held up a hand. "I call for a judgment of blood debts."

Semiazas stilled. Lucifer would preside if he agreed to the judgment, and he was trying to stay under the radar since he'd technically escaped. Normally having Lucifer preside wouldn't guarantee a fair hearing, but with current circumstances being what they were, Semiazas might not be so willing to bet on that.

"If I agree to let you use the argument of blood debts owed, you won't be able to use it again. The next time we meet, everything will go to me."

Raphael smiled. "I agree that once used, the blood debts can't be reused. However, that doesn't mean our next meeting will go in your favor, Semiazas. I won't give up without a fight, and neither will you. It will be up to our Father to decide."

Semiazas snorted. "Our Father. He would have to be paying attention for that to happen." He gestured with a flourish. "Take those who owe you a blood debt and go. Leave the rest for me."

Amalya stared across the room at her sister and wondered who would be the last person in the room when they were gone.

Raphael smiled and waved as everyone except for Semiazas and the elderly butler hiding in the corner disappeared.

* * *

As soon as the group rematerialized in the large receiving cavern in Lilith's lair, Levi looked around to get his bearings. The entire cavern was in chaos, their small group scattering faster than Levi could find them.

He glanced behind him to find Raphael gently holding Caldriel in his arms. She was pale, but the deep wound in her throat was no more than a healed red line now.

Levi wasn't sure about the blood debt his mother owed to Raphael, but her life was forfeit for what she'd done to Amalya.

"She didn't summon Semiazas."

"Excuse me?" Levi heard Raphael's words, but they wouldn't

make sense inside his brain. "I saw her standing over Amalya back in the ballroom."

"One of the guards called Semiazas when he recognized Amalya. Your mother was trying to protect Amalya and had tried to summon me several times, but since she and I share no blood ties, she couldn't invoke a strong enough summons. It's extremely difficult for demons to summon any type of angel, let alone an Archangel."

A large hand squeezed Levi's heart until he thought it would explode out of his chest. "She didn't . . ." He couldn't bring himself to say the words.

"No. Despite everything, she loves you and wants you to be happy. She knew if she didn't follow Semiazas's directive, she would be tortured for eternity, but if she did, you would hate her. So she chose to take herself out of the equation."

"She's dead?" Levi's gut knotted at the thought. He'd assumed even after that horrific injury that Raphael wouldn't have wasted time healing a dead woman. Was this really just her human host's shell that Raphael held?

"She's very weak. But alive."

Levi laughed as relief washed through him. "Stubborn, resilient wench." He laid a hand on Raphael's shoulder. "Thank you."

Raphael smiled. "I'll let her know to come and see you when things are sorted out?"

Levi nodded, grateful that he'd get another chance to speak with his mother. Another chance he'd make sure neither of them wasted.

"The queen wishes to see you at once."

Levi turned to find an incubus several inches shorter than himself dressed in the male version of an *I Dream of Jeannie* outfit.

Levi hadn't expected any different. Lilith had let him go after

Amalya, thus living up to her side of their bargain. Now it was his turn.

Hopefully whatever Lilith required of him wouldn't require him to never see Amalya again.

* * *

Amalya was almost entirely healed by the time Raphael brought them all back to Lilith's lair. She wasn't used to Raphael's potent blood pumping through her veins, but she couldn't deny she appreciated the benefits.

She turned to find Levi, craning her neck to see over the milling crowd that had gathered in the main cavern at the news of their return. She and Levi had a lot to discuss and she refused to wait until something else could happen to stop her.

"Lilith wanted him taken straight to her."

Amalya whirled to find Jezebeth standing behind her with a frown. "He made a very open-ended deal with her to be able to come after you."

"He what?" Something like panic squeezed Amalya's heart as she stared at her sister. "What was the deal?"

"Lilith told him he could go after you for a price to be named later, and he agreed."

The implications of such a deal froze all Amalya's blood to an icy sludge inside her veins. "No!" Amalya pulled away from her sister's concerned grip and ran down the hall toward Lilith's rooms. She had to stop this somehow, even if she had to offer herself in his stead.

Lilith already owned Amalya, but in the supernatural world there were always deals to be made.

When she reached the queen's rooms, she resisted the urge to pound on the door. Pissing off the queen wouldn't help her cause. Instead, she knocked and tried to slow her breathing while she waited for permission to enter.

When Lilith's soft invite finally came, Amalya forced herself to slowly turn the knob and open the door rather than slam it open.

Levi stood before the queen, his bearing regal and proud even in the still-disheveled and blood-covered clothes. He turned when she entered, his hungry expression raking over her as if to ensure she was all right.

"My queen, I seek an urgent audience." Amalya bowed and waited for Lilith to acknowledge her further.

"Rise and come forward."

Amalya breathed a sigh of relief and walked forward to face her queen.

Lilith lounged back more comfortably in her chair, her bare feet peeking out from under her long, flowing dress. "You seek an audience to what end? To save this man from his promise that he used to save you and bring you back?"

Amalya wanted to bristle at the unfairness of the deal, or find some loophole that would set Levi free, but she didn't see one. The deal had been for Levi to be able to come after her for a price to be named later. Lilith had fulfilled her part of the bargain and would now require Levi to fulfill his. "Yes," she said anyway. "My queen, I wish to purchase the cost of his payment with whatever you would require of me for such a concession."

Lilith raised her brows. "You love this man?"

Amalya hesitated. Admitting such a thing in front of Lilith was tantamount to admitting an indiscretion. But at the same time, Amalya's willingness to offer anything needed to relieve Levi of this debt he'd taken on for her did require some explanation. Besides,

Lilith wasn't stupid. The queen tended to know much more than she let on, which was one of the reasons she and her kind had prospered as well as they had within the supernatural realm.

Amalya glanced at Levi and Caldriel's words rang through her mind.

I should've told him while I had the chance.

Amalya held Levi's worried dark gaze and forced a small smile. "Despite all my better judgment, I do, my lady."

Levi's expression of concern faltered as surprise flashed across his face, quickly hidden behind a mask of nonchalance. He dropped his gaze and turned to face Lilith. "This payment is mine and mine alone, my queen. I took the deal and I'll pay the consequences. Amalya had no part in this, so should have no say in its payment."

"Damn it," she snapped at the man's high-handed dismissal of her. She'd just told him she loved him and he couldn't even speak directly to her. She winced as she realized she'd cussed in front of the queen. "My apologies, my lady. This man makes me crazy. He only took on that debt because of my stupid decision to leave. The least he can do is let me pay it."

"Amalya, be quiet," Levi warned, "and let me handle this."

His condescending tone fed all the fear and anger she'd endured over the past several days and she rounded on him as the dam holding back her anger broke. "The hell I will." She stepped forward and poked her finger into his chest. "I've put up with your condescending, chauvinistic bullshit quite long enough. I'm a fully grown woman, *Your fucking Grace*," she said stealing one of Jethro's expressions. "And I expect to be treated as such. If we're comparing life spans and experience, you're a toddler compared to me, so stop treating me like I don't know anything. I know that despite my better judgment I've gone and fallen in love with you, and God help me, I won't stand by and see you ruin your life because you tried to save me from my own stupidity."

"You daft woman. Don't you realize I wouldn't have done this for you in the first place if I didn't love you as well? I can't live with myself unless I know you're safe and happy."

Amalya stumbled back as if he'd slapped her. Levi loved her too? She'd never expected him to return her feelings. And judging from the shock still frozen on his handsome features, he hadn't expected to tell her in such a way. "What did you say?"

The queen cleared her throat, which had the effect of a cold bucket of water being tossed in Amalya's face. Heat burned into her cheeks as she realized the scene they'd both just created in front of the queen.

"I can see there are some issues the two of you would still like to discuss. However, I have other things to attend to today. Levi, your payment to me has been purchased by Uriel. He requires your services and assistance, and in light of recent developments with the journals and horsemen, I would like to extend your protection of Amalya indefinitely. Uriel has agreed to that stipulation."

The information was delivered as an edict and not a question. Levi owed the debt to Lilith, which allowed her to set the terms as she liked. The fact that there was still ambiguity within the terms did nothing to dampen the initial relief Amalya felt, but she remained cautious. "My queen?"

"I suggest you two return to your quarters and rest and recover. Levi, when Uriel summons you, Amalya will accompany you. You are responsible for her continued safety. Any other . . . attachments . . . will be discussed when the current situation plays out." Lilith rose and turned her back on them.

Thus dismissed, Amalya found herself preceding Levi out of Lilith's rooms in silence as she slowly tried to digest all the possible nuances of what they'd been told.

* * *

"Amalya . . ." Levi began, not willing to waste another second without talking to her and telling her everything he'd realized.

"Not here." She grabbed his hand and half dragged him down the hall toward her rooms.

He bristled at the delay, but since their "attachment" still hadn't been officially approved, he knew they had to continue to publicly act the part of protector and protected. Anything else would require somewhere more private.

When she made it to her room, Levi reached around her to open the door for her, but when he tried the knob, it remained stubbornly locked.

A smug smile pulled at Amalya's lips. "I haven't invited you inside yet." She turned the knob easily and swung the door wide, stepping inside and staring back at him over the threshold.

He started forward, smacking into some type of invisible barrier. Pain radiated up and down his injured arm as well as his nose where he'd taken the brunt of the hit. He stumbled back cursing as he studied the air between them for any telltale sign of what he'd run into. "Amalya, what's going on?"

"Sorry," she said with a guilty smile. "Only the queen can enter everyone's quarters without permission. All others need to be invited and can have that permission revoked at the will of the rooms' assigned occupant at any time."

Levi frowned as he tried to work out what point Amalya was trying to make. "You don't want me to come in?" He tried not to think about all the other things she might not want by extension.

She huffed out an amused breath as she faced him. "For once, will you stop thinking you know everything and pay attention?" Her words were teasing, which flustered him even more. "Ever since you walked into my bathroom back at Sinner's Redemption, you've made decisions for me, assumed you knew best, and even though I think you've come to learn that I can take care of myself in a lot of situations, you still act like you're living in Victorian England when it comes to how you treat women."

"Amalya, I—"

"Stop." She sliced the air in front of her with her hand. "Just be quiet for once and listen to me. If I invite you inside, I want to do it willingly."

He had the distinct impression she was speaking about more than just inviting him inside her quarters.

"I want to have the choice and thus the responsibility for anything that comes as a result of that choice." She stared into his gaze, her expression pleading for him to understand. "I want you to trust me enough to know what's best for me and to allow me to make my own decisions."

He thought back to all the decisions he'd made for her and winced as he realized that the majority of the time she would've made better choices for them than he had. He'd assumed he always knew better and had made not only circumstances much harder for them both but also hadn't given Amalya credit for being the smart, capable woman he knew her to be. He cringed as he realized this was just another example of how he'd been an arrogant ass.

Her intense gray gaze burned through him and he sighed. "I can't promise to change overnight. But I will do my best. I want you to invite me inside willingly because you know I love you, and you're willing to let me be a part of your life no matter what happens in the future."

A long silence stretched between them as she studied him. Levi's stomach knotted as he waited for her answer. He wasn't sure what he'd do if she turned him away. It had taken him so long to realize that his place was by her side, he hoped it wasn't too late.

What felt like an eternity later, a smile curved Amalya's lips. "Come in, Levi. I've been waiting for you."

He let out the breath he'd been holding as relief and anticipation flooded his system. He stepped slowly forward, reaching out with his good arm to gently cup Amalya's cheek and feather his thumb over her silky soft skin. "Thank you." He knew she would take his whispered words as more than just gratitude for inviting him into her room.

She was his salvation from a lonely life spent in pursuit of nothing. She made him a better man, and he wanted to spend every waking moment he could with her, no matter if the world self-destructed around them. "I love you, Amalya. No strings, no stipulations, just me telling you you've captured my heart."

She reached up and traced gentle fingers over his stubbled jaw, the slight touch sending gooseflesh rushing over him and warmth growing inside his chest. "I know you do, Levi. I love you too."

"Despite your better judgment?" he teased, parroting her words inside Lilith's chambers. He'd been shocked when she'd said those words, but now that he was past the first spurt of surprise, they humbled him. He vowed to spend the rest of his life trying to be worthy of such an emotion from such a woman as the one who stood before him.

Her smile widened and she stood on tiptoes to brush her lips over his. "Definitely against my better judgment, but since I was the one who left the safety of the lair to follow you, I think my better judgment is impaired when it comes to you."

He laughed against her lips and captured her close with his good arm. "Thank God." He leaned down to meet her kiss, and she surprised him by wrapping her arms around his neck and kissing him like she had back at the farmhouse—as if she were trying to brand him as hers.

Levi growled low in his throat as his cock hardened and blood rushed through his veins. It had been too long since he'd touched her. He needed to be inside her, to lose himself in the sweet heat of her surrounding him.

He let himself bask in the warmth of her soft curves against him, her hungry mouth against his, and the wondrous sensation of her fingers running through his hair.

Levi slowly walked her backward toward the bed as a wave of dizziness stole through him making him stumble. He probably needed to eat and sleep, but all that could wait until after he'd left Amalya boneless and satisfied. Right now there was only her.

She pulled back with a laugh. "Careful of that arm." She turned him around until the backs of his legs hit the bed and then she gently undid the button and zipper on his trousers sliding them down his legs until the fabric bunched around his ankles. The cool air from the room hit his skin and he felt exposed and at a disadvantage standing in his silk boxer shorts as she raked her hungry gaze over him.

"Let me." She grinned up at him as she sank down to her knees in front of him. She laid her small hand over his cock and arousal slammed him in the gut like a sledgehammer.

He sucked in a breath and prayed for strength. This woman had a way of stripping away all his control and she hadn't even touched him skin to skin yet. When she leaned forward and laved a hot wet line over the silk, he stiffened.

"Relax, Levi. Let me pleasure you."

Those simple words sent fire shooting through his veins and he had to swallow hard to maintain any semblance of his composure.

As she nibbled and stroked him through the boxer shorts, he allowed his eyes to slip closed and he threaded his fingers through her thick, silky hair. The honey gold strands were warm against his skin and he had a sudden vivid image of all that hair sliding over his skin, taunting him, teasing him.

A strangled sound escaped from his throat before he could stop it and Amalya's throaty laugh told him she was enjoying every second of her erotic torture.

She fished her fingers up through the leg of his boxers to gently cup his balls, and the first hot bead of pre-come leaked out to be absorbed by the silk that still separated Amalya's seeking mouth from his cock.

"Mmm. I can taste you."

Those dark words burned through him and combined with the erotic sensation of the warm, welcoming heat of her mouth teasing him through the cloth barrier, he had to fight hard not to come.

"Not yet," she murmured. "I want to feel you come inside me. I want to watch your face as I take you deep and see the ecstasy in your expression when you lose all control and spill inside me."

He groaned, a low, plaintive sound that sounded much more desperate than he liked. Through pure willpower he fought back the slow tingling that had already begun deep inside his pelvis. He gulped in another breath as the sensation slowly receded but didn't disappear. "Amalya." He laid a gentle hand on her hair. "I can't last like this. You're going to kill me."

Her pleased laughter feathered over him like gentle kisses and his entire body tightened. But then she slowly stood, whisking off her T-shirt over her head to reveal a simple white cotton bra that lovingly contained her ripe curves.

Levi fisted his hands at his sides to keep from reaching for her.

She'd made it clear she wanted to lead, and he would do his bloody best to let her.

She unbuttoned the top several buttons of her jeans and pushed them down over her hips to puddle on the floor where she kicked them away.

His hungry gaze followed her shapely calves back up to her lovely thighs to find her smooth-shaven mons and the wonderful warmth that beckoned to him from between her thighs.

"Have I mentioned I love that you don't wear knickers?" It was said in a worshipful tone that didn't bother to hide his admiration.

When she laughed again, he traced his gaze up past her gently rounded stomach to the pale expanse of skin between her belly and her breasts. He had a sudden urge to kiss and lick every centimeter of that expanse until she was panting and begging him to plunge inside her.

The movement of her reaching between her breasts to unhook her bra caught his attention from that tempting expanse and he found himself riveted as he waited for her shapely breasts to be revealed to him.

As the material fell away and she dropped the bra to the floor behind her, the full creamy swells of her breasts were bared for his view. "Lovely . . ." he said in a reverent whisper.

Her large areolas were light pink with tight nipples that beckoned for him to suck them into his mouth and taste.

He must've leaned forward to do just that because she placed a restraining hand against his shoulder. "Not yet. Sit."

Levi obediently sat, taking a moment to adjust his position to give his aching balls enough room so he could sit comfortably.

Amalya came forward and leaned over him to slowly unbutton his shirt. Her tempting scent rose around him, taunting him, just like the proximity of those lovely pink-tipped breasts that were close enough to reach out and touch. When she slid his shirt off his good arm and realized she couldn't pull it off his injured arm without moving the sling, she left it and crawled on top of him, straddling him and grinding against him.

Her heat beckoned to him through the damp silk of his boxers and he reveled in the sensation of the smooth skin of her breasts sliding against his chest.

With his good arm he slid his fingers deep into her hair while she captured his mouth, kissing him hungrily until his head spun and he thought he might pass out from the exquisite sensations she sent shooting through him.

Amalya arched against him, rubbing her wet slit over his aching cock again and again until they were both panting and Levi was left once more fighting not to explode inside his boxer shorts.

When Amalya finally pushed up on her knees and reached through the fly of his shorts to fish his cock through the opening, he wanted to shout out his anticipation, but she continued to kiss him, devouring his mouth as if she would never get enough of him.

Finally, she guided him to her entrance, the tip of his cock brushing against the silky wetness of her pussy. She gasped as she sank down on him until only the head of his cock was inside her beckoning warmth.

He wanted to thrust up inside her, to feel her sheath his entire aching length, but he held back, letting her lead and enjoying the erotic torture she had decreed for them both.

Amalya slowly moved, teasing him, but not taking him any deeper.

Whenever she sensed him getting close, his breath backing up in his lungs and his body tensing under her, she would stop and allow him to regain his control before she would begin again.

She gasped, her skin shimmering with the golden glow from his pre-come as she continued to tease him.

He closed his eyes as the world began a slow spin as if he'd drunk too much brandy. His body suddenly felt sluggish, like it had tripled in weight, so heavy that he had difficulty keeping himself upright. Only Amalya's warm weight kept him anchored.

What a wonderful way to die . . .

The thought teased through his muddled thoughts just as a loud knock sounded on the door, startling them both. "Levi, Amalya. I need to speak with you immediately."

The urgency in Uriel's voice made Levi's gut clench. What had happened now?

Amalya frowned and brushed a quick kiss across his lips as she climbed off him and grabbed a silk robe off a hook fastened to the side of a large wooden wardrobe cabinet. "Stay right there. I'll see what's happened."

Levi tried to reach out and grab the edge of the comforter and flip it over his lap to cover his erection that stood proudly where it protruded out of the fly of his boxer shorts, but his arms refused to respond to his commands. Panic threaded through him as he tried to move any body part and failed. Instead, he slowly sank backward onto the bed.

24

"*The universe had* better be on the brink of collapse," Amalya grumbled as she stalked to the door. Her body still hummed with arousal and the wonderful pulsing energy from the skin-to-skin contact with Levi and the amazing bursts of power from his pre-come that always felt like mini-orgasms churning through her body.

She yanked open the door with more force than necessary just as Levi slumped backward on the bed, his cock still protruding from his boxers.

"I'm too late." Uriel pushed past her as panic flashed through Amalya.

She rushed back to Levi's side as Uriel laid a hand over Levi's forehead. "What's wrong with him?"

"The amulet that made him immune to your succubus nature doesn't work inside Lilith's lair. Only inside the human realm."

The implications spilled through Amalya, sending icy shards of fear through her veins and squeezing her heart. "Dear God. I could've killed him." She took Levi's hand in hers, his skin cool to the touch. "I remember him swaying, but I thought . . ."

Uriel pulled the corner of the comforter over Levi's lap. "He's lost a lot of energy, but he'll be fine with a few hours of sleep and some food. If it wasn't for all that Archangel blood pumping through his veins, he would already be dead."

Amalya sucked in a deep breath as Uriel's words sliced through her.

He glanced back at her with a kind expression. "You didn't know."

She swallowed hard and sat down on the bed, not sure how to digest the information that she'd nearly killed Levi. "How did you know?"

"You might want to ask your sister. She and Noah found out too late when they returned to the lair."

"Too late? But I thought Noah—"

"He's fine but now indebted to Lilith. Talk to your sister, she can tell you everything. When she found out you'd both already left Lilith's rooms, she was frantic. I told her I'd take care of it." He glanced back at Levi. "As for him, I've bought his debt to Lilith for my own purposes, so I can't have him dying on me." He leaned down and brushed a gentle hand over Levi's forehead and eyes.

Something glittering and golden seemed to pass from Uriel's fingers into Levi's skin, and Amalya watched Levi expectantly waiting for what would happen next.

Uriel's low chuckle made her glance up. "You'll be sorely disappointed if you're waiting for some visible sign of the gift I've given him. I've made him wholly immune to succubus and incubus powers for the duration of his service to me." He straightened and shrugged. "After that, it will be up to Lilith."

As he said the queen's name, pain flashed across his features and then disappeared. Amalya studied him with a frown. "She loves you, you know."

Uriel stiffened and wouldn't quite meet her gaze. "Yes, I know."

When he didn't say anything else Amalya slowly stood. "Thank you for helping Levi, and for . . . the gift," she finally managed.

Uriel nodded and walked toward the open doorway. "Treasure each other," he said before leaving and softly closing the door behind him.

* * *

Levi woke to the tantalizing smells of bacon and fresh bread. His stomach growled and he stretched as he realized he lay naked between soft sheets. He opened his eyes to find Amalya fully clothed, sitting by the bed watching him.

"Good morning." The happy relief in her voice confused him until he remembered falling back in a boneless heap on the bed. He searched for some time reference to tell him how long it had been but found none.

"Morning." He pushed himself up to sitting, leaning back against the wooden headboard as he motioned for her to join him on the bed.

She scrambled up beside him, her vulnerable expression reminding him of a little girl.

He traced his fingers over the soft skin of her cheek and couldn't resist brushing a gentle kiss over her lips before sitting back to face her. "What happened?"

She swallowed hard, making him sure that something more than him passing out had gone on.

"I nearly killed you." The last word ended on a choked sob and he reached for her, but she pulled back holding out a hand to stop him from touching her. She gained her composure quickly, taking a deep breath before meeting his gaze again. "The amulet from Lilith that gave you immunity to my succubus nature doesn't work inside her lair."

What a wonderful way to die . . .

His own thought came back to taunt him as he realized what had happened. A vague memory of Uriel at the door came back to him. "Uriel came to warn us."

She nodded. "Apparently, Noah found out the same way, only he wasn't as lucky."

"Wait. I thought Noah—"

"He is. And it's a long story for another time."

Levi caught sight of his clothes draped across the end of the bed and he remembered the box he'd retrieved from his room at Ashford House. "Can you hand me my suit jacket?"

Amalya frowned but did as he asked, handing it to him and then sinking down next to him on the bed.

Levi reached inside and found the picture. He cringed as he thought of the water damage, but when he pulled it out, it was pristine and perfect as the day he'd drawn it.

When he handed it to Amalya she frowned. "Where did you get this? It's me."

"I drew it. I saw you all those years ago stepping inside a carriage, and I couldn't get your face out of my mind." He smiled as he gazed into her beautiful eyes. "And now, several lifetimes later, here you are, and you're real."

He reached deeper into his pocket and pulled out the tiny box that rested there. "And I meant what I said in Lilith's rooms. I love you, Amalya. I don't know what the future holds for either of us, but if I—we," he quickly amended, "can work out the details with Lilith, would you do me the very great honor of becoming my wife?"

Levi opened the box and watched a look of surprise and delight flow over Amalya's face. However, when he followed her line of sight, he realized she was looking at him and not the ring.

Moisture glistened in her eyes and she smiled at him. "You want to marry me?"

He laughed. "Hundreds of women would've given their right arm for this ring alone, attached to me or not, and that's all you can say?"

She glanced down at the ring as if seeing it for the first time. "It's beautiful." She reached out to gently trace the royal blue rubies and sparkling diamonds with her fingertip before raising her gaze to his. "But so are you. And I'd rather have you."

"Is that a yes?" he pressed.

A smile curved her lips that didn't reach her eyes. "If you don't change your mind before this is done, and we can work it out with Lilith, then . . . yes. Right now, you need to eat." She motioned toward the table that was filled with more food than Levi could eat in an entire day. "I had them make a wide assortment since I wasn't sure what you'd be craving when you woke up."

His body was already hard and ready and he started to reach for Amalya and then stopped.

"What is it?"

"What I'm craving is you, but after the last time—"

Her throaty laugh cut him off midsentence.

"Since you now have a debt to Uriel, he's granted you immunity to all succubi and incubi powers until your service to him is done. Then it will be up to Lilith."

His cock hardened further, apparently as happy about that news as the rest of him.

"Levi, I feel horrible about—"

He grabbed her around the waist, toppling her backward and falling on top of her in a tangle of covers.

Amalya gave a surprised squeak followed by a throaty giggle. Then his mouth was on hers, with both of them wriggling and squirming to push the covers as well as Amalya's clothes out of the way.

He wanted his skin against hers and her welcoming body around him. "Don't you bloody mention any of that again. It's all behind us now."

When Amalya tossed the last scrap of her clothing aside, Levi rolled them over so he was on top of her, pressing her into the mattress while he claimed her mouth in a desperate kiss.

She spread her legs, welcoming him into the cradle of her hips as she arched against him, spearing her fingers into his hair and holding him close while she returned his hard, urgent kisses with a fervor that made him light headed. But this time it was all Amalya. No succubus energy or other supernatural force at work.

He shifted and slid into her hard and fast, ripping a gasp from both of them as her tight muscles welcomed him and held him like a gentle fist. She arched against him, urging him on.

The urgency surging through his body heard her silent plea and roared to comply. He began to thrust inside her as their tongues still mated and dueled. The frenzy of arousal surging through him faster and faster as the exquisite friction of Amalya's supple body on his drove him higher and harder.

When their panting breaths became too choppy to continue the kiss, Levi buried his face against the side of Amalya's neck, losing himself inside her body as he allowed himself to let go and just feel.

Amalya stiffened and cried out, her nails scoring his back and neck as the internal walls of her pussy contracted with her orgasm.

A flash of power spilled through him making him cry out as every nerve ending fired and contracted.

He continued to thrust, dimly realizing through the haze that he was still close and hadn't come yet. Several thrusts later, the tingling deep in his pelvis exploded sending spirals of lava through his veins while jets of his hot come spilled deep inside Amalya.

She cried out and tightened her thighs around him as his essence was absorbed inside her body and converted to energy.

When his mind cleared he found himself slumped over Amalya, still buried inside her, her arms and legs wrapped loosely around him as if she couldn't bear for him to move just yet.

"Did you come twice?" Her words sounded sleepy and sated but voiced what he hadn't yet had time to wonder.

With effort, he raised his head to look down at her. "No, not exactly. When you came, it was like I absorbed the energy."

With shock, he realized the implications of what he'd just said and frowned down at Amalya. "What did you say Uriel did to make me immune?"

Amalya's lips curved in a sated smile that made Levi's cock harden inside her. "He brushed his hand over your face."

"He what?"

"He kissed you and something like a golden ball of light passed from his fingers into you. He didn't elaborate, but apparently, he's given you a way to recharge your energy just like I do."

Levi let the ramifications of that churn through him. "So every time I make you come, I gain energy?"

She grinned and traced her fingers down his long sideburns. "I think I could really grow to enjoy this, but you need to eat."

Levi brushed his lips over hers, inhaling her fresh scent and imprinting it in his memory for all time. "Until Armageddon or Uriel come knocking on our door, I say we see just how long we can live on energy alone."